'Jimmy! The bastards! Did they kill you?'

'My throat was pierced,' he confirmed, his sullen voice sounding far away. 'My head was shot. I tired and died.'

'What shall I tell Rosey?' cried Pelling. 'What about the kids?'

Copper stretched his mouth to make a smile. 'Tell her I preferred her sister,' he said. 'Tell them I don't miss them.'

Fred was shocked to silence. His friend had been the kindest of men, a faithful husband and loving father.

Adam would have interrupted him anyway. There was no time for domestic chit-chat.

'Who took you?' he said, loud and clear and confident. 'Who killed you? Where did you go? Where is the King?'

'He . . .' said Copper – and then said no more. His body remained but *he* was gone, snatched back as though pulled on a rope to whence he came. A new voice spoke from his mouth. The water in the trenches began to boil.

'I did it,' said the voice, the sweet sound of a giggly young girl. 'It was me. What of it?'

Also by John Whitbourn in VGSF

A DANGEROUS ENERGY

POPES AND PHANTOMS

# JOHN WHITBOURN
# TO BUILD JERUSALEM

**VGSF**

First published in Great Britain 1995
in hardback and paperback
by Victor Gollancz
A Division of the Cassell group
Wellington House, 125 Strand, London WC2R 0BB

A catalogue record for this book is
available from the British Library.

ISBN 0 575 05871 4 hb
ISBN 0 575 05873 0 pb

Typeset by CentraCet Limited, Cambridge
Printed and bound in Great Britain
by Cox & Wyman Ltd, Reading, Berks

Protestantism required more than personal conversion and the throwing away of what were regarded as the props and sops, the placebos and hypnotics of the old creed. . . . They had to face up to their own vile sinfulness and to the awesome fact that they were already predestined to Heaven or Hell by the irreversible and unmerited decree of God.

For those who had seen the great light the issues were clear. The path had been laid out. The struggle to build Jerusalem was on.

*The Reformation and the English People.*
J. J. Scarisbrick
Basil Blackwell, Oxford, 1984

# Contents

*And did those feet in ancient time*
  *Walk upon England's mountains green?*
*And was the holy Lamb of God*
  *On England's pleasant pastures seen?*

*And did the Countenance Divine*
  *Shine forth upon our clouded hills?*
*And was Jerusalem builded here*
  *Among those dark Satanic Mills?*

*Bring me my bow of burning gold!*
  *Bring me my arrows of desire!*
*Bring me my spear! O clouds, unfold!*
  *Bring me my chariot of fire!*

*I will not cease from mental fight,*
  *Nor shall my sword sleep in my hand,*
*Till we have built Jerusalem*
  *In England's green and pleasant land.*

'Jerusalem', by William Blake (1757–1827)
    The National Anthem of United England, approved and sanctioned for use at public gatherings by His Majesty King Charles III in the year 1870.

## From: THE PIOUS CHILD'S GARDEN OF WISDOM

By E. Blyton
Published Coventry, Auto-da-fé Press, 1942.

Page 23: *A Rhyme for Recalling the Rulers of England*

*When the Romans departed,*
*there were Saxon Kings,*
*till William slew Harold,*
*at the field of HASTINGS.*                5th–11th century

. . . .

*Richard the Bad,*
*and Henry the Worse.*
*Then Henry his son,*
*whose name we all curse.*                15–16th century

*Edward his bastard,*
*and Mary the Great.*
*Black Betty, her sister,*
*the vile apostate.*                16th century

*Mary the Second,*
*(less Darnley the clot).*
*Then Essex, then James,*
*the blown-up Scot.*                16–17th century

*Saint Charles the Victor,*
*and Charles his son.*
*Then James the True,*
*and the battles he won.*                17th century

*Joseph the Wizard,*
*and Peter the Brave . . .*

*We gather today to honour one of the great men of English history; a true son of the Church, a patriot, a soldier and a martyr. Recognition of his rare qualities was put beyond doubt when, a hundred years ago to this day, Mother Church sanctioned his canonization. Distinguished by a life of selfless sacrifice to his country, Church and the cause of justice, he now sits in a deserved place of special exaltation in Heaven. We who venerate his life and example, have come together on this, his feast day, to add our more humble, purely English, but no less fervent honours to one of our land's finest sons.*

*When, in a few moments, I unveil this statue, we will add a small but sincere contribution to the chorus of acclamation and approval which our brother, his earthly tribulations over, now enjoys in Paradise. The English people, who by their generous donations to a subscription fund enabled this statue to be raised, will be joining their prayers to both those of Christ's Church-in-Pilgrimage on earth, and those of the Church-Triumphant beyond. Our veneration will surely not go unrewarded, both in this life and the one to come.*

*We know surprisingly little of the man: the times in which he lived were not conducive to fulsome declarations. His baptism, at least, is a matter of record; we read of it in the records of St Michael le Belfry, York, for the sixteenth of April, the Year of Our Lord 1570. Likewise, we can hardly fail to be unaware of his untimely grisly end, here in London, in the churchyard of St Paul's Cathedral, on the thirty-first of January, 1606. But what of the years between? we ask. We know that his father was a lawyer and that he attended St Peter's school in York. It is said that he grew tall and stately,*

11

*over six feet in height, and had long, light brown hair and a reddish beard. His commanding officers praised him for his courage, loyalty and integrity. And that, my friends, is more or less all. We have no clear glimpse of his life and works until that fateful night, three centuries ago, when he smuggled 'two hogshead and thirty-two small barrels of powder', as Black Robert Cecil records, into the old Parliament building. Aided by spells of silence cast by accompanying wizards, the perilous task was accomplished. We are all familiar with the heart-stopping incident of their discovery by a yeoman of the guard, and his nick-of-time felling by a conjuration of 'anathema'. I doubt that at any time in the thousand years since its discovery and codification has magic been put to better use in these Isles. Fortunately, after many such adventures, all went well.*

*Modern engineers have reconstructed events for us. The usurping Scottish King, his arrogant Scottish courtiers, the lickspittle lords and 'protestant' Parliament; they were struck at first by an enormous blast. Then they fell into the blazing cellar beneath, hotly followed, in every sense of the word, by the burning wreckage of the House of Lords. Those few who survived this treatment had to contend with the famous black cloud, which all London saw, rich in choking smoke and gas. Together it was sufficient to send every single one to give account of themselves to their Maker. Indeed, those same engineers calculate that the Saint gathered twenty-five-fold more explosive than was needed for the job. That may be so, but we today applaud his painstaking caution.*

*True, he was betrayed and taken. True, he was subject to undeserved torture and a traitor's painful death. However, that is a mere sad postscript to a great mission fulfilled. He had done his duty and now has his reward in Heaven. Meanwhile, those of us still concerned with earning our place in Paradise, may look at this man – together with his fellow conspirators – and say never, in the field of human conflict, was so much owed, by so many, to so few . . .*

Extract from the address given by His Majesty's Chief Minister, Lord Winston Spencer Churchill, upon the unveiling of the statue to St Guy Fawkes, Parliament Square, London, 5 November 1940.

# Part the First

*England's pleasant pastures*

One morning in 1995, Jonah Ransom, clothier, was going about his normal business, only to find that 'normal business' was over for ever.

'Hello,' said the woman.

Jonah was going to ask her what she was doing in his store cupboard – and where was his stockpiled cloth? But not after that 'hello', not after . . . that voice. The sound of her went right through body and soul and shook him to silence.

One of Jonah's hands fell from the door handle, the other with its accusing finger dropped to his side. He looked into her face and wanted to sink to his knees.

She seemed as puzzled by her location as Jonah. It took her a while to notice the middle-aged man beholding her, amidst the other strange surroundings. Eyes flashing beneath a boyish fringe of coal-dark hair, she licked her black lips.

'Hello,' she repeated with indecent relish, her voice transcending normal female range. Then Jonah noticed that the colours on her dress were all a-dance and flowing.

When he raised his eyes again they directly met her extended hand, mere inches from his face. Her nails were nibbled and glossy black. He sought soundless permission for his dearest wish and it was given with a coquettish tilt of her head. Jonah seized the hand like a drowning man (which in fact he was), and all but consumed it with burning kisses.

The woman drew him into the cupboard and the door slammed shut on them, of its own violent accord, as final as judgement.

~

'You did well to tell us,' said one of the white faces in the shadows. 'We can understand the temptation to silence.'

Jonah sobbed and the panel standing in judgement of what he had to say shifted uncomfortably at the display of emotion.

'I am ... torn,' he wept. 'I didn't call her. Chance brought her to my house. I've never felt so ...' He shook his head in frustration, unable to find the words.

'We know,' said the man who had spoken before, 'or we can imagine, at least. You are prey to the strangest of afflictions, and that being so I do not think the Lord will hold you liable.'

'You take too much upon yourself, Brother Zeal,' said a bitter-sounding woman in a clerical collar. 'This is a twenty years married man, I believe, and such a tie is not so lightly to be ...'

She trailed away into silence beholding the widespread and manifest hostility to her intervention.

'Special times, special cases,' said the first speaker, rebuking her.

'No, she is right,' said Jonah, earning himself equal but more muted disapproval. 'My wife and I were one flesh, as is enjoined, knowing no other since youth – but now ...'

'Now ...?' said his interrogator, urging him on as gently as he knew how.

'Now I don't care,' blurted Jonah, 'not since ... *she* came. I don't care for the opinion of spouse or God and be damned to both.' Suddenly he was calm again. 'That is the worst of it,' he added.

Half-suppressed gasps and angry retorts filled the dimly lit barn. Outside in the night the nervous guards heard the sounds and grasped their pikes and pistols, fearing the detection that would, one day, surely come. Tense moments followed, waiting for the enemy to issue from the dark and silent fields before they could relax and resume their patrols. Meanwhile, within, the first speaker regained order with difficulty.

'He does not speak his own mind,' he said, raising his voice as much as he dared, 'but betrays the influence of another. Deploy charity, I implore you, and recall the great work in hand.'

This had the desired effect and discipline was restored.

'Do not fear,' said another panelist to Jonah, 'we do not take your words as yours. We know this thing that you embrace is . . . perilous.'

Jonah laughed bitterly. 'Embrace!' he said. 'I would give my soul and the life to come for an embrace. I am not so favoured.'

Again his words caused a ripple of embarrassed unease.

'I spoke in metaphorical terms,' said the pale man who had prompted this outburst, 'and of spiritual considerations. We know you for a Godly and sober man in normal times, a steadfast patron of our cause. Your presence here is proof that person is not wholly lost.'

'Though you were not always so forward, sirrah!' commented the first speaker.

Jonah did not hear their words of comfort or reprimand; he was lost in thought, exploring the strong emotions shaking his frame. One of the inquisitors signalled to the armed men by the door and the little clothier was led away.

Once the door was re-barred, the initial speaker, first among equals there, stepped forward in the meagre light of the few candles that security permitted. Needing no other cue, the two dozen assembled men and women, old and young, armed and not, assumed attitudes of prayer.

'Lord,' he intoned quietly but with passionate intensity, 'unworthy, crawling creatures that we are, we beg Your guidance in our deliberation tonight. This is a sharp sword that You have permitted us to find. All good things come from You and we thank You for the weapon stumbled upon by our humble brother. Broaden our understanding to comprehend Your gift. If it be Your will, let us find in this lowly clothier the means to smite Babylon hip and brow. Grant us, we beseech You, the great favour to avenge our slaughtered brethren and thus show Your strong and righteous arm upon the land. Permit us the privilege of establishing Your rule. Through Jesus Christ, our Earthly King in waiting, amen.'

The others echoed 'Amen' with a will.

'So?' said the first speaker, fingering his pastor's collar and looking inquisitively around.

'It might just be possible,' said a snowy-headed man with a Cornish accent. 'I really think it might just be possible. Preliminary tests—'

'Judgement,' interrupted the first speaker fiercely, 'not argument!'

'Then yes!' snapped the old man, unable to purge the excitement from his voice. 'Yes!'

A murmur of irrepressible joy flourished briefly in the barn. One or two present raised their voices to say 'Alleluia'.

The first speaker looked at each person in turn, pursuing unknown private paths of thought or prayer. Then he nodded.

'So shall it be,' he said quietly.

The soldier caste there, the so-called 'Gideon Bands', held gun or blade aloft in acclamation. The rest smiled and shifted on their feet as if limbering up for the struggle to come.

'The matter then goes to the Joint Grand Council,' said the first speaker, 'for the affiliates to approve. We shall speak also to the Unitarians and Agnostics.' Here some of those present turned aside and spat heartily. Noting this, not disapprovingly, the first speaker raised a placatory hand. 'We do not know,' he went on, seeking both to calm and conclude, 'the nature of this thing that brother Jonah has met. We are not aware of its provenance save that, like all things, it comes ultimately from Almighty God. May He then make it a blade in our hands to pierce the breast of our enemy. We must not fail this time, for time is something not in infinite supply. Matters are drawing to a close for good or ill, and it is given to us to have a civilization to build. Go forth to save your souls!'

Straight away, well practised over long years, the conspirators filed silently away under the vigilance of the military cadres, out into the night, back to their homes and shops and families; and all the many and various social pretences in which they bided their time.

It was that very same day that Adam (who was just plain 'Adam', no longer having any other name) first heard about Jonah the clothier and his discovery in the store cupboard. True, he didn't hear of it spoken plain or direct, but he was used to that. Very few of the things he was asked to deal with were ever simple or what they seemed.

The Mameluke escort had been dismissive of him to start with – he was just another infidel 'Frank', here on the Caliph's sufferance. However, Adam's easy show of horsemanship on the hot and dusty ride into Fez, the way he reined in his unfamiliar steed as a train steamed across their path, the confidence with which he bore arms – and then surrendered them to their captain – enabled them to

21

warm to him. They had much in common, after all, both being taken from family and homeland at a tender age into lifelong service to a distant lord. Adam belonged, mind and body, to the great Christian Father, they to Allah's appointed, the Caliph. The nature of their elite calling contained more similarities than differences to such military men.

So the Mamelukes smiled benignly on Adam as he slid lithely off his borrowed mount at their white-walled destination in the Foreigners' Quarter. They forgave his plain red clothes, so dull compared to their dazzling silks, and wished him well in various tongues. He ignored them.

Adam was expected – after a fashion. The Bey of Fez, ever whimsical in his favours, had warned Sir Michael Clarke to expect a 'Frankish' guest, who should be received with such courtesy as he saw fit. Accordingly the interview took place beside the cool and private courtyard at the centre of the house. Here, belying the plain exterior walls, were flowers and running water, greenery and effigies in marble. At its sides were shadowed cloisters to contrast with the brassy light of the sun. Aside from the works of his pen, Sir Michael considered such a ... sympathetic place amongst his greatest achievements.

Clarke had entertained hopes of a similarly sympathetic visitor from 'home', but little dreamt the extent to which he was mistaken. His lightly painted face fell as Adam strode into the receiving room and seemed to occupy it as if by right of conquest. He did not acknowledge the lavish decorations laid on in his honour. However, Clarke's recovery was swift and he made a *salaam* of welcome. It elicited no response from the soldier. Neither did the Christendom-style proffered hand which followed.

Sir Michael shrugged gracefully. 'Well, hello anyway,' he said, lolling back on to his divan. 'Mr ...?'

Adam remained standing, pointedly foregoing the colourful and inviting couch provided for the expected visitor.

'That's irrelevant,' he said, in a voice surprisingly quiet and gentle. 'We shan't be meeting again.'

'So you are here to kill me?' Sir Michael asked, averting his eyes.

'No, I'm not.'

Clarke restrained his fluttering breath commendably. 'Well then,' he said, raising his gaze to the soldier again. 'If we *are* to converse, I must call you something.'

Adam shook his head. 'Not necessarily. Our conversation need only be short and sweet. Stop your writing.'

'Ah,' said Sir Michael, 'now I understand. Yes, short certainly, but sweet? Alas, no. Mind you, it could be worse: there was the fear, just for a moment, that you were one of those appalling "Earthly Judgement" people that your master retains. Of course, had you come to do away with me, the Caliph's dashing Mamelukes would certainly dispatch you in turn – and in a most horrible manner. However, that consideration wouldn't deter those addled colleagues of yours, would it?'

'No,' agreed Adam. 'Their efficacy is deliberately exaggerated, but what you say is broadly true. Look on me as John the Baptist to their Christ. They follow in my footsteps should I fail. Stop your writing.'

Sir Michael frowned, not angrily, but as if puzzled. 'I had illusions of the Caliph's protection, you see,' he said. 'As with all the exiles of Christendom here, I fondly dreamt we were now beyond your sordid command. It was, for instance, said that what I scribble amuses the Cairene Sublime Porte.'

'Possibly so,' answered Adam, 'but matters now move on apace and it seems His Sublimeness is more ... *amused*

by certain trade arrangements that are offered him; more
... *amused* by the prospect of Christian "volunteer" artil-
lerymen to assist him against the Benin horse tribes of the
south. Thus, by the ever-shifting sands of statecraft, our
way to you is cleared and I am able to deliver my request.'

Clarke stared hard at Adam, pursing his scarlet lips.
Several long moments passed in such strange communion.
Then Sir Michael spoke, as though making a fresh start.

'Well,' he said, 'what you say may be so. And since
you've come all this way to recite your piece, perhaps you
would care for some refreshment?'

'No.'

'I suspected not. You'll permit me, then?'

Adam shrugged, but Sir Michael courteously awaited
even this sign of indifference before sounding a tiny silver
bell which lay beside his divan.

A stunningly beautiful pale-skinned boy, dressed in a
parody of the Clarke family livery, appeared directly,
bearing a flask and goblets.

Sir Michael made a great play of being served his iced
lemonade and then beckoned the boy to join him on the
wide couch. With ease of practise, he snuggled alongside
his master and turned black-lined limpid eyes upon the
stranger before them. Clarke rested one hand on the boy's
rump and smiled at Adam.

Adam did not respond other than to avert his glance,
taking in the quiet courtyard with its water music and
unexpected fecundity. It would be easy – for some – he
thought, to desist from ... everything here, to lay down
duty and burden and forget time and place. Happily, for
his part, he was beyond such weakness. He did not need
earplugs to shut out the siren song. Moreover, that
triumph over self was doubly pleasing when, as now,
temptation was strengthened by Sir Michael's magic.

Clarke, closely observing the outward signs of inner debate, mistakenly saw some faltering of Adam's resolve. He pounced.

'Tell me,' he said, 'are you not just the slightest bit ... seduced by what you see?' He waved five scarlet-tipped fingers to encompass the light and shade of the courtyard, the villa and the painted boy. 'Not the minutest bit?'

Adam shifted his head from side to side, a gesture of equivocation. 'A little,' he pretended, 'should I choose to permit it.'

Sir Michael could not judge whether his covert spell had worked. There was an Achilles' heel there for him to sink his fangs into, he was sure; but had his venom found a vein?

'Then permit!' he said swiftly. 'Don't condemn yourself to a life of desiccation. Warm the flesh *with* flesh, before the lasting chill of the grave!'

So saying, Clarke playfully squeezed the servant boy's velvet-covered bottom and the lad giggled.

Adam answered with a humour-free smile and Clarke realized that both he and his magic had quite failed.

'I recognize the quotation from your latest *opus*, Sir Michael. Oh yes, don't be surprised. I have read what I've come to silence. Your use of it brings me back to my purpose – and conveniently clears the air of your sorcery. Now, may I convey to my superiors news of the immediate cessation of your literary endeavours?'

Sir Michael sighed theatrically. 'Since you seem proof against all charms – both of this world and beyond – I suppose I must consider your nasty proposition: particularly since you reveal my host has forsaken me. It's a great shame, though. I consider my *Cupid Given Poison* a work of minor greatness. Not only that, it developed points quite essential to restoring mental health and wellbeing to European civilization. Surely you can't wish to abort that?'

'I surely can,' replied Adam.

'But it was so well received!' protested Clarke.

'In certain clandestine circles,' Adam said dismissively. 'Among certain sad agnostic chatterers such as yourself: no one of import.'

'Important enough to bring a senior bully like you all the way to the Caliphate,' Clarke countered. 'Important enough to incite the trading of diplomatic favours!'

'You annoyed a certain significant few,' Adam conceded. 'Perhaps you disturbed a modicum of sleep. If you'd written in Latin – as I know you can – instead of a minority tongue like English, you'd have stirred things even more – though maybe not to your benefit.'

Clarke appeared to agree. 'I have this emotional attachment to the old country,' he explained. 'And English is greatly neglected as a literary medium. Besides – Church-speak – that's the tongue of the enemy, isn't it? I have nothing to say to *them*.'

Adam was starting to warm to Sir Michael's foundationless courage. In a detached way, he wished the man well.

'Taken out of context,' he pressed on, 'your arguments and teasings possess some illusory weight. And so here I am' – his voice suddenly hardened – 'awaiting your answer.'

By contrast, Sir Michael's feelings towards the Papal emissary were heading in a less charitable direction. Seeing the ruin of his great project, that very work which justified his play, he visited his disappointment and impotent rage on the bearer of the bad tidings.

'There is only one answer I can give, isn't there?' he hissed, pushing the startled servant off the couch on to the cool tiled floor. Apparently used to such rapid mood swings, the boy scuttled away into the courtyard's shadows. Still unwilling to offer unconditional surrender to the civilization he hated and had fled from, Clarke set to feverish work on last-ditch defences. 'There's always the possibility of a nom de plume,' he muttered.

Adam, fully committed to his mission, took this throw-away face-saver with a seriousness he knew it didn't really merit.

'I think not, Sir Michael. Your style would be recognized by the experts retained by the College of Ideological Vigilance, and retribution for your deceit would soon follow. Do not treat your last chance so lightly.'

Clarke glowered at him. 'You already knew I was a magician, didn't you?' he said, changing tack.

Under the combined protection of both Pope and Caliph, Adam felt secure enough to stand and face Sir Michael's barely controlled anger.

'Of course,' he answered. 'I know more about you than your mother does. My prior research and briefing were quite exhaustive.'

'Well, they would be, wouldn't they?' sneered Clarke. 'You world-deniers have so much excess energy to sublimate. And leave my saintly mother out of things.'

Adam sighed impatiently. 'Have you got anything to actually say, Sir Michael, or can I skip the parade of pique?'

Clarke, who seemed very grave all of a sudden, sat up straight. 'Oh yes,' he said, 'I've got something to say – and it ought to interest you.'

'Fire away,' said Adam.

'Oh I *would*,' said Sir Michael, 'if I didn't think you might be faster with the concealed firearm you have trained on me . . .'

One up to you, Sir Michael, thought Adam.

'... if I thought I might get away with it, if your theocracy didn't have infinite more monsters like you to send in your place. So, no, I won't seek to cover you in balefire or similar; I'll let you go home, alive, infected with something else.'

'Which is?'

'You're aware that I have what we call "the Talent" and what my hosts term "the Blessing". Quite a few of my fellow escapees from repression here do. My personal gifts don't amount to much, I confess; I was never good enough to merit recruitment by your grim organization – thank Zeus. Still, I practise a little, I commune with ... powers and ferret out things of interest. Do you follow me?'

'Yes – but with mounting impatience,' answered Adam.

'It's just this,' said Sir Michael confidingly. 'I have reason to believe that you and yours will not always be so – ' here he gritted his teeth – 'unanswerable. I suspect your dominance might, at long last, be under challenge.'

'The Mamelukes?' offered Adam. 'The Golden Horde of Muscovy?'

'Oh, no,' said Clarke, worryingly confident, 'nothing that obvious. What I speak of is something new and not at all to your taste. You see, just recently my conjurations have been thrown awry. The magical geometry is ... displaced and no longer quite predictable. Everything works but there's some major new factor to be considered. I sought the reason why that should be and purchased an answer of sorts. It transpires there is something fresh and unprecedented in the world, master soldier. Ask your own thaumaturgists – Zeus knows you've contrived to have the best ones: something *new* in the world!'

'I shall ask,' replied Adam, fully meaning, in his hyper-cautious attention to detail, to do so.

'You do that,' said Clarke, considering his future life of literary celibacy. 'And whatever it is I hope, with all my mistreated heart I *hope*, this new thing brings down your horrible certainties. I hope you personally get to meet it. I hope it . . . destroys you – as you have me.'

# From: THE BOOK OF CEREMONIAL MAGIC

By Sir Arthur Waite
Published London, Auto-da-fé Press, 1911.

## Introduction: For laymen and novices: the nature of that faculty commonly called magic

Magic is a child of faith. Some small segment of mankind (within which I also include the fairer sex) is able, after training, to so *believe* in their God-given 'talent' as to render reality a plastic, pliable commodity. If a wizard can but convince himself, with the faith of a saint in Christ, that a bullet speeding towards him will do no harm, then it will not. If it is his will to wreak harm on an enemy then so shall it be: if his wish is strong enough – and stronger than his enemy's desire to live. In effect, the sorcerer is permitted to take some little part of the Deity's creative power and wield it with human hands. It is desirous therefore that this hand be linked to a humble and pious heart, which is why Mother Church takes all magicians under her wing for nurture and instruction.

There is, it is true, the necessity of what is termed the 'algebra' of thaumaturgy, of constructing 'power words', spells and incantations, but these are only the means to an end. The true essence of the matter is the triumph of the will.

However, although it defies exact calculation, there does exist some correlation between a spell's 'impossibility' and the drain it exerts on a magician's strength. Sorcerous stamina varies amongst individuals just as does physical strength (though there seems no relation between the two). A mighty spell might prostrate its caster for many months. Conversely, minor conjurations and lesser marvels can be performed a dozen times a day without undue strain.

In short, from beginning to end, the practice of magic

is a working upon a mystery. Its very existence hints at the limitless potential of mankind and the illusory nature of the perceived universe. Therefore, in permitting sorcery, our Heavenly Father is passing us a message. Sad to relate, even after a thousand years of usage, we are little nearer to discerning what precisely it might be.

A. W.

London, Bognor, Jaffa. 1902–10

'Oh yeah,' said Frederick Pelling, 'our lot say that too: the magic's gone askew.'

'You overstate the case,' said Adam, ever precise. 'The Thaumaturgic College's report merely notes a significant disturbance in the "Numinous Ambience" – whatever that may be. Magical cause and effect aren't affected; they can still operate.'

'I'm just repeating what I've heard,' said the slight, youngish man beside Adam, staring morosely out over Calais. He was clearly less than enamoured with his present company and circumstances.

'Possibly so, but I require you to be less colloquial in future,' replied Adam, trying to make it sound a polite request rather than a rebuke. 'I need to assimilate what you have to tell me quickly and accurately. I don't wish to do so through a filter of chitchat.'

Adam's acquaintance with Frederick Pelling was only five minutes old – he had been sent to meet Adam on the Channel ferry and brief him during the crossing – but already things were none too good between them.

The Papal Officer knew that the qualities his vocation required of him made his company hard going. He'd confessed his impatience with the slack and careless ways of ordinary people on numerous occasions, and always obtained easy absolution. He was, he'd been consistently told, going about *higher* works, serving the Church Universal in invaluable and specialized ways. Others had to make allowances for the social graces he was thus obliged to sacrifice. Accordingly he had an easy conscience about prodding civilians into efficiency. However, for the moment Adam needed the full cooperation of this Pelling person because of the information he alone bore, and a second attempt at cordial relations was merited.

'Look,' he said, trying to remember exactly how it

was that one sounded friendly, 'let's start again, shall we?'

Pelling's large and melancholic eyes registered an unlikely mix of surprise and indifference.

'Suits me,' he said in his soft voice.

By now the ferry was starting to steam up for the trip. Economical as always with precious time, Adam had delayed his arrival on board to the last moment, thereby making space for additional study of the English news-sheets in the Bishop of Calais' Castle Library as well as a rosary in the adjoining chapel. Accordingly it was a mentally and spiritually prepared Adam who'd met Pelling on the *Our Lady of Walsingham* that morning.

Association with the red-coated soldier had secured the infinitely less exalted Pelling early access to the ship along with the few other high-status passengers. Lesser function-aries, the scattering of middle-class tourists and, lastly, the unwashed hordes of pilgrims and itinerant Church work-bands, were coralled away from the quay to permit their unhindered boarding.

The first, less than happy, exchanges between Adam and Pelling had taken place on the Church and First Class Viewing Platform overlooking the flotsam-marred water and neglected harbour fortifications. Seeking a fresh beginning (and noting the advance of the proletarian passengers) Adam tore Pelling's attention away from a particularly forlorn-looking cannon and directed their steps below deck.

In the appropriate lounge, comfortably seated and waited upon by acolyte stewards with French brandy and comfits, they returned to the fray.

'You're too sallow for pure English,' said Adam to Pelling. 'What's your lineage?'

It was honestly meant to be small talk and to Adam's

unpractised ear sounded so. Fred Pelling merely heard sad confirmation of a rough time to come and sank deeper into his chair and discontent.

'My grandfather did four tours with the English Chapter of the Knights of St John,' he mumbled, 'in the Jaffa Citadel. He married a local girl out there. Also there's meant to be some Spanish blood from way back.'

In their world a degree of cosmopolitanism was almost expected from all but the peasant classes. The rule of the Church in Europe had quite deliberately striven to mix nation and race, with the distant aim of welding the warring tribes into Christendom.

'From Civil War days, perhaps,' observed Adam politely – as he thought. 'There was considerable fraternization between the English and the assisting volunteer troops, so I understand. Anyway, it sounds very acceptable.'

Pelling alone registered the innocent solecism.

'I'm also English, you know,' Adam ploughed on, 'by origin.'

'Goodness, really?' said Pelling, sailing as close as he dare to sarcasm.

'Yes, indeed. I was resident there – in the county of Sussex – up to the age of ten. Then my family received permission to volunteer me for the Apostolic Guardianship and I had the good fortune to be accepted. Since that time I have lived mostly in the Italian States.'

'An Italianized Englishman is a devil incarnate,' recited Pelling to no one in particular.

'*Inglese Italianato è un diavolo incarnato*,' translated Adam perfectly. 'Yes, I have heard that ancient saying. It is based on the falsest of prejudices, of course.'

'Of course.'

Adam judged that this was sufficient social exchange to

34

constitute friendship and returned to the real matter in hand with the abruptness of a guillotine.

'So, you witnessed the abduction. Relate it to me now. Do not leave out any detail without prior reference.'

Pelling bridled at the tone. 'Is is all right if I breathe whilst I do it?' he asked, raising his voice.

Adam sighed and quietly studied his companion. The next thing Pelling was aware of, aside from half sighting some vague blur of motion, was his awaking, groggy and confused, on the floor. Adam was gazing impassively down on him.

'Are you conscious? Fully conscious?' he asked briskly.

Pelling somehow found the strength to raise himself a little and nod. Then he sailed up into the air, courtesy of Adam's fist gripping his collar, and was casually flung back into his recently vacated seat. In the privacy of his rapidly developing thoughts, Pelling offered unconditional surrender to the unmatchable brute strength just manifested.

'I *do* hope,' said Adam in a measured tone, 'that I'm not wasting my time with you.'

Pelling signalled he wasn't.

'Good.'

Adam suddenly turned his attention to the agog audience attracted by the brief cabaret.

'Carry on with what you were doing!' he snapped, entirely sure of himself. 'This is none of your concern.'

The other passengers, high-office holders, Churchmen and nobility, all hastened to comply and find a new absorbing interest in their refreshments or companions. Pelling, in his provincial innocence, hadn't realized quite the dizzy heights he was perched upon. Everyone else in the elegant lounge was less naive and fully appreciated the power represented by Adam's smoky red attire.

To make (slight) amends, Adam leant forward and straightened the dazed man's lapels, brushing his jacket shoulders free of imaginary dust as he did so.

'There will be no permanent damage,' he said. 'Certain long and stringy filaments in your body, of unknown exact function, have the capacity to cause pain, oblivion or even death, if struck precisely. In Rome we were taken to observe the dissection of cadavers by the Sacred College of Surgeons, thereby to learn where these features run close to the skin. It comes in handy. Would you like another brandy?'

Pelling nodded absently and Adam's confident click of slim fingers brought the steward, and thus the restorative, in ship-record time. Frederick Pelling drank it down with gratitude.

'You must understand,' said Adam, as kindly as he could, 'that this really is no game, no mere . . . job. My presence here is a sign of that. I deal in the ending of lives, of careers, even, on occasion, of places – never anything less: that's what I'm trained for. Am I getting through?'

'Absolutely,' answered Pelling, now just about able to speak again, never taking his eyes off the soldier.

'I don't know what your grievance is,' Adam continued, 'whether you're "England-First" or anti-Church or just plain put out by life. It doesn't matter and has to be put aside for the duration. *Has* to.'

'It is – put aside – whatever.'

'Good. Right, now you know who I am, more or less, let's get things crystal clear about you. You work for this lord . . . Onslow – the head person where it happened. Correct?'

Pelling carefully replaced his glass on the table. 'Correct. My dad was a town constable for him. I got his job, of course, and then got promoted. Also, *Weston*-Onslow's the name they prefer.'

'What's the difference?' Adam was genuinely anxious to learn.

'The Westons kept the faith in our area during the bad times; you know, the "protestant" days. The Onslows married into them afterwards – and just in time. The association saved their bacon. Now it adds lustre.'

'Interesting. But your man'll answer to Onslow, will he?'

'Oh yes, and I answer to him – when he's around, that is. His Lordship's been away on Crusade in Estonia the last two years. I'm deputy head of his Cabinet of Temporal Welfare.'

'Which is to say security. Right?'

'Well, yes, amongst other things; there's not that many of us so we have to double up with other functions. Still, by our standards he's a pretty big man – Parliament and all that. In south-west Surrey he's pretty much the law.'

'I'll bear that in mind.'

'Also I'm acting Head of the Cabinet. My boss went ... well, when the others did.'

There was a pause whilst Adam looked out of a nearby porthole at the grey and heaving horizon. Despite the thick wall tapestries (genuine Persian 'Armada-weave') and teak panelling in the lounge, the struggling church-sized engines below were obstrusively loud.

'So, granted, you're out of your depth,' he said at last, as though musing on the strange vagaries of a man's fate. 'But that needn't be a material consideration, as long as you keep your sense of proportion. Don't be awed by the gulf between present circumstances and your normal life. Regard it as a dangerous opportunity.'

'I'll certainly try and recall what you've taught me,' said Pelling, carefully extracting all intonation from his voice. His fingers unconsciously reached up to probe the pinpoint bruise between neck and shoulder.

'It was necessary,' said Adam, noting the movement even if Pelling didn't. He sounded sincerely regretful. 'You needed to appreciate my authority. Different people can be reached in different ways. I can tell you're not a person of violence, but I'm on a cruel schedule here. I can't spare the time to be subtle or considerate.'

. 'No,' replied Pelling – and in the privacy of his own head that answer could have meant a great many things.

'No,' 'agreed' Adam. 'Now, having lost five irreplaceable minutes, let's begin again. As I said before, tell me the whole story. Do not leave out any detail.'

And so, as the giant *Our Lady of Walsingham* made its noisy, smoky way through choppy seas, causing the fishing fleets and sailing ships to give it a wide berth, Fred Pelling told Adam how the King of England and most of his court had vanished into thin air.

# A FRESH COMMANDMENT TO THE PEOPLE OF ENGLAND-THAT-IS-TO-COME

BE IT KNOWN THAT HIS MOST GRACIOUS AND CHRISTIAN MAJESTY, CHARLES, THE FOURTH OF THAT NAME, KING OF ENGLAND, WALES AND CORNWALL; PROTECTOR OF MANNIN AND THE ISLES; PATRON OF THE JERUSALEM AND JAFFA CITADELS, HAS BEEN RESCUED FROM HIS SEDUCTION AND SERVITUDE TO THE EVIL INFLUENCE OF ADVISORS AND CONFESSORS (CONTRARY TO GOSPEL TRUTH) OF THE CHURCH OF BABYLON. TRUE BELIEVERS, PATRIOTS AND JUSTIFIED SOLDIERS OF CHRIST NOW ATTEND HIM IN A PLACE OF UTMOST SAFETY FROM WHERE:

HE DOES DIRECT, COMMAND AND PROCLAIM, BY THE ANOINTED AUTHORITY INVESTED IN HIM BY ALMIGHTY G*D, THAT ALL HIS SUBJECTS OF WHATSOEVER CLASS AND CONDITION DO OVERTHROW AND OVERTHROW AND OVERTHROW THE BEAST! THE WHORE OF BABYLON! AND BRING IT TO UTTER RUIN.

ENGLAND ARISE! ENGLAND ARISE! THE SPIRIT OF AN ANGRY G*D IS MOVING AMONG US. DO NOT BE FOUND WANTING AMIDST THE DAY OF WRATH!

Adam threw the broadsheet back on to the table.

'Nailed to the main door of Westminster Abbey? They were taking a chance – or don't people go in there to pray any more? Is the Royal Seal genuine?'

The tired-looking Churchman sitting opposite shrugged. 'Either that or so good a copy it hardly matters,' he said. 'The notice itself is pretty typical of the dozen or so examples we've retrieved, all secured to prominent places. And, no, we never see anyone putting them up. In my opinion, for what it's worth, the seal's the real thing, God rot it.'

'So,' said Adam, quite casually, 'whoever produced this ... outpouring has the King.'

Father Brian Bancroft, Grandmaster of the Archbishop of London's intelligence service, nodded his grey and weary head.

'So it seems. The King, a Papal Legate, a bishop, various assorted nobles and courtiers ... And before you ask, we haven't been able to trace the printing apparatus. I *can* say it's not from any printing press we've licensed or from any of the illegals we're aware of.'

'The latter have been visited?' queried Adam.

'Of course,' replied Bancroft, a touch peevishly, 'every one. Dozens of promising surveillance operations and years of work down the drain just to catch a few miserable heretic print monkeys.'

Adam imperiously waved these regrets aside. 'Irrelevant,' he pronounced. 'This is a bigger game altogether and takes precedence over all others. If you feel that way, you should have taken better care of your King in the first place.'

The atmosphere had been tense ever since the *Our Lady of Walsingham* had docked at Dover. Adam's reception committee had been waiting on the quay, hardly bothering to conceal their impatience with the pilgrims whom ancient custom allowed to disembark first (a reversal of the boarding process, the better to speed their grace-bound footsteps). As he watched the spectacle from the armoured bow, Adam had noted with amusement the furtive glares up at him and pretended to be fascinated with the looming castle on the cliffs above. Its walls fairly bristled with newish-looking cannons and the blue uniforms of the regular army. A cage full of dragoons was ascending the heights in the great ox lift at that very moment.

Typical provincials, he'd thought. Either passive or panicking – nothing in between.

In fact, he ought to have been flattered by the company gathered to welcome him to England. As mentioned, the Archbishop of London, the Church Universal's senior figure in the British Isles, had dispatched the coordinator of his eyes and ears (and occasionally his strong right hand). Aggrieved by the hysteria of the times and at being ousted from his spider's web in the capital, Father Bancroft had dragged two deputies (both of them magicians of the Roman School) along in his wake. There was a no-nonsense, flaxen-haired military man, called Colonel Longstaff, from that shadowy branch of the army which tried to muscle in on the affairs and secrets of the State (it knew better than to try the same with the Church). From the lonely Sussex palace that was home to Baxter, Grandmaster of Magic for the South-East, had come his Chief Assistant, Mr Hillaire, to represent a different, though equal, set of interests. Major link with continental Christendom and the Church heartlands though it might be, it was a while since Dover had been so greatly honoured.

Pelling, a mere lackey of the old land-based aristocracy, shrank to infinitesimal insignificance in such exalted surroundings, but Adam noticed his shying away and drew him along with them.

'You're in now,' he said with a gallows smile. 'The only way out is right on through to the end.'

Frederick Pelling well knew the very real perils of high company but, to his credit, marched along with them through the port, along the city walls and into the vast shadow of the cathedral, his sensitive face remaining quite expressionless.

Security (of a sort, thought Adam) was provided by the

41

pike and shot of the Bishop of Dover's black-coated Cathedral Guard. They surrounded the hall in the minster where the initial council was to take place and made a passable show of military efficiency. But for the cool silence that greeted the suggestion, the Bishop and his Dean-Temporal would have graced the gathering inside with their presence as well.

After the two junior magicians present had cast complex spells over the venue (Hillaire was above such things), ensuring they could not be overheard or spied upon undetected, Adam introduced himself. He was, he said, an officer of the Vatican Outer Cabinet (which was obvious), he hinted at rank sufficient to merit their respect and plainly stated he had been appointed to head all such investigations as the Holy and Apostolic Father might care to make into 'the present matter'.

That put some noses out of joint, for English nationalist sentiments ran at a discreet level in not a few hearts present there. However, they had imbibed acquiescence to the Church's rule along with their mother's milk. Unassailable, eternal, supernatural and confident in its cosmic role, that edifice stretched back beyond the memory of mere nations and would survive still, they knew, when 'England' and 'Europe' were just names in a history book. As with rain from heaven, they might on occasion be annoyed or frustrated by the Church Universal, but it was pointless to protest its right to fall on them. Top men in their little national and personal spheres, they were obliged to listen diligently to this representative of a higher and older order.

Seated at his ease at the head of the Bishop's banqueting table, Adam helped himself to the cob bread and spiced beef provided, fashioning a rough, soldier-style sandwich. Then before he partook, judging that this with a little red wine would be refuelling enough, he beckoned Pelling forward into the limelight. The other men huddled round the top half of the table looked at the unimposing Guildfordian with mild interest only, as if he were about to sing or juggle.

'This is Pelling,' Adam explained. 'Doubtless he's cropped up, at least as a footnote, in the reports you've received. He saw what happened and is going to recount it to you.'

'We've heard this,' protested Colonel Longstaff brusquely. 'Why don't we—'

'And now you're going to hear it again,' interrupted Adam, with quiet and marvellous authority. 'Proceed.'

Quite unabashed by the presence of the others, Adam then attacked his snack and seemed to be entirely absorbed in doing so. Pelling took one rather furtive look at the faces around him and henceforth restricted his gaze to the floor.

'I'll take it from when they got to Guildford Borough boundary,' he said, and hearing no opposition to this took it as approval. 'The Mayor and the Corporation met His Majesty out on the Portsmouth Road, down below St Catherine's and the ford. His Majesty had just paid his respects to the Prioress up there. The Papal Legate and his entourage was with him so the road was a bit hectic. Eventually I found the Gentleman Pensioner and Papal trooper jointly in charge of security and discussed arrangements with them. My boss, Lord Onslow's Head of the Household Cabinet, was with us. Then after the Loyal Address we supervised the progress up the High Street, right to the cathedral steps where the Bishop and Chapter were waiting. I think it took thirty or forty minutes. My job was the windows and roofs, so I didn't get much of a look at the crowd on the ground.'

'You're to be commended, then,' said Longstaff, too sarcastically for his own good. 'At least His Majesty wasn't dispatched by a crossbow-sniper from behind a chimney.'

He looked round for the laughter which never came and then had to slowly disengage the humour from his own face.

Adam, who was evidently listening after all, waved Pelling on.

'There are steps leading off the High Street,' he persevered gamely, 'to the cathedral main door: big broad steps you could get a carriage up – sideways. The Bishop and the Church people were at the top of them. The King started to ascend and most of the security ring contracted, except me and my few scanning the skyline. The Pensioners, my boss and his chosen two or three, some cathedral guards and so on moved with him. That made some space on the street and the outer ring of military closed on it. Naturally the crowd followed and pressed forward. They like to get as close as possible, you see.'

'Yes, yes, we see,' said Bancroft impatiently. 'Most of us have observed His Majesty amidst his subjects on occasion. We're not convert aboriginals fresh off the boat, you know.'

'No indeed, Father,' apologized Pelling. 'It's just that I was instructed to leave nothing—'

'He was indeed,' growled Adam. 'And he's doing exactly as I asked, if only you'd let him.'

Father Bancroft wasn't accustomed to being rebuked but, being a subtle man, he managed to give no sign of the white-hot rage he momentarily felt. He would ponder on it later; at his leisure, and in private.

'Well, it was after that . . .' Pelling faltered.

'In your own words,' ordered Adam. 'Doesn't matter if it sounds nonsense.'

Warming to his subject, Pelling shrugged. 'The first I knew, there was a sort of ... nothing. I mean a lot of the noise suddenly stopped – that was obvious – but also ... it was like a load of air was rushing in to where the King was – or had been. That was when I looked over and saw that they'd gone: King, Legate, Bishop, cathedral steps and all – they'd ... gone somewhere else. There was a second or two of silence and then the screaming and shouting started. And that's about it. Can I have a drink?'

'No,' said Adam. 'Continue on a little further. Cover another quarter of an hour or so.'

Pelling didn't seem to mind. In fact, he'd just recalled that the next instalment reflected well on himself. With things in their current state of flux it might be wise to impress as wide a range of people as possible and maximize his career options.

'By that stage I had two Onslow retainers with me,' he said. 'Ex-gamekeepers with rifled fowling pieces for picking off anything untoward. I got them to clear me a way through the crowd – people were panicking and stampeding away, you see – to where the action was. Only it wasn't. Like I said, there was nothing left, right down to the bare earth the steps had rested on. Actually, it was pretty nasty because whatever happened had come down like a knife ...'

'Now mark this,' Adam advised, looking up from his cup of wine.

'Some of the people on the edge of ... what happened had been cut,' Pelling went on. 'It was like they'd been under a blade that'd dropped. There were hands and toes missing, a few nose tips sliced off and a couple of poor devils cut in half like a joint of beef. Believe it or not, we had to put one of them out of his misery 'cause he must have been sideways to—'

'Proceed,' ordered Father Bancroft brusquely, applying a cologne-drenched kerchief to his nostrils and waving Pelling on.

'Um ... well, it chanced I was the most senior security person left so I got a cordon together out of the remaining cathedral guards and Onslow people and we sealed the area off. Then I searched the ground where the personages had been but found nothing. It wasn't hot or cold or anything like that; just completely normal. After that I tried to get the town isolated and sent a messenger to—'

'That'll do,' said Adam, pushing aside the remains of his meal. 'There's no more that can particularly help us. Now then, assuming no one's proposing a purely natural cause for this occurrence ...?'

He looked round the table and ascertained that no one was. Pelling meanwhile took the opportunity to resume his proper and obscure place at the side of the hall.

'Right. So we are left considering an *un*natural causation. I understand there's a team being assembled in London for me to consult regarding this specific aspect when I get there. In the meanwhile, let's hear from the thaumaturgists present – by way of a preliminary opinion. I'm asking you: is this any magic you could reproduce or have you ever heard of anything similar?'

The two Archbishop's men didn't even need to confer.

'Never,' said one, an enormous, hard-eyed lout rendered even more imposing by his scarlet magician's gown. 'Magic is merely a product of the mind and it's only as powerful as the will behind it. No mortal's as strong as that. No single mind could generate so widespread or profound an effect.'

'No *single* mind?' asked Adam, alive to the slightest whisper of ambiguity.

'Nope!' replied the giant, entirely confident. 'And since,

46

as you must surely know, we are frighteningly alone in the prison of our own intellect – save for the presence of Almighty God – such tricks as you're implying will for ever remain unperformed.'

'To put it as bluntly as one can, sir,' interposed the second magician, a Turkish convert by the look of him, 'team sorcery exists only in myth and hope. Each generation of thaumaturgists strives for it and each has always failed. Sad to say, like all men, a magician must think his thoughts – or work his magic – quite alone.'

Hillaire, a tall and cadaverous man possessed of a chilling amount of reserve, was sitting bolt upright in his seat toying with his cigarette case and lucifers.

'I concur with what has been said,' he advised – and that was that. Adam could be satisfied this particular avenue was fully explored and found a dead-end if so eminent a magician declared it so.

'Right then,' said Adam, once again acting as chairman. 'It's nothing we know of or can do ourselves. However, assuming it didn't happen by chance, *someone* can do the trick and that's distinctly worrying. Moreover, this some-one who's cleverer than we are has the King of England and a Papal Legate in his probably far from safe-keeping.' He held up the subversive broadsheet between a disapproving thumb and finger to illustrate his point. 'Any ideas?'

'We thought that's what you're here for,' said Longstaff, eyeing Adam challengingly. 'We didn't come to the edge of a kingdom that's half ablaze to hear ourselves speak!'

Adam pointedly let the remark die stillborn in the embarrassed silence that followed. He'd seen countries that were *really* afire, and complete nations on their way out. He couldn't share in the excitable mood. Hillaire, the Master of Magic, went so far as to grimace in displeasure at such . . . unprofessionalism.

Adam got to his feet. 'Has anyone else got anything – vaguely useful – to add?'

Father Bancroft rushed in to rescue the meeting's reputation. 'I can give you some negative evidence,' he said.

'It's often as good as the other sort,' said Adam, donning his smoky red greatcoat.

'We have even the hard-core apostates and heretics riddled through and through with agents,' said the priest-cum-spy chief with not a little pride. 'We know what the poor wretches have for breakfast – except this time.'

'No, not *this* time,' agreed Adam rather mockingly.

'We've not had the ghost of the embryo of the genesis of this episode,' Bancroft persevered. 'This is not the doing of any of the old organizations. I tell you, there is some new thing abroad!'

Adam did not directly respond but nodded his thanks to them. Then, beckoning Frederick Pelling to follow in his wake, he set off for Dover Station. The others could catch him up or not, as they wished.

As he strode along he wondered why the mention of 'new' things sounded strangely familiar – and disturbing. Then, amidst the market-day throng in the High Street, beside the famous forty-tiered monument to the Unknown Recusant, he suddenly remembered.

How odd, he mused, that there should be any subject on which Father Bancroft and Sir Michael Clarke could agree.

~

'Do you mind if I give you a word of advice?' said Pelling.

Adam smiled insincerely at him. 'Of course not,' he said. 'I need all the counsel I can get.'

Pelling looked from side to side but needn't have feared. Father Bancroft and his party were well out of earshot, further down the train. Aside from an ear-trumpet-wielding, deaf-as-a-post dowager lady in a mourning-black crinoline, Adam and he had this part of the carriage to themselves.

'Well, it's this,' he said softly, leaning across close to Adam. 'You're making too many enemies here. People like Bancroft and Longstaff aren't spoken to like that – not ever. I'm frightened of being associated with you.'

Adam smiled again, this time more genuinely. He stretched back into his seat and regarded Pelling.

'I owe them nothing,' he said eventually. 'There's some crucial factor in this that they're not disclosing: some information being wilfully held back. I don't know what it is yet but I'll rectify that in London. At the same time I'll convey my low opinion of such treatment to their superiors—'

'I'm not sure they have any,' interrupted Pelling. Adam was unperturbed by the suggestion.

'Everyone has a superior,' he said. 'Everyone. It's merely a matter of finding him. As for you and your consider-ations – well, you'll just have to take your chances tagging on to me. After all, we've each of us got to die sometime!'

Pelling pretended to laugh but then realized to his horror that Adam really meant what he said. That ended conversation between them for a while as Pelling explored the rich and heady world of his jangling emotions.

Adam's behaviour at the station had been of a piece with that at the minster conference. Flinging some golden sovereigns (whose value he clearly did not appreciate) across at the railway clerk, he had seemed to expect that a locomotive would be directly put at his disposal.

Disabused of this notion by the station master and monarch-of-all-he-surveyed representative of the Kentish and Wealden Railway Joint Stock Company, Adam and Pelling waited for the next London express train in the comfort of the patrician-class lounge. Adam's physical needs were apparently fully met by the minster repast, but Fred Pelling sought comfort in a quart bottle of Harveys of Lewes Armada Ale. Adam disdainfully paid the bill with, by way of variety, Vatican lire – good currency wherever His Holiness had been heard of.

It was through the ornately engraved scrolls and whorls of the lounge window that they observed Father Bancroft, Longstaff and the two wizards arrive at the station. Hillaire was not of their party. He would be on his way to Sussex by now, to report to his master by the sea at Pevensey Bay. To make up for that loss there were three other men whom Adam hadn't seen before. He studied and then dismissed them . . . mere messengers and muscle of the English Church, unworthy of any significant place in his deliberations.

When Adam and Fred were summoned at last on to the appropriate platform, the two little groups could no longer ignore each other's existence. In a momentary clearing of the smoke and steam Adam locked eyes with Bancroft and smiled politely. The priest returned the compliment but sought to board the train just that bit more speedily than necessary. Longstaff, too honest or proud for dissemblance, glared at the Papal Officer and caused Pelling to wish himself somewhere, anywhere, else.

Oblivious to any embarrassment, Adam made himself comfortable on one of the train's upholstered couches, stowing the carpet bag that was his only luggage on the rack above. Shortly after, the whistle was blown by a liveried rail-servant and the black and gold *'Bretwalda'* class engine, with its four first (and only) class carriages pulled away.

It was shortly after this that Pelling had proffered his unsolicited advice and Adam's response had so unnerved him. Accordingly they'd passed through the fourteen-hundred-yard miracle of the Shakespeare Cliff Tunnel, one of the marvels of English Christendom engineering, in unappreciative silence. Conversation wasn't in fact resumed until they were crossing the sturdy ironwork of the Stour River Railway Bridge, a dozen or so miles out of Dover – and only then because, embarking on a fresh adventure, Adam felt light-headed and playful.

'Not far from here,' he said, gesturing out of the left-hand window, 'is the village of Lympne, the *Portus Lemanis* of the ancient Romans. Evidently there are the remains of an antique *castella*. I should like to see that.'

Pelling listlessly followed the line of Adam's hand but was unable to observe any such thing.

'And will you?' he asked.

'No,' answered Adam succinctly. 'There will not be time. Also, will we be passing Tonbridge?'

'No idea,' said Pelling. 'I'm a south-west Surrey man. This Kent and Sussex business is as foreign as Jericho to me. Why do you ask?'

'I'm sure we do pass through Tonbridge,' Adam said, as though thinking aloud. 'I distinctly recall there being a large railway terminus there.'

'You know it?'

'I was born there – or nearby,' said Adam. 'In a hamlet called Forest Row. I believe my family still reside there.'

'Won't you visit them?' asked Pelling, puzzled.

'No,' replied Adam, it being his turn to be puzzled. 'What for?'

An hour or so out of Dover they did indeed roll into Tonbridge town. Adam looked about the dozen acres of sidings, offices and warehouses which flowed over the illegally neglected defensive walls with no more interest than he'd reserved for any other part of the journey's unfolding scenery. His monster status mounted to a new high in Pelling's eyes.

Entering the long dark stretch of the Bletchingly Tunnel, Adam chose to readdress his partner of the moment.

'Just for the record,' he said, smiling, 'what was your problem back there on the ferry? Why the unmerited hostility?'

Pelling felt it safest and easiest to be honest. 'It's the culture I grew up in,' he said. 'The one I work in. All my family were staunch Albionites: Lord Onslow's set-up's pretty much that way too. It's been in the air I've breathed.'

'That's all right,' said Adam. 'They're a legal party; an ancient point of view.'

Pelling wished very much that the tunnel would end so he could see Adam's face.

'It's nothing personal,' he rattled on. 'And I'm straight-down-the-line True Church myself, really. It's just that ... well, when you Papal types come over here and start—'

'Telling you what to do – I know. So you're a nationalist with a small *n*. There's nothing unique about that: we can still work together.'

'Oh good.' Pelling was agonized by the stupidity of saying such a thing even as he said it. Then, at the moment they suddenly re-entered the light, he found to his horror that an idiot, placatory grin was occupying his face. The visage of the Vatican emissary opposite, however, was sadly unreadable.

Pelling's embarrassment was mercifully short-lived, for directly after leaving the tunnel the train slowed dramatically, hurling those who happened to be on their feet forcibly into the nearest seat, lap or floorspace. Then, with a great sound of mechanical protest, the locomotive was brought to a shuddering halt. Adam, attentive to the babble of passenger bewilderment, queried the stop by raising one eyebrow at Pelling.

'I dunno. I don't think there's a station near here.'

'No, nor do I,' said Adam evenly, rashly indicating a greater study of their route than hitherto revealed.

A few minutes of unexplained waiting went by and passengers were becoming restive (rail travellers being of a social class unused to delay) when, above the noise of the engine's restrained energies, several very distinct popping sounds were heard.

'No, no station, I think,' commented Adam, a frown on his face. 'Go and get Bancroft and the others.'

Pelling rushed to do so but met the priest with his wizards and bodyguards heading in his direction. He and his words of explanation were brushed aside as they and Longstaff pushed by.

In the meantime Adam had undergone a transformation. Now he was equipped with a stubby-barrelled, 'pepper-box' pistol and a short sword was tucked into his belt. Most startling of all, his broad-brimmed hat was discarded and the resplendent greatcoat of smoky Papal red had been reversed, as it was evidently tailored to be, to reveal a buff-brown material such as might adorn the coat of any well-to-do artisan.

'Are any of you armed?' he asked peremptorily. In their astonishment at his transfiguration they all meekly answered. Longstaff had his sabre; one of Bancroft's bodyguards carried a *lady pistol*.

'Pathetic,' said Adam. '"A Kingdom ablaze", eh?' He turned to the carriage door. 'Follow me.'

'What did you expect?' remonstrated Bancroft to Adam's back. 'This isn't Poland, you know!'

Maybe Adam did know, maybe not, for he was already

gone, swinging lithely down to the ground and setting boldly off up the track, apparently indifferent to whether he was supported or not. The rest followed, assisted down or otherwise, as swiftly as age and vigour would permit.

From the convenient obscurity of the smoke and steam about the engine's steel wheels, Adam sought and found all he needed to know about what was going on. The barricade of logs up the track and the armed men behind it were plain speech in a universal language well known to him. For the sake of fullness, however, he went to seek out the driver.

He and the stoker were exactly where he expected them to be: well under cover in their cab. Adam swung up beside them.

'Any idea?' he asked concisely.

The driver recognized authority when he heard it and knew what was required of him.

'Enemies of God!' he snapped, narrowing his eyes at the dark matchstick figures up the line. A typical locomotive man, an artisan-aristocrat, proud of his uniform and long training, the driver was consumed with rage at this affront to his train, company and calling. 'We've 'eard of it 'appening in other places,' he said, 'just recent, like, but not here, though – not on the Kentish and Wealden . . .'

'They're Gideons,' confirmed the stoker, as brawny and confident as his mate. 'Madmen! They've killed railmen before, it's said – and damaged engines!'

The driver spat with impotent rage into the open firebox and looked to Adam for guidance.

'How long till we're missed – by someone who matters?' Adam asked.

The driver didn't need to think. 'We're thirty-three minutes out of Babylon, that is to say, London, begging your pardon. They'll give us an extra quarter-hour before making enquiries.'

'So between one and two hours before anything worth-while comes to help?'

'That's about the shape of it – and even then it'll only be a couple of men on horses with maybe a carbine apiece. Anyhow, you *are* train security, aren't you?'

'Is there such a thing?' asked Adam in turn.

'A few handy sort of blokes,' replied the stoker, 'but we don't see much of 'em. The company's been cutting back, sort of, and—'

The driver didn't like the tone of even this mild disloyalty. 'There's been no call for 'em!' he cut in. 'Not until recent, anyway. The last apostates or demi-demons round here were hung or burnt out while I was still training. *This* is the train security!'

He tapped the workman's knife strapped to his belt. Adam took no notice.

'Could we push that barrier aside?' he asked. 'Burst it asunder at speed?'

'No,' said the driver, badly affronted. 'We'd derail, and/or explode. You don't understand the ways of locos, mister. And anyway, if you're not train security, then who are you?'

Adam turned back the collar of his coat to show the smoky red side below.

'*Sicarii*,' the man muttered, turning his head away.

'Keep the steam up,' Adam instructed. 'We're not stopping.'

He leapt to the ground and made his way back to where Bancroft's party were sheltering.

'It's hours before we can expect help,' he told the priest, 'and I can't wait that long. Besides, they'll be on us long

55

before that and we've not enough firepower to lay them low – not rushing on in those numbers.'

'We could reverse the train,' offered Bancroft.

'Away!' said Adam. 'Last resort only. No wonder this country's in a mess if you cave in that quick. Anyhow, they'll have people at the start of the tunnel by now – stands to reason. I need something white.'

'Why, may I ask?' said Bancroft, icily cold, his face a mask.

'I'm going to parley with them. See what they want and buy some time. Here, take these.'

He retrieved his pepper-box and sword and handed them over to Fred Pelling. The Surrey man held them at arm's length as if they were hissing grenadoes.

Clearly wishing it were a viper instead, Bancroft unfastened and gave Adam his white silk cummerbund.

'You'll get it back, don't worry,' Adam reassured him, insulting in a way that couldn't really be acknowledged or countered, roughly tying the object to the end of his empty scabbard.

'Now, you two,' he said, not looking up, but signifying by a nod of his head that the two magicians were addressed, 'bide a while here but keep out of sight. Your gowns are too conspicuous. I want to retain the shock effect of there being two Rome wizards aboard; they won't be expecting that. Also, by the time I get back I want you to have raised a demon.'

The over-sized of the two thaumaturgists stared in horror at the Turk before speaking.

'We can't,' he spluttered. 'It's too dangerous!'

Adam looked up from securing the sign of parley. 'And this is safe?' he said, his blue eyes suddenly as cold and compelling as a shark's. 'Don't worry, I'll get you the time you need.'

56

The Turk, willing as he was to serve, felt obliged to support his colleague.

'We are in the open,' he protested, 'and prey to all manner of distractions. One slip in the conjuration or the binding—'

'Or the dismissal – anything!' the giant interrupted to confirm. 'Even splitting the job between two you have to be at peace, in seclusion, in finite surroundings. Besides, there's got to be an offering – and preparation!'

'So prepare,' was Adam's glib reply. 'Just be doing something conspicuous by the time I get back. Be seen and be seen at work. If you can't raise the real thing then improvise. Wizard us a sentient smoke shape or something. God knows, there's enough of that around!'

Actually, since the train had been at rest for some time now, its smoke and steam were beginning to settle and clear. Great patches of sunlight were punching through the cover, threatening to expose them to universal view. Noting this, Adam waved those about him back into the recesses of the train.

'Keep out of sight until the sight of you is some use,' he said. 'Meanwhile, I'm off.'

Colonel Longstaff looked as if he wanted to say something, but in a second's hesitation lost the chance for ever. He was thus left with the second string task of mustering the train's feeble defences and keeping its furious passengers aboard.

By then Adam was a dozen paces up the track, beyond the engine and very alone. He slowly waved his instant flag from side to side and was careful to show his other arm held well away from his body. Not *too* confident, still less too afraid, he covered half the distance to the barricade and waited patiently. The situation wasn't entirely unfamiliar to him – it was not so different from his vigil below a Druze citadel in *Syria Secunda*, the wait before the 'protestant' log stockade in Iroquois-League country. Whatever the relative strengths of the situation, those in cover had to be given time to assess the person petitioning their kind attention. Seeing the glint of distant perspective glasses, Adam tried to look suitably intimidated and yet inoffensive. Human curiosity being what it is, he was fairly sure they wouldn't just shoot him down.

At length, three figures detached themselves from the barrier, muskets held across folded arms in pointed defiance of the strict rules of parley. If he hadn't suspected himself to be under telescopic scrutiny, Adam would have smiled.

Close up, in their own, unhurried sweet time, the three men were slightly more worrying than as distant nuisances. He recognized the type straight away – as well he might, for he saw a fair example of the breed each day in his mirror.

There was one obvious leader, a stocky yeoman in farmer's-best black, and he stood a little forward of his henchmen, a dozen or so paces off.

'Hello there.' He smiled. 'And who might you be?' The Kentish accent was rich and assured.

'Train security,' answered Adam, deliberately keeping his responses both crisp and sufficient so as to placate. He hoped his long-discarded Sussex tones had been revived convincingly.

The yeoman smiled again and shifted the heavy musket further up his broad chest. One of his men was signalled forward and with the minimum of deft pats and strokes it was determined that Adam was unarmed. This man then resumed his former station, thus allowing his partner to lower his rock-steady gun from its beeline on Adam's head.

'I see,' the leader said. 'Took your time coming, didn't you?'

'The passengers were frit,' said Adam. 'Come to that, so was I.'

This time the man of Kent failed to smile; he'd clearly set humour aside from his life. The soldiery remained similarly unamused.

'There's no cause for their fear,' he said eventually. 'Nor yours either, I think. We're not apostates or savages. We'll recognize your parley.'

'Praise be,' said Adam, trying to sound oh-so relieved. 'So what can I do for you?'

The chief ambusher sucked upon his teeth, and gazed into Adam's face. 'Any priests aboard?' he asked. 'Any religious – that is to say monkish folk or nuns?'

'A few I've noted,' said Adam cautiously.

'Or any men of Rome? Any arms and eyes of the Church Universal?'

'Likewise.'

The man nodded. 'Right, we'll have them. Otherwise you're free to go.'

'What will you do with them?' asked Adam.

For the first time, proper suspicion clouded the man's eyes. 'That's for us to know and you to wonder,' he said. 'Be thankful for what you're offered.'

'I am. I am,' Adam said hastily.

The man nodded. 'That's good. Their fate is none of your business – in this world or the next. It's no one's business. You go and gather them and then move off. That's all. Otherwise we storm the train. We'd prefer not to. Contrary to what you may hear, we're against free effusions of blood – not even in these, the last of days.'

'Thank God for that!' said Adam, audibly relieved.

'Be sure you do just that,' replied the man. 'And while

you're about it, you will distribute these words to those who remain on your loco.'

So saying he released one hand from his gun and drew a sheaf of printed sheets out of his frock coat.

'Tell them to read and learn and act,' he said.

'I will, I will.' Adam stepped forward to receive the offered pamphlets. The step turned, too fast to be registered let alone prevented, into a pounce and a leap and Adam's outstretched hand, now a rigid lance, rocketed into the man's cravat-covered throat. He fell back like a toppled idol, croaking horribly.

His compatriots hefted their muskets, barely delayed by surprise. However, Adam's momentum carried him into one before anything more positive could be done. As he went, his right hand moved to his belt buckle and withdrew the stubby blade concealed within its design. He planted this firmly into his enemy's eye socket and embraced the corpse as a shield against the survivor's revenge.

As he'd feared, those sent to meet him were no mere bandits, no income-supplementing farmboys reviving a style of crime a century dead. The last of the parley party took Adam's treachery and the death of his companions entirely in his stride. Whatever he might have felt about the matter was not allowed to affect his reaction. With all the time in the world, he took calm and careful aim at Adam's head.

'So much for parley,' he said, advancing step by cautious step to make sure of a killing shot. 'So much for honour. And so much for "train security"!'

Adam was shifting the body of the man he'd killed, the silver buckle blade protruding from its face, trying to cover himself from the inevitable shot. Against such an unflustered foe, he knew it was an outside chance, barely worth the humiliating effort. Worse still, from the corner of his eye he noted figures piling over the railtrack barricade and heading in his direction.

The man with the gun suddenly moved, perfectly poised and balanced, crablike to one side. Adam could not heave his dead assistant so deftly and for a second the man had a clear shot to Adam's temple. He made good use of it.

Adam did not permit the thunder of the musket or his wonder at still being alive to delay him. Dropping the dead man, he closed with the puzzled survivor and swiftly broke his neck in the way he'd been taught as a child.

Pausing only to pick up one of the discarded pamphlets, Adam set off at speed for the train. Once or twice the projectiles of those pursuing him, a musket ball or two and what felt like a crossbow bolt, disturbed the air around his ears and spurred him on to greater efforts.

He had to take these particular shots more seriously than that which had gone before. The Vatican-provided amulet round his neck would not work a second time. It took several hundred magician-hours and high-level skills to imbue an object with sufficient attracting and disabling thaumaturgic force to protect its wearer from shot and shell. None but the most favoured were provided with more than one from the jealously guarded stock in the armoury at Castel sant' Angelo.

He would have preferred to husband it and save his life in some more conventional way, but the man had been too blasted . . . good for that. But such was life. Accordingly, what was once worth a prince's ransom on the open market now hung spent and useless on Adam's chest, the ambusher's musket ball lovingly attached to it. He had no time for things that had served their purpose and, snapping the holding cord, he flung the glass bauble aside.

61

Let some yokel find it and brighten the life of his lady-love.

Adam's life happened to be bright enough as it was at that moment, for all his frivolous thoughts. Strong legs and hard-won stamina had added a score of paces to the distance between him and the mob behind, but they would be with him soon enough. Dashing past the loco's head, he called out for his companions to show.

Only Colonel Longstaff and the two magicians answered the summons but, in the event, even that poor display proved to be sufficient. With a passion that commanded obedience, Longstaff ordered Adam to stand behind him and he was very happy to comply. Only then, stationary and mildly winded, did he notice that they were in the bounds of a crudely drawn pentagram. In the space of time that he had gained, it had been etched with a stick in the gravel and earth partly in the shadow of the first carriage, its hasty construction largely out of sight of those on the barricade, even had their attention not been diverted. Adam was now gratified to note how the onward rush had been checked by the first glimpse of the magicians.

Sight of the scarlet robe of a Rome-trained thaumaturgist gave universal pause for thought throughout Christendom – and wherever else His Holiness's expanding interests reached. This was doubly true if the wizard was clearly about his unnatural, otherworldly work. Seeing the two magicians acting in unison, perhaps hearing the distant sound of chanting, two dozen armed men were prey to grave consternation. They slowed, looked around and began to consult.

'I've beheaded them,' advised Adam, his even breath fully restored. 'They've no officer. Just one push and—'

The magicians 'pushed'; the Turk's upheld hand

crashed down like an executioner's axe to point four-square at the enemy a hundred paces off. The giant gestured frantically at the pentagram.

'Now,' said the Turk, his face deathly pale and running with sweat. 'They are yours!'

Something . . . rose out of the trackside, fashioning itself into a giant parody of human form from the dirt and dust and stones. Its rudimentary head slowly turned to regard the halted men up the track and two almond-shaped gaps that might have been eyes glowed with pale yellow light from . . . somewhere else.

Like the flight of a bird of prey, it ascended, ponderously at first, leaving behind a scatter of earth, but then ever more graceful and speedy as it arced towards the ambushers. A scream in its own octave-leaping demon voice added to the cries and screams of those it was approaching. A few diehards loosed off shots, punching holes in the insubstantial body, to entirely no avail.

Adam and company watched, fascinated, as the demon's shadow covered the clump of men, darkening their frightened, upturned faces. Then the beast itself fell upon them, as sudden and final as a plummeting anvil.

A few, the more individualistic or percipient, had already detached themselves from the group and so escaped the demonic nemesis. The rest howled and fell writhing amidst the scattered remains of the creature.

Adam studied the escapees and judged them to be beyond all bar the flukiest of shots. Accordingly they were permitted to go and obligingly spread news of the terror to their compatriots. The vast majority of his former opponents, however, were going nowhere as death and stillness claimed them one by one. He watched the mound of dirt-splattered men until it was finally quiescent, and only then did Adam feel it quite ... proper to say anything.

'Is it safe to step out?' he asked, indicating the homely pentagram.

The giant and the Turk were past sensible words but the latter nodded an answer even as he sank to his knees, exhausted. The giant, determined to show as little weakness as he could, looked equally fit to drop but resisted his body and mind's pressing demands. His sense of grievance lent him strength.

'You don't know,' he gasped, pointing feebly at Adam, 'what we've done. You've no *idea* how close . . .'

The Turk had recovered a little and he raised his right hand to display the fresh and bleeding stump of a severed index finger.

'We had no offering.' He heaved out the words, one by one. 'But they have to be appeased . . .'

The giant showed a similarly maimed extremity. 'Have *you* ever severed a part of your living flesh?' he asked angrily. 'Have you ever been asked to do that and had seconds to decide?'

'No,' replied Adam, splendidly unmoved. 'But in my occupation I don't rule out the possibility . . .'

'It's painful, I can tell you that.'

'Doubtless.'

'And even so, we barely held the creature. You can't *do* outside, ad-hoc summonings! It only just swiving worked!'

'But it did,' said Adam, indicating the subject was closed. 'What do you want? A medal? All right, bravo and all that. Pat on the head. You did what was asked, what was necessary – you survived. Let's move on.'

By now, Bancroft and Pelling and the more intrepid of the passengers were emerging to investigate matters. Adam didn't want to get involved in a lot of chat and paused only to recover his arms from a shock-silenced Fred Pelling before walking off.

In approaching the dead men strewn across the track, Adam kept his pepper-box to hand in case the demon hand hadn't been laid on heavily enough in some instances. He needn't have worried. Close up, it was clear that the earth with which the creature had clothed itself had burned and seared whatever it touched. Those not killed outright had choked on lungfuls of the demon stuff. Every eye, ear, nose and mouth had been clogged full of it and burned to the bone in consequence. Adam had seen whole towns of dead in his time, but had to admit to being mildly impressed.

There was nothing left for him to do and nothing worthwhile taking, so, as the train crew and Bancroft's security gingerly organized the clearance of the track, Adam went and resumed his seat.

~

'Good,' agreed Colonel Longstaff, 'but not invincible.'

'I was not alleging that,' said Father Bancroft, fingering the crucifix about his neck: the only outward sign of inward agitation. 'No one but God is . . . insurmountable. What I do maintain is that our laborious calculations must be assessed anew.'

'More your side of things,' said Longstaff, looking out of the train window. 'Let me know what you come up with. Meanwhile I'll watch over him. In London, between my military observers and your network, we have him snuggly sewn up. On the plus side, at least he kills Levellers and saves us the trouble. There's little new harm he can do.'

The priest shook his ever-troubled head. 'Wrong. I expected bad but this is worse. I know his kind better than you. He is capable of unstitching anything we have "sewn". Our best hope is that not too much escapes from his unravelling.'

Adrift amidst the needlework metaphors, the Colonel fell silent. Bancroft, he thought, was lost in his distorting-mirror existence of spies and triple plots. He lacked . . . ballast. Longstaff's universe was more solid, more weighty. It didn't really wobble. Studying the – his – world streaming past, he remained confident that all he saw could not be undone (there he went again – more sewing) by a single madman from nowhere.

# A SECOND BLAST ON THE TRUMPET TO THE PEOPLE OF ENGLAND-THAT-IS AND ENGLAND-THAT-IS-TO-BE

WHEREFORE HIS MOST GRACIOUS MAJESTY, CHARLES, THE FOURTH OF THAT NAME, KING OF ENGLAND, WALES AND CORNWALL; PROTECTOR OF MANNIN AND THE ISLES; PATRON OF THE JERUSALEM AND JAFFA CITADELS, HAS BEEN FAVOURED BY ALMIGHTY G*D WITH A FRESH REVELATION LIKE TO THAT VISITED ON ST PAUL (SAUL THAT WAS) ON THE ROAD TO DAMASCUS, HE DESIRES HIS SUBJECTS TO *KNOW* THAT HE ABSOLVES THEM OF ALL USURPED LOYALTY, OBEDIENCE AND FEALTY TO THAT *APPARATUS* KNOWN TO THE JUSTIFIED AS *THE BEAST, THE GOVERNMENT OF THE WHORE OF BABYLON*. THEREFORE IT NOW DEVOLVES TO THEM AS THEIR BOUNDEN DUTY TO WRESTLE MIGHT AND MAIN WITH THE PRESENCE OF *SATAN* IN THEIR MIDST AND BRING ALL SUCH TO RUIN DIRECTLY – THIS BEING THE WISH, COMMAND AND FERVENT PRAYER OF THEIR SOVEREIGN LIEGE, CHARLES, REX.

HIS SIGNATURE AND SEAL HEREWITH.

SMITE THE PRIESTS, DASH OUT THE BRAINS OF *BABYLON'S* CHILDREN. THOSE DAMNED BY ALMIGHTY G*D HAVE NO TITLE IN THEIR PROPERTY OR LIVES.

'They couldn't resist that last bit, could they?' commented Adam, passing the pamphlet he'd taken to Pelling. 'It was semi-sane up to there but the strain of being normal got too much, poor things.'

Fred Pelling scanned the document. He might well be of mildly patriotic sympathies but had no time for this full-scale attack on the world-as-it-was.

'They're brain sick,' he agreed dismissively, handing

the tirade back to Adam. 'Brain sick, but dangerous with it.'

'Dangerous certainly,' confirmed Adam, musing to himself.

'Though you dealt with them rapid enough,' said Pelling in as uninflected a tone as he could manage. Adam had been frustratingly reticent about the ambush, ignoring the passengers' inquest. He seemed to regard it as nothing of any great import, whereas Pelling and everyone else were polishing the story to tell to their grandchildren.

'Only because I'm that vital bit better trained in a specialist line of work,' Adam said. 'And also because I'm a man in a hurry and willing to take risks.'

Pelling gazed out of the window at the cottages of Coulsdon as the train steamed by. Some beaming churl children were waving wildly to the loco from the village crossing. A kindly man at heart, Pelling would ordinarily have waved back, but today he looked through them. By the time Coulsdon and its friendly junior inhabitants were dots in the distance, he had made an important decision.

'It was the Levellers,' he said, turning back to Adam. 'That's the thing you've not been told. Those men you killed, the ambush, that blasphemous pamphlet – Leveller-stuff, all of them.'

Adam smiled, as reassuring as a crocodile. 'I was wondering how long it would be before someone could bring themselves to say that name,' he said softly. 'You're the first honest man I've met in England, Frederick Pelling. Maybe you won't end up on a rope when this is sorted, after all.'

'Another joke?' asked Pelling, his jaw set and face grim.

'Probably,' answered Adam, unintimidated. Being who he was, he had no call to fear even the anger of patient men. 'You've spoken aloud what I already guessed but was waiting for someone to mention. If it'd taken till London to do it, you'd have been included in the fate I have stored for some others. Why all this bashfulness, I wonder? That's probably the key to it.' His face hardened and his voice altered from its previous amiable amble. 'Are you a Leveller, Fred Pelling? Do you know anything else you should have told me?'

'Certainly not!' blurted Pelling, knowing this was no moment to stand on dignity. 'And all I was going to add was – well, maybe they have the King!'

The terrible mask of anger threatening action to follow lifted from Adam's face like a shift of scenery. 'Oh no.' He grinned. 'I don't think so. That would just be politics. You lot could deal with that. No, the Levellers don't have the King – though they might think so. Something bigger has them both.'

Other than that he would say no more and was soon asleep, as contented and easy as a happy child. Past the vast Addington Park Citadel of the Archbishop of Canterbury, past the permanent 'Pride of Christendom' exhibition in the Crystal Palace and the Society of Jesus' Dulwich College, over the Surrey Canal, right to the railway's breach in the walls of London, Fred Pelling watched the unlined face opposite him and searched it for signs of humanity.

London Bridge Station and journey's end found him still entirely bereft of comfort.

*ENCYCLOPEDIA BRITANNICA 2020 EDITION*

LEVELLERS: a heretical and subversive movement current in England since the closing days of 'the Great Civil War' (1642–1649), but at its most widespread and active in the middle to late 20th century. The Levellers' belief was formed during the final years of the great 'Protestant heresy' and if this enormity lives on anywhere it is amongst the underground activists, or 'pastors' as they call them, of the Leveller groups. For all its egalitarian dogma, the Leveller heresy was and is sustained and propagated by an intensely secret and tightly knit group of these pastors whose numbers were never very large.

Their undeniable organisation and high degree of motivation from time to time allowed them to take advantage of discontents and grievances among the people and thereby transform their elitist heresy into a popular assault on the proper orthodoxy and the divinely ordained status quo. By far the worst of these attempts was the so-called 'Thames Valley Crusade' of 1990 [*See cross-reference*] where Leveller elements cleverly took control of what had started as a minor breakdown of public order (caused by unpopular troop levying for service in the Ukraine). The situation so deteriorated that by the summer of that year much of the Thames Valley was avowedly 'Leveller' and several major towns were in their control, including Reading. Two separate detachments of royal troops had been soundly beaten in the open field and the rebels (for such they were) had framed a number of impudent demands regarding desired changes in the Church and State, and the system of taxation.

Anticipating such a serious turn of events, the Archbishops of London and Canterbury had jointly called for a crusade to restore proper order and religious freedom to the faithful in the area. This was ratified and confirmed by Pope Simon Dismas when the news reached Rome in the early summer, whereupon volunteers from all nations . . .

. . . and in the chaos which unavoidably followed the capture and sacking of the town, elements of two Leveller regiments were able to make a fighting retreat and then disperse, thus escaping the fate visited upon their colleagues in rebellion. From this sad remnant, and those few cadres not committed by the Levellers' elder-pastors to their 'all or nothing' gamble of the Reading debacle, there later arose the fanatical Gideon Bands: cell-based underground groups which practised increasingly random terrorist attacks on what they termed 'Babylonian' society. Whilst productive of a plentiful harvest of horror, they achieved little and recruited less, only rising to prominence in the troubled latter years of the reign of Charles IV . . .

Fresh from her eventful train ride, the 'deaf-as-a-post dowager lady' stood in front of the Whitehall Citadel and hesitated. No matter how favourable the light or season, the great squat edifice always appeared grim. That was the builders' intention in the seventeenth century and in each successive expansion and strengthening over the years. Looming black and baroque over the puppet Parliament and Royal Palace, it made the required point with ease.

In lingering even briefly, the 'Dowager' came to the attention of the guards at the gate. Their hard eyes challenged her to advance or flee and obliged the woman to come to a decision. Thoroughly frisked by a rare female trooper retained for such occasions, she was then led into and through the siege-proof walls. Overhead, the shrivelled heads on spikes gibbered and cried, obliged by magic to speak of the crimes and opinions that had brought them there.

The Papal troops had every right and reason to be vigilant. Mere months ago, a crazed terrorist had driven a coach and four packed with powder against Norwich Cathedral, blowing himself, the Bishop and half the building into the next world. Even someone as patently harmless as the 'Dowager' was tracked on her way by the eyes of hidden snipers as she progressed from search to search and each new interrogation. Eventually she emerged from the chambers and crooked ways into the courtyards beyond, where she was coralled with a mob of other low-grade supplicants and visitors, covered by a culverin complete with attendant crew. Just beyond the roped off area stood a line of red-coated Papal soldiers, men from every land of Christendom (except, this being England, England itself), observing pilgrim and priest alike with neutral expressions.

When her turn came, she made herself known to the clerk in charge and settled down to wait, sitting on a huge, barred drain cover, an antique from days past when London's sewers sheltered demi-demons. From time to time a diversion presented itself, a resplendent bishop's coach and escort or a clattering formation of dragoons back from patrol, but these aside the hours passed slowly. The woman declined to take part in the full rosary organized by a crippled negro priest.

Finally, when the sun was almost set and she was definitely depressed, a captain of the Palatine Grenadiers, no less, came to take her to the Archbishop of London.

His Holiness's senior representative in the British Isles was quite some way shorter than the 'Dowager' – but that was his only disadvantage. The floor behind his titanic desk was subtly raised for maximum intimidatory effect. The desk's freedom from paper and clutter served the same purpose, indicating that the whole attention of the Church Universal was being brought to bear on each and every visitor.

Behind the Archbishop loomed two great portraits, one of Simon Dismas, the present, 111th, holder of the Apostolic throne, the other a lurid treatment of the Sacred Heart. The 'Dowager' looked briefly at all three and averted her eyes.

The meeting began with prayer, a few words seeking blessing on what was to come. The woman crossed herself at the appropriate point but didn't otherwise participate. Like many other of her fellow actresses she was, in private, an agnostic. Now was not the time, however, to make it a point of discussion. She was not invited to sit down.

'Right then,' said the Archbishop, suddenly becoming

relaxation itself, 'to business. I've heard the bare bones of what happened, but you can tell me your version. Would you like a coffee before you start to wet your whistle?'

She smiled gratefully but shook her head. People of her class and profession didn't get offered such expensive refreshment every day of the week and ordinarily she'd have jumped at the chance. Now, though, she wanted to get it over with and be safely on her way.

'Suit yourself. Off you go then.'

The woman tried maintaining eye contact as she spoke but gave up in short order. The Archbishop's probing, asiatic little face, with burning eyes and nodding goatee beard, unsettled her. None of her stage training would be of any value before such fully justified confidence.

'I got the train with them and really played my part,' she said, with the tiniest hint of pride in her abilities. 'They spoke quite freely in front of me, taken in by my ear trumpet and lack of interest.'

'So he's careless then?' interrupted the Archbishop eagerly. 'A man who doesn't pay attention to detail?'

The woman thought hard, knowing it was in her best interests to be scrupulously honest.

'No ... I don't think so,' she replied. 'I'd say, off hand, he's more a man who doesn't care, and that's a different matter.'

'He frightened you?' hazarded the Archbishop.

'Oh, yes,' said the woman, glad she'd not had to make that point. 'He's a cold one all right.'

'That effect can be learned,' butted in the Archbishop, somewhat tetchy. 'It doesn't necessarily signify anything.'

The woman happily conceded the issue and her mistake, if any.

'The rest of the party didn't join him and the Surrey man,' she went on. 'I judged there'd been a falling out at

Dover Cathedral, not that it seemed to concern the Roman. He talked about the journey and the places we went through – though he knew more about them than he let on. Apparently he has family there – Tonbridge way – though not planning to visit them. That shocked the Surrey fellow.'

'Interesting,' mused the Archbishop, noting something with a golden inkstick in a little pad that hung about his neck. 'Discretion prevented me asking information on that score.'

'He also was talking about the Levellers. There was something he'd worked out for himself and he was annoyed he'd had to do that. I think some heads are going to roll if he has any say in it.'

The Archbishop remained silent; significantly so in the actress's attuned judgement.

'Then there was the business with the ambush,' she continued. 'He just took charge there, like he was used to such things. And it was horrible, really horrible . . . I don't like to talk about it.'

The Archbishop raised slightly widened eyes at her.

'Though I will if you require, of course,' she added hurriedly.

'Yes, I'm sorry to be the cause of your subjection to such an experience,' he said, with genuine – or at least courteous – regret. 'Tell me, what was it that most distressed you, the demonic manifestation, the deaths or what?'

The actress was not so sure that his concern sprang from compassion as from a collector's interest in human responses to extremity. She decided to play it safe and short.

'All of it, Your Grace. I'm not used to such barbarities.'

The Archbishop, who had a low opinion of the stage in

general and who knew (or had heard) of the ways of actresses, took leave to doubt she was quite such a sensitive flower. He felt sure the woman was no stranger to moral 'barbarities' of one sort or another.

'Indubitably,' he said in a dry tone. 'Still, at least our "man of action" from Rome saved you from ravishment or worse.'

Now it was the actress's turn to be of a differing opinion. She thought it unlikely that loco bandits would behave much worse than some of the more respectable organizations she knew of. The Church had been known to lay a heavy hand on some of the wilder exuberances of the acting profession.

'Praise God for that,' she said, however.

The Archbishop looked out of the window, apparently distracted by the arrival of some technologically trendy bishop's armoured steam wagon in the inner courtyard far below. In reality he saw nothing, for the computer precursor he had made of his mind was processing facts and opinion, and had no time for other diversions. A brass clock on the wall noisily ticked the minutes away and the actress pondered on the glorious liberation when she would be out from this spider's web.

'And so?' he said eventually, turning back to regard her with surpassing interest.

The actress knew exactly what was meant. Her judgement of human nature, together with her dramatic skills, was what she'd been hired for.

'He's formidable,' she said, concisely and with confidence. 'And I don't think there's much "self" left in him either: someone's done a very thorough job.'

The Archbishop nodded acknowledgement of the half compliment.

'And since all normal ambition's been burned away,'

she pressed rapidly on, 'he'd be hard to stop or mislead. Bancroft and the others there were just hanging on to his coat tails – out of their class and depth. That's the problem of provincial societies like England: you can always come up against people forged in fiercer fires.'

The Archbishop looked again at the red and gold steamer from which armed retainers and priests were issuing in profusion. He appeared to have no dispute with what had been said.

'Right,' he said, not bothering to look at her, 'that's good. You did well. Collect your engagement fee from the secretary outside. Tell him I said to add ten lire to it – the silver sort, not paper. And leave your latest address. We may require your services again. We also need your utmost discretion, but I don't have to stress that – do I, Redgrave?'

'No, indeed, Your Grace,' she replied and leapt forward to kiss his proffered hand. Her crimson painted lips lightly brushed the raised cross keys on the ruby of his seal and ring.

Then she hefted her heavy black dress and rushed away, glad for once to be heading for the anonymity of home and the east end slums.

Left alone, the Archbishop of London sat and relished the silence, aside from the salutary warning of the ticking clock. Life was short, it said to him, and of finite duration, ever slipping away. He would not always have to be here in this fortress, in this world, wrestling with the consequences of Original Sin. There would one day be an end to it, and rest of some or other kind.

In the meanwhile, though ... With heavy heart and furrowed brow, he unlocked the desk drawer and fetched forth, for its umpteenth study that day, the latest threatening letter from the King of England.

~

'It's not exactly Rome the Eternal, is it?' said Adam.

Neither he nor Pelling had ever been to London before, but Adam was as unimpressed as Fred was, metaphorically speaking, slack-jawed with admiration.

For reasons he'd not divulged, the Papal soldier had chosen to pass the night at an inn near to London Bridge Station rather than report to higher authority right away. Since this would certainly involve visiting the famed Westminster Citadel, Pelling was happy to go along with the delay. They'd attended evening mass in a little church by the terminus, and then passed the time till curfew in a random wander through the streets of the capital. Unbeknownst to Pelling, Adam was reconnoitring, taking soundings from every conversation he could overhear, making judgements from the looks and manner of the ordinary people. Professionally speaking, he'd been reassured. This was no pot on the point of boiling over. Aesthetically, though, he was distressed, and since this didn't matter he felt free to talk to Fred about it.

'Doesn't anyone wash or clear the streets?' he asked as they sat together outside an Ale and Chop House the next morning. He indicated a particularly offensive dead dog (or large rat).

'There's no need,' protested Pelling. 'The rain does that – eventually. Why bother about a bit of muck? It never did anyone any harm. Do you have people going round sweeping up after you in Italy, then?'

'Yes, of course,' came the answer. 'That way you don't get the almighty stink I perceive here. Do you want another drink?'

Conscious of where they must go sooner or later, Fred Pelling declined the offer. He didn't want to be weaving about and slurring his words when they got to meet the ogre awaiting them.

'Suit yourself,' said Adam, and called the waiter over to order yet more brandy and water. They were receiving suspiciously excellent service, even for this hub-of-the-city hostelry, but the soldier seemed to regard it as nothing less than his due.

Pelling continued to sip at his mug of Fullers porter and wondered if and when he would be able to spin the sights he'd seen into anecdotes for the people back home. The unsleeping activity of London Bridge: those ceaseless trains and the nearby and prosperous Hebrew quarter – they'd been wonder enough, but here was ... something else. He'd heard about the Guildhall and Exchange beforehand, but, for once, reality put tales to shame. He could well believe, as was often said, that the Mayor and merchant princes who resided in each were the equals and more of dukes and earls. The latter, after all, only had the lands the Church saw fit to permit them. The new gentry he could see about their business before him appeared to be lords of a new dispensation, captains upon an ocean of money that was not so easily tamed. You only had to look at the suits they put on their backs and the clouds of retainers that followed their heels to see that. Then there were the buildings. Pelling had never seen so much gold and marble and fine carving. Not even the four centuries of favour which had graced the Weston-Onslow family in Fred's homeland had permitted them to accumulate such fine accommodations. He stored the lesson therein away for future consideration.

Still, even here, the Church had the final – and definitive – say. Watt's world-famous 'The Defeat of Mammon' loomed on its massive column high over even the Guildhall's golden cupola, and made such point as was thought necessary. On the entrance to the Exchange there were blazoned the words 'All the World is the Lord's and the glory thereof'. The masters of the money machine passed under that message every day of their prosperous lives.

Adam, true to his nature and calling, was more capti- vated by the column of troops passing by the Guildhall in review, on their way to the Bishopsgate gap in the walls. There were a couple of regiments of the line, decently trained and clad in standard blue, some troops of heavy cavalry, in 'lobster' and plate and an unusual amount of artillery. Bringing up the rear sauntered a rag-tag of mercenaries – Burgundian *gendarmes*, Scottish archers and Irish 'gallowglasses'. They'd been paid in advance and didn't feel the need to put on much of a show.

The delegation of aldermen on the Guildhall steps smiled and saluted, pretending to cast a professional eye they didn't possess. Such ceremonies maintained the fiction that no soldier left or entered London but with its rulers' consent. After burning the place down, Charles I had felt granting such empty honours the least he could do to make amends. Then, rather than force the issue and cause embarrassment, his successors (and their Church masters) had continued the quaint practice.

A largish crowd of ordinary Londoners, obtrusive and out of place in such surroundings, cheered the soldiers on and waved little flags of St George or the red and cross keys of His Holiness.

'I think they might actually do it this time,' said Adam. 'There's some decent big guns there – cannon-royal and demi-cannon. Someone's been spending money at the foundry at long last.'

Not feeling desperately involved, Pelling nodded his agreement. The efforts to capture Caernarfon, and thus terminate the insolent existence of Free Wales, had been going on half-heartedly since he was a child – and before, for all he knew. Secure in his own world, he couldn't see the need to hold a place where you weren't welcome and where he'd never go; somewhere gaspingly poor and rainy, where the elves walked openly in the streets – such as they were. He wondered that the Church (studiously neutral on the issue) didn't veto such madness of kings.

'Happen so,' he agreed, for the sake of it. 'A chap in the bar last night said there were upward of five thousand gathered in the camp at Hendon.'

Adam smiled meaninglessly. 'Yep, that should suffice,' he opined. 'Then guerrilla warfare for a few generations – if you lot keep your nerve and don't go soft about tit-for-tat murder.'

'"You lot"?' queried Pelling.

'You English,' Adam answered.

Pelling's face couldn't help but fall. His only claimable affinity to the madman was gone. They weren't even fellow countrymen.

'Still,' the soldier continued, not noticing his companion's dismay, 'you'd think they'd have better things to worry about. Caernarfon will still be there when our little problem's sorted one way or another.'

'The show must go on,' ventured Pelling weakly. He'd had an aunt who – to the family's horror – had made her way in music hall.

'There is that,' conceded Adam. 'What we're about doesn't require great quantities of soldiery – not unless it goes wrong. This drink is vile, by the way. Do you put dead bears in the vats here?'

'Then why have any?' said Pelling, flaring momentarily, his nerves overriding wisdom. 'Keep a clear head and your mind on what you're doing – whatever the hell it might be!'

Adam finished the tumbler of alleged bruin-brandy.

'That's well said. You've a fair grasp of what's going on, even if the details escape you. I'm too relaxed. That's what you reckon, isn't it?'

'Something like that ... maybe,' said Pelling, bracing himself for another blow and period of darkness. The seconds stretched on but it failed to arrive.

'That's how it should appear,' said Adam eventually, plainly in confessional mood. 'You're looking at a happy man, Frederick: I've laid my burden down. My masters and patrons—'

'The Church?' hazarded Pelling, happy just to be awake.

'The same,' confirmed Adam. 'They've been very open with me, they've told and shown me exactly what it is they have in mind: for me, for you, for everyone – for history. Accordingly, I don't worry any more or trouble my head at all. It's a very great gift. I've seen the future and agree with it. I've every reason to seem relaxed.'

'I see,' said Pelling.

'No, you don't,' Adam corrected him, not unkindly. 'If I'm told to threaten murder in the Egyptian Caliphate, I do it. If on my return an archbishop – bearing letters from Rome – says go and straighten out the state of England, I go. Never mind that I wasn't meant ever to see that land again. There's need of a native Englishman and so that's it. I don't worry, I don't ask questions any more. There's no cause for me to be concerned again, not this side of the grave – or the other. You won't be able to see that. You were merely being polite. It's okay. Just bear in mind what I've confided.'

Pelling nodded, eyes downcast, not knowing whether to feel envy or pity.

'Right,' smiled Adam, rising to loom above the pavement table. 'I've seen and said all that's needful. Let's pay our respects to the Archbishop of Toytown.' He was in no hurry, confident that the *deaf* spy on the train had already recounted the juicier parts of recent events.

On the way, along the spacious and leafy Cardinal Wesley Road, their hansom cab passed the Royal Palace. The Lion and Unicorn flag was lowered. His Majesty was not at home.

~

They'd got the idea from the Janissaries, the elite troops of the Great Turk. Before the Ottomans were thrown out of the conquered Greek and Balkan lands, there'd been a tax in flesh on the subject Christian peoples. Boys around the age of ten were taken as tribute to the Sultan to be trained – to either perfection or death – as devoted soldiers of the Caliph and Allah.

Kept secluded and celibate in the monastery barracks of the dervish religious orders, free of family ties or national feeling, those that lived emerged into the world as masters of the military arts, despising mere death or injury and thirsty for conquest in the name of Almighty God.

The armies of Christendom came to fear them like no other enemy. After the bombardment of the famed Ottoman artillery, so thoughtfully provided for the generous Sultan by renegade Christian specialists; after the human-wave assaults of the expendable Bashi-Bazouks, soldiers knew to expect the silent charge of the Janissaries. The one ensuing certainty was that the struggle would be grim and to the finish. Christian generals learned that only the best and staunchest of men – the Knight Templars or Hospitallers of St John, for instance – would stand to face such a challenge.

It was the Janissaries who had breached the walls of

Constantinople and made it Istanbul, burnt Vienna and killed the Christian land of Georgia. They returned 'home' time and again to tear to shreds the Sparta-reborn of the Grecian despots and Gemistan Republic. Only the severe bloody nose dealt them in Adam's great-great grandfather's time, by the Blessed George Gordon, Baron Byron of the Peloponnese, had reversed the myth of invincibility. That had been a great and surpassing deliverance, in both military and psychological respects, and it was solely what he'd done to the prisoners taken that prevented the baron's rapid, posthumous, ascension to sainthood.

Even now, when they'd lost a few more battles and recruited from far and wide, from any Christian family who wore their religion lightly, from anywhere save amongst the Turks, the Sultan's fair-skinned elite remained a worry to the mighty. Visions of their battle-lines of rainbow silks and black chain-mail, their characteristic spiked fezzes and scimitars and the thunder of their kettledrums, popped unbidden into the dreams of popes and kings. One of the former, around the time the first steam engine was being banned, was musing in this way and then thought to himself: Why can't *we* have people like them? And thus Adam's fate was sealed.

A captured Janissary captain revealed (under torture, naturally) the basic mechanics of making another such as himself and a 'school' was opened on the edge of the marshes near Ravenna. It started with orphans and strays from the great European War that had just whimpered to an exhausted end. Within a quarter of a century the first carefully selected graduates of what was now the Monastery of St Peter-of-the-Sword were committed to experimental battle.

They were set against a mixed force of Ottomans and apostate Croats who were extirpating the remnants of civil

84

society in disputed Kossovo province – and dealt with them as a sabre would a lamb. The precisely detailed report of events revealed how a mere one or two Christians had been wounded in the back – and even these could be honourably accounted for. They had not mourned their dead, they had not even buried them: for why, they asked, do anything but rejoice about those who had gone to Paradise? Prisoners were taken, but for one reason only. One man in each hundred was left with a single eye, the better to lead his ninety-nine blind brethren back in chains to deliver warmest greetings to the Sultan. They looked forward, the message went on, to meeting him – albeit briefly – in person.

This event, and all the subsequent successes, were skilfully publicized along Christendom's lines of communication: the nerve system that led from Rome and ended in the Church in every village. As a result, there was never the need to extract recruits from weeping parents as the Sultan had done. Within a generation, families, rich and poor alike, were vying to offer sons to the new elite and its presiding brains could afford to pick and choose. True, the donating kin would never see or hear of their son again and he would come to forget or deny them. The compensation for that was that some part of their flesh and blood was earning prodigious grace for them and certain glory besides. Whatever else might befall the chosen son, for good or ill, his family were entitled from that day hence to append to their name and coats of arms the symbol of the Roman *gladius* sword as token of their sacrifice.

There arose the question of devising a name for this new and sharp tool in the hands of His Holiness. A cardinal, with more honesty than care for ill omens, came upon the ancient term *Sicarii* in his readings of Josephus.

Derived from the Latin *sica* for dagger, the name described the armament and *modus operandi* of some famed and feared Jewish terrorists murderously operative in the first Christian century. What started as a private after-dinner Vatican joke spread and stuck, and by Adam's day held nothing but honourable associations to all but malcontents such as Sir Michael Clarke. In popular parlance, with blithe disregard for correct Latin forms, the name was applied to them both jointly and severally, and only the most pedantic grammarians demurred. Adam was infinitely proud to be called 'Sicarii', a 'daggerman', even though he rarely had cause to ply one – and even then only with just cause.

In 1900 the legion born in Ravenna, now some twelve thousand combatants strong amidst a larger army, fulfilled the promise of their forebears and called upon the Sultan. The first Christian soldier on the walls of Istanbul (soon to be Constantinople once more) was a wild-eyed young officer of that unit-cum-crusade who happened to be born in Fulham. The man who planted the cross atop the dome of St Sophia (the church that was and would be again) as the sultan hurriedly left the Sublime Porte for the last time was also of their number.

They did not list battle honours on the giant flag they carried into war; instead place names were subtracted from those already there. In 1901 the entry for 'Istanbul' could be unpicked to leave another glorious plain patch of Papal smoky red. Only the names of Cairo and Mecca remained to be removed before they could present a blank banner to His Holiness to place fresh objectives on.

It was all very well, even laudable, for the Sicarii to be so ambitious and implacable, but Pope and Sultan, each being emperors in all but name, came to see that they had problems in common, headaches made worse by perpetual war contrary to the separate but similar gospels they upheld. In time, an ... understanding was reached. Each culture had arrived at the stage when they wanted to relax and enjoy the benefits that were the only arguments for the constraints imposed by civilization. The Pope of the New Rome, the rival Sultans of Baghdad and Cairo, began to speak to each other like reasonable men. They each had their own fish to fry at home. There would always be Sicarii, Janissaries and Mamelukes but they were more and more for internal use only.

Ever obedient to their masters and He whom they represented on earth, the elites slowly changed and developed more subtle skills. By the time the boy Adam came out of Sussex, there were still two names on that ancient flag but no real thoughts of removing them. Events had taken another path, one which would lead him not to plant the cross in Mecca, but to the politics of Lilliput in London.

Jonah was cutting a bolt of local blue Kersey into useful lengths when she came back. Ordinarily that sort of Monday morning job would have been done by his apprentices, but of late he was glad of anything simple and none too important to occupy his floundering thoughts. It wouldn't matter that much if his no-longer-trustworthy hands hacked and spoilt such plain stuff. The silks and cottons he had to leave to his helpers. They didn't know what was going on; only that *something* was. He saw that in the sidelong glances they were giving him. He no longer cared.

Suddenly she was just ... there. Jonah didn't have to see her, he knew by the crackling charge in the air, the indefinable sparkle her presence grafted on to mere reality.

She was standing by his shoulder, deliberately invading his space and allowing her warmth to flow over him. He paused in mid-cut.

'It's time,' she said – and her voice stamped on the fingers by which he clung to normality. He gladly let go and fell free from the bonds of the satisfactory life he'd built up with such pains.

No one else heard anything, no one else saw her, not unless she so chose it. She'd laughingly complied with Jonah's pleas to show herself to the Leveller High Council – and done it in such spectacular fashion that they'd not lightly ask again. Whilst she expanded to fill the appointed chamber and awed the terrorists to silence, what she called 'aspects', smaller replicants of her, had detached themselves from her body and ravished three of the company (and one of them a woman) to death. The frenzied mountings had gone on throughout 'negotiations', when the braver, unafflicted souls found courage to speak and frame their requests.

'I perused their minds and gave them what they truly wished,' she'd 'explained' towards the end, when the three were plainly dead although the swiving had not ceased. 'And if Jonah permits' – this with a wry, three-foot-wide smile – 'I'll grant your spoken desires as well.'

Then, by sorcerous means, she'd whisked him back to his shop in the blinking of an eye and wickedly tortured him by permitting the kissing of her hand. When she'd gone, he knew not where, Jonah had hauled himself up to bed and envied the three who'd expired through joy. Their journey was over; his, he sensed, had barely started. There was a long path of degradation yet to tread.

This time she joined that long white hand to his – quite literally. The ivory flesh of her extremity melted and fused with the calloused pink of his. Even if he'd wished to –

and he did not – Jonah could not have resisted the woman's summons to follow.

The apprentices, his customers, observed only half of the story. Today it was her caprice to appear only to her chosen Jonah. All they saw was the poor, distracted tradesman advance, slack-jawed and arm outstretched, into the stockroom. No one cared to follow. They knew they'd get no thanks for it. The paying public left without buying anything, off to spread further stories and hasten the shop's demise. Already Jonah's assistants and bonded men were looking tactfully around for alternative placements. The Clothiers Guild didn't like such transfers of underlings, but soon they'd not be able to refuse.

Once through the cupboard door, Jonah was beyond such thoughts; beyond even the reproach of the God-like guild. He was joined, in flesh and blood communion, with a more genuine divinity. There had been the merest second when his stockroom was just the stockroom, and then it became ... a new world. Drawn willingly along behind the woman, he was taken into a darkened landscape that paid no respects to the confines of his shop and house.

He paid little attention to his new surroundings; concerned himself little enough even with his footing on the long, slick grass through which they trod. Jonah would have been content to be dragged bloodily alongside her bare feet, if it would have increased his proximity to her.

There was a feeble light, from no readily obvious source, to render the scene a shade less than inky. He used it gratefully to study the movement of her narrow back and haunches under the shifting, kaleidoscope dress. Seemingly aware of the appreciation, and not in the least disapproving, she turned once to favour him with a saucy smile and smoothed her free hand over the taut globes of her behind. Without the least feeling of shame, he discovered he was drooling.

After a few minutes' march Jonah suddenly stumbled forward, finding his hand had been disengaged and was his own again. Those one or two paces carried him to stand beside her and they stood shoulder to shoulder, gazing into the featureless murk. She, plainly able to discern more than he, was looking about with unconcealed rapture, noting features in the far darkness very much to her approval.

Then there was another eye blink of dislocation and Jonah found himself on his back, half covered by the sopping grass, with the woman looming to her full five feet height above him. She seemed uncertain, ebony eyes perplexed under the low black fringe of her bob. He shook his head, desperate to show that he did not know what was required of him, but that she only had to ask . . .

'Oh yes,' she said abruptly. 'I remember.'

In an instant, the area in which they stood (or lay) was flooded with the light of a summer's day. The grass was suddenly dry and dotted with wild flowers. From nowhere came the gentle warmth of a favoured August evening. Outside the ten-yard radius, 'night' continued as before.

She smiled, abnormally wide, down at Jonah, and the red inside of her mouth made her face seem all the more pallid.

'That's better, don't you think?' she said, wild-eyed. Jonah nodded, not caring what he was agreeing to.

'They told me to ask if you'll really do it,' he blurted out in a tormented voice. Jonah's long history of loyalty to the cause still exerted some pull. He wanted to get business out of the way whilst some fraction of his mind remained fever-free. The woman knew exactly what was meant.

'If that's what *you* want, I will,' she said. 'These "Levellers" are nothing to me, but I'll take your King if it's *your* wish.' Her smile no longer seemed natural to her; it was too manic and threatening.

Jonah nodded again; his breath was coming out in noisy gusts. The constricting tightness about his chest increased.

'And is that all you want?' she went on. 'Everything for them, nothing for you?'

He couldn't say anything. She knew his inmost thoughts already. He wished his body would hurry up and explode.

'Is there someone else?' she asked, tilting her head to one side; a very girlish gesture. 'Have you a mate?'

There was a noise from beyond the radius of summer light. Something monstrous and even blacker than its surroundings reared up at them. A blast of leathery hot air swept over Jonah and the woman, and their ears were assaulted by a howl, more echo than sound in its own right, resounding in a place impossibly far away. In its two long arms the creature hefted some sort of bladed weapon, and, with a swish a dozen feet above the couple's heads, had drawn it back for a sweeping blow.

The woman wasn't in the least perturbed. 'Not now,' she said, barely deigning to pay the thing attention. The words were no sooner said than the nightmare burst into smoke and flame. Explosions of smoke gouted out from the forks of its body, and the thing permitted itself the liberty of an agonized scream. Stumbling away, tongues of fire decorating its flapping form, it was swiftly lost to sight.

Jonah's recovery from the incident was infinitely speeded by the woman leaning forward to within inches of his face. Her lips hovered above his and he knew, but didn't care, that those black eyes were observing his study of her cleavage.

'I asked you a question,' she said.

Jonah tried to recall, and sluggishly, like a puppy being dragged to a bath, the answer came to him.

'A wife, for twenty years,' he said, 'but—'

'No buts,' she said firmly. 'I won't have that.'

With one slim, black-tipped finger extended, her hand lightly touched his forehead, brushing over his eyes to close them. It carried on down, gently parting his lips to flick the dry tongue within. It pressed upon his Adam's apple and lingered on the grey-haired barrel chest. Journey's end was the buttoned flap of his moleskin breeches, which expanded and strained as never before.

'I'll perform all that's – nicely – asked of me,' she whispered to him, straightening up and leaving him prostrate. 'But I'll accept no buts. You and your kind must learn that.'

Jonah learned the lesson when he woke, in his home over the shop, another mere split-second of nothingness after she had spoken those words. He must have been with the woman for some hours in the place she had taken him, for it was now night and the undercroft was shuttered and empty. His long-suffering saintly wife had left a note for him on the kitchen table beside his salt-beef supper. 'Where have yo bin?' it said. 'I have bin scurred to deth. Luv Naomi. XX.'

She'd been alongside him all the way; right back to apprenticeship days. Without her the lean, make-do times would never have been turned into prosperity. They'd not been blessed with children, true, but he'd had no other cause to rebuke her, not in all those years. Not once had she complained about the hard work, or their earnings being lavished on the Levellers. How then was it Naomi's fault if she lingered on after their make-believe, second-rate life was ousted by *her* arrival? Jonah's hardness of heart fuelled self-disgust.

As shattered as if he'd done ten days' work, no answer prepared for his wife, he trudged upstairs to their room. Once inside, the merest glance by candlelight told him no answer was necessary. Jonah's problem had been solved for him, and Naomi had her reward for her devotion.

The poor woman's face had ... rotted away, although she still lived, unable to protest save by the feeble waving of her hands. When Jonah arrived the corruption had so far left her body alone, but by the time the surgeon and priest were summoned most of Naomi's flesh was on the bedclothes and she was beyond the help of either. By morning, to the astonishment of all who saw – and the scandal of the town – she was just a dry skeleton.

As if that were not bad enough, suspicion was flamed to new heights by the fact that Jonah did not weep or even seem surprised. In due course he would have been put to the inquisition of Church and State – and would have had an interesting story to tell. By then, however, things had moved on apace and the authorities who ran the – normal – world had more to worry about than the death of mere clothiers' wives.

Whilst a Mohawk steward offered them sherry wine and biscuits, the Archbishop of London looked blankly out into the inner courtyard, as he had done whilst considering the words of the actress-cum-'dowager'. Adam meanwhile contemplated the commendable likeness of His Holiness, framed on the wall before him. All it lacked was the glint of wry, Levantine humour that adorned the eyes of the real item. He then moved leisurely on to wonder at the presence of artistic excellence in such a provincial back-water. Neither Churchman nor soldier entertained any great hopes of benefit from their meeting.

Fred Pelling was seeking to perfect his impression of inconsequential invisibility. If he dared, he would have hidden behind the cloak stand. Even his biscuit lay untouched for fear it might crunch too loudly.

Once the steward was gone, conversation could not politely be postponed any longer. The Archbishop turned his intrepid little face towards the two visitors.

'So, is there anything I can do to help?' he asked. The notepad and gold inkstick were poised aloft, awaiting the formulation of the merest whim.

'Not really,' said Adam. 'Thanks all the same, Your Grace. I'll obtain assistance from the garrison here—'

'Won't that take time?' the Archbishop interrupted. 'You haven't any prior acquaintance with the Roman troops. I would be happy to provide—'

'That's the great thing about the Papal forces,' Adam pressed on, entirely unfazed. 'You can assume a universally high standard. I might well just pick the first lot I see. It's more in the line of information where I could do with some help. I presume it's you who's handling the English side of this business?'

'In strategic terms, yes,' agreed the Archbishop, a trifle warily, combing his goatee beard with delicate white fingers. 'Save that all things are in abeyance for the seven days His Holiness has allotted to your exclusive control. I shall then inherit the consequences of whether the King comes back or not, which is to say your success or otherwise. A regency in the name of myself and His Highness the Prince of Wales has been arranged. What-ever transpires, I think we can be confident in the

94

continuance of proper authority. Meanwhile, my man Bancroft will be dealing with day-to-day affairs.'

'Yes,' said Adam, putting a wealth of underwhelmed reaction into that simple affirmative. 'Actually, there is one thing unresolved, to my mind. What exactly was the Papal Legate doing in this country? Admittedly, I got this assignment with maximum haste and minimal briefing, but you'd think I'd have had a straight answer to that question by now. Do you know it, Your Grace?'

His Grace considered whether he did or not as the brass clock ticked out the seconds of uncivil delay.

'I think so,' he said at last. The silence then continued.

'Would you care to share it with me?'

'Not particularly,' came the reply. 'It impinges on high politics, which I would take to be beyond your remit.'

'I disagree,' said Adam, respectful before the dictates of proper social order. 'My entrustment was quite open-ended. That can be checked with the Archbishop of Paris-and-Versailles, who spoke to me as the messenger of Rome.'

'That won't be necessary,' said the Churchman, waving Adam's offer away. 'The times we live in mean that soldiers deal with statecraft and I must handle wars. The devil turns the world topsy-turvey, Sicarii, and so I'll confide what I know to you.'

'I'm indebted, Your Grace,' said Adam, bowing his – quite genuine – thanks. He had not disagreed with one word of the little man's world view.

'"Something rotten in the State of . . . England",' recited the Archbishop. It was well known that a love of the works of St William Shakespeare was his one anomalous concession to a life of the mind beyond his calling. Adam was also familiar with the English playwright-saint whose early conversion and driven pen had done so much to reconcile his people to the Church Universal.

'*Hamlet?*' he hazarded. '*The Merry Road to Rome?*'

'The former,' confirmed the Archbishop. 'A paraphrase from therein. There's been too much trouble here, this last generation. The Church, in its infinite wisdom and compassion, wondered why it was Englishmen in particular who should so hate their social betters. It questioned why, time after time, mere peasants and artisans – not normally the home of high or self-sacrificing sentiments – should throw all away to slit the throats of a few gentry. Mother Church was saddened and puzzled – hurt even. It did not seem likely to them that the English were intrinsically more wicked or bloodthirsty than the general run of man. Even I, with my excess of unfortunate and souring experience, do not hold to that theory. After stately consideration – and endless English pervarication – a Legate was sent to probe the infection of evil. It may be that he discusses it with the King at this very moment – though I doubt it,' he added soberly.

Adam worried at the frayed top of his boots with thumb and forefinger. 'And what do you think his conclusions might have been?' he asked, not actually looking at the Archbishop.

'Might *still* be,' he was corrected.

'If you like.' Adam was none too convinced, but happy to humour an optimistic stance.

The Archbishop first thought of a suitable answer, then considered if he should express it and, if so, the most advantageous way to do so. This potential reply was then measured against his estimation of the literal truth, to check any discrepancy wasn't too shocking. It was the standard process he applied to each and every statement that passed his lips.

'If I were he,' he mused slowly, inclining his head benignly in Adam's direction, 'I would meditate upon this country's position at the periphery of Christendom, its distance, both in leagues and cultural achievement, from the calming influences of high culture. Secondly, I should cogitate upon the island's less than happy history – its merely tenuous and partial Roman conquest in ancient times, for example; its disgusting and morally ruinous "protestant" interlude and so on. Combine all these with uncertain weather and the Anglo-Saxon addiction to an excess of beer, and I would conclude myself surprised that the nation is not worse than it is.'

Adam smiled and nodded. 'You may have a point there, Your Grace,' he said, meaning *though not a good one*.

'You can observe the material signs of that national malaise in these adornments,' said the Archbishop, indicating the accumulations of Papal-red files around him. The normally clear desk had been piled high in order to impress. 'A bad harvest in the Vale of Evesham leads to attacks on the gentry – with what possible aim one cannot guess. This thick tome relates to labour unrest in Coventry with undertones of heretical Neo-Druid incitement. A minor-gentry probate dispute of quite impenetrable complexity – not to say pettiness – leads to bloodshed in Stratford, Castle Lichfield, Nuneaton and Market Bosworth. I was obliged to send a full infantry regiment to conclude that little fracas, though the report, as you see, contains more pages than people were involved. In these files you will find anything from West Country scrumpy riots that boil up out of nothing to some shadowy figure called Spartacus Penrose, if you please, who deals in assassination and subversion amongst the factory artisans of Birmingham. There's nothing special about us or the tasks I've inherited: it's in our blood and history, you see.

I don't doubt the Legate would have concluded the same, had he been given the chance.'

'Doubtless,' agreed Adam smoothly. 'I expect you've got plenty about the Levellers in there as well.'

Fred Pelling straight away made it his business to be looking out of the window. The Archbishop's face revealed nothing – not that Adam had expected it to.

'Some,' he said. 'Though much less so since they received their richly merited deserts in 'ninety. I can devote precious little time to the activities of dead terrorists, you'll appreciate. Is there some particular point to your singling them out?'

'None,' said Adam. 'Some colleagues of mine served in the Thames Valley Crusade, that's all. I'd heard the name.'

'Yes. They used to shoot at me on a fairly regular basis,' said the Archbishop. 'Consequently, I was glad to see the back of them.'

Adam downed his sherry in one. 'I'll be off then, Your Grace. By the way, where's Father Bancroft at the moment?'

'At Guildford, much to his disgust, settling matters down there. I suspect he feels physically unwell out of the sound of Bow Bells. One was obliged to convince him that the site of His Majesty's disappearance was the mandatory starting point for his enquiries.'

'Which are now superseded by mine, of course,' said Adam guilelessly.

'Naturally,' agreed the Archbishop, just as blandly. 'Though we stand poised to offer every assistance and counsel. Are you sure you don't require some secondments from my people?'

'No, thank you. I'll travel light and travel fast.'

'Very wise, Sicarii. A week is such a short time for all that you are asked to do.'

'I couldn't agree more, Your Grace. When does the Thaumaturgic Inquisition convene?'

'They are here and waiting, Sicarii. They've come from everywhere, awaiting your word.'

Adam bowed over the Archbishop's hand. 'Then consider it given,' he said.

From: THE BOOK OF CEREMONIAL MAGIC

By Sir Arthur Waite
Published London, Auto-da-fé Press, 1911.

## Chapter 2: Before Corbishley, even before Ibarra

... of that lingering period of 'sub-Roman' culture termed the 'Patrician era'. For all their heated differences in emphasis, within each of the three principal schools of thought concerning the initial 'discovery' of 'magic', there is rare concurrence for the timing of the event. Few now dispute the notion that it was somewhen in the opaque centuries following the fall of Rome's Western Empire that man initially found ways to make matter malleable. Whether it was actually some obscure Balkan shaman or cultured senator who first burst the bounds of reality looks likely to forever remain unknown. All we can say for certain is that humanity spent most of its history only dimly aware of the supremacy of the mind.

And yet ... and yet, in the light of retrospection, it is clear that the way was long pointed out to us. We were blind and could not see. It is now agreed that what we term 'magic' is nothing but the working of certain strong minds upon the fabric of the universe. A few men and women can be made so *convinced* of their puissant abilities that they are able to impose their will on Nature's laws and ways. Mankind had but to stop and reflect to realize it, but our eyes were closed to this example of the Lord's generosity and favour. Whenever I read Matthew, Chapter 17, Verse 20* I realize with a shock that our Blessed Saviour could hardly have dropped a heavier hint ...

A. W.
London, Bognor, Jaffa. 1902–10

* 'And Jesus said unto them ... If ye have faith as a grain of mustard seed, ye shall say unto this mountain, Remove hence to yonder place; and it shall remove; and nothing shall be impossible unto you.'

At the heart of the Westminster Citadel there was a secret patch of green. It had served four centuries of the Church's highest echelons as a place in which to stroll, rest and conspire. The fate of England had often been decided there.

Around the edges ran tiled cloisters with marvellous magically enhanced sound-suppressing properties. These were used on inclement days or occasions requiring particular discretion. It was not, however, altogether wise for ambitious but still comparatively junior Churchmen to be noted conversing there *too* often.

In the centre of the mossy lawn an ancient statue of St Augustine, much discoloured and afflicted by London's polluted air, reminded those who saw it just where and from whom their status came. The seventeenth-century Archbishop who'd placed it there had thought it no bad thing to instil that calming sense of historical perspective, the sense of being mere part of an immortal chain, in his successors. It had partly worked – and far more gently than any set of rules with the same aim.

Around the four sides towered window-dotted walls, holding the more spacious of the citadel's offices and chambers. Inside worked the most favoured of the English Church's officials. It was their privilege, in rare moments of ease, to be able to look down on the hidden lawn, and aspire to the day when they, too, might walk there. That also was conscious policy. 'The donkey with the carrot before it,' opined that same shrewd seventeenth-century Prince of the Church, 'works all the harder.'

The night that Adam and (at Adam's unshakeable insistence) Fred Pelling were admitted to the hallowed square, the windows of the Church's 'fast-stream' administrators were shuttered. However trusted they might be in the wielding of St Peter's delegated power, it was not desirable that any late worker should observe the enquiries about to be made. Those few so privileged were ushered in by soldiers of the Papal garrison of London and, once in, the heavy door was locked behind them. When finally gathered together, the small party spread out to their appointed places, aided by the dancing light of the torches hung on the cloister walls, and waited for the word to begin.

In the course of paying his respects to the Papal *Gonfalonier* in his separate offices within the Westminster Citadel, Adam had acquired the assistance of two Rome soldiers. Sharing the same higher loyalties, the *Gonfalonier* and Adam could meet like brothers and ask anything of one another. There'd been not the least problem in detaching a Swiss and a Palestinian, both highly recommended, into Adam's service. The unacknowledged Lord of London had five thousand such at his disposal, more than enough to ensure His Holiness's will be done.

Among others of their number, these two made a brisk job of getting the participants in and then guarding the approaches. However interesting or intriguing events unfolding before them might become, they could be relied upon to direct their attention elsewhere. Adam was confident that, whatever else might transpire, they would not be interrupted or observed. No one was taken in by the troopers' lazy stares or casually carried arms.

The Archbishop was there to observe. So were the half-dozen vaguely identified members of his inner cabinet that swarmed about him and stooped to whisper in his ear. The others were magicians and instantly recognizable as such.

It wasn't so much their various emblems and armbands, symbols of the schools that trained them, that marked them out for what they were. Adam discerned the men's nature from the set of their faces, their bold stance and the tigerish pacing which accompanied the slightest pause. They were of a type: elderly young men with appraising glances and excessive self-control. Being Masters of Magic in the thaumaturgic hierarchy, etiquette dictated they were individually introduced – Morris of Verulamium, Al-Khorbouri of Windsor, Oakley of Reading and so on – but Adam let the names drift on and through him. In common with the majority of normal mortals he retained a quiet distrust of those who dabbled in 'the realms beyond', particularly men as experienced as these in the craft. He might respect their powers and skill, might be grateful for the service they rendered the Church, but he'd never, ever, warm to them. Deep inside, the things they'd learned had turned them wild. They often wore secret little smiles – which failed to reach their eyes.

Only the magicians crossed the tiny trench freshly dug around the sides of the central lawn. It was filled with copiously blessed holy water, intended to restrict what was to come to those best equipped to deal with it. Most of the day had been spent preparing the cloth and paint pentagram within that square, infinite painstaking care being devoted to its complex thaumaturgic algebra. Final approval had been pronounced at dusk by the Middlesex region's Grandmaster of Magic, no less, and after that any further scrutiny would have been an insolence.

If the Archbishop had dared, he'd have gathered more grandmasters to perform this unique summoning, but mass movement of such exalted creatures would have drawn attention to the deed. Grandmasters rarely left the castle-palaces in which they wove their high magic, grew strange, and awaited the consultations of kings and cardinals. It had been difficult enough to excuse a gathering of 'mere' masters without announcing the news to all the spies and factions which abounded in the capital. Already he'd had to advise an over-curious earl of the Albionite persuasion to attend exclusively to his own business for a while – preferably on his remote Essex estate. No, what he'd brought together here would have to suffice.

The men in question seemed confident enough, to be sure. They'd taken their agreed positions within the pentagram like young blades at a barndance – not that one could ever imagine any of them performing something so light-hearted. They turned as one to look at the Archbishop and he, with a movement he instantly regretted, turned to pass the silent request to Adam. The Sicarii shrugged, meaning, 'If not now, when?'

Anxious to regain the authority he'd just freely relinquished, the Archbishop paused as if in thought, and only then gave the signal to go. No one had spoken aloud since they'd arrived at the secret lawn.

The magicians raised their arms in unison, an outward sign of an inward adjustment. That undefined force, part thought, part energy and part ... something else altogether, the thing that was termed 'the Talent' and marked them out from the mainstream of mankind, was being directed beyond themselves. They were each separately reaching out into the night, stretching beyond the visible world, probing into the whirling ambience which magicians knew lay just beyond and carried on for ever. Tentatively and with exquisite care, they were searching for the new and displacing power which magicians now perceived in the universe.

To date, it had ... sat there, in a way that wizards could not explain clearly to normal men – not even if they were angry kings or subtle Church lords. In making their spells and working their wonders thaumaturgists had come to take account of it, inputting a new constant to the algebraic calculations so as to arrive at the old results. It was possible to work your way around the ... obstruction without any great difficulty and soon enough magic had become reliable again. In time, if it (whatever it was) chose not to shift, it would become part of the landscape, something 'normal' and long-standing. Wizards, by their very nature and training, were well suited to getting used to the incredible. Even after a millennium of practical use, the nature of the realm in which magicians moved and into which they reached to twist reality to their wishes was only dimly understood.

Together they gingerly reached out, touching with magical talons the 'something new in the world' that Sir Michael Clarke had spoken of to Adam. It did not move or stir to acknowledge their presence. They glanced at the Archbishop for further indulgence and it was given. The magicians shifted their stance and moved on, as previously agreed at the highest level of Church and State, to administer mild shocks to the invisible target. The sorcerous needle thrusts, delivered around its boundaries, were designed to provoke a reaction – any reaction. The governors of Christendom wished very badly to know what this 'new thing' was. They were willing to court catastrophe to find out.

For a second time the magicians looked back to the Archbishop, signalling that their efforts had produced no response. To return to the 'landscape' analogy, they could not discern whether the shape blocking their way was animate or lifeless; a sleeping lion or a fallen rock. In the absence of any response, it didn't really matter either way. There was no way round it.

The Archbishop had hoped to avoid stage two of the agreed plan but there seemed no alternative. He could not afford to come away from this gathering without any answers.

There was a blanket ban on necromancy, dating from the earliest days of practical magic. Those 'Dark Age' Popes who had arrived at the Great Concordat had demanded that as the price of peace. They feared that false confusion might arise between the mere corpse-prodding of wizards and the Resurrection, the central mystery of faith. Likewise, communication with those who'd already left the world behind was too subversive to be permitted. When they did come back, the dead often had strange and disturbing tales to tell, unsuitable for any but the most sophisticated audience.

Happily, the Church's theological concerns were met and matched by the desire of emperors and kings that their darker deeds remain obscure. It did not do for a murdered man to be able to return and name the culprit. Accordingly the practice was enthusiastically suppressed and even in the modern age, when more relaxed attitudes usually prevailed, it was still one offence which could land the delinquent in the fiery embrace of the auto-da-fé.

However, an archbishop, being a trusted shepherd of the flock, could, on rare occasions, sanction an exception to this iron law. In dire need he might issue a dispensation, stripping the sin from the deed, and allow, under supervision, the construction of a bridge over the great divide. This particular archbishop didn't like doing it. A copy of the dispensation had to be rushed by messenger to Rome for after-the-event ratification. The rough and tumble and high Church politics meant that sometimes this wasn't granted, leaving the man who'd requested it in rich varieties of trouble. He'd heard of occasions when that ploy was used to unseat out-of-favour Princes of the Church. That didn't currently apply to him, he thought, but all the same it wasn't the kind of entry he wanted on his Vatican file. The Archbishop was very far from the summit of his ambitions and had to be careful.

Reluctantly he recognized that need was now must and waved them on. In the ill-humour the decision produced, the Archbishop wondered how the magicians came to be so familiar with a forbidden act.

The lines of the pentagram lazily stirred and came in and out of focus. Though there was no breeze, tiny waves and tides appeared in the channels of holy water around it. At the lawn edge away from them a rectangle of sickly yellow light now shimmered, free-standing and man-sized: a 'door' opening into somewhere other than Westminster, London or earth. The stone Augustine stood stark and black against its otherworldly glow.

It was only the fancy of the presiding magician; the Archbishop knew that. At the one other summoning he'd witnessed, as a young and frightened priest (a stranger now, from another age), the portal had appeared as a cave mouth. Doubtless the thaumaturgist on that occasion had the underworld of classical fable in mind. Oakley of Reading, the caster tonight, was clearly a more prosaic man. He'd envisioned the entrance to Heaven as a cottage door. The Archbishop disapproved. Pearly gates would have been more appropriate – and respectful.

The call had to come from someone who had known the man in life. For reasons of their own, the dead only answered to voices they knew well. The Archbishop stepped forward.

'His Majesty King Charles the Fourth of England!' he said as loudly as he dared.

Everyone watched the portal and long seconds went by. The door remained firmly closed.

'So he's still with us, then,' said Adam. 'I'm not sure if that simplifies things or not.'

The Archbishop ignored him and pondered whether to press on. No one here had ever met the Papal Legate who'd accompanied the King off into limbo and so there was no way to call on his testimony. He grudgingly saw that there was little option but to try Adam's suggestion and bring on his provincial buffoon.

'Very well,' muttered the Archbishop. 'Let him speak.'

One didn't have to be a psychic to sense Pelling's overwhelming desire to blend in with the brickwork. Adam overcame this shyness by giving the man a firm push forward. All eyes were now on Pelling and the only way out for him was to say his lines.

'James Copper,' he shouted with commendable vigour. 'I want a word with you!'

Pelling was uncharacteristically impatient in waiting for a reply. He gave the man only a few instants to respond before turning back. Even so, to his visible disappointment, he was answered before he'd gone two paces.

The door hadn't 'opened'. The door was no longer a door. It was now simply a gap, a tear communicating between different places. Those on its far side did not enter into the games and pretences of men.

Adam and the others could see into the yellow light beyond. Within its glare they detected a spot of dark. The 'spot' grew steadily larger and developed legs and arms and, worst of all, a face. In less than a minute, Fred Pelling could recognize the man with whom he'd worked long years in the service of Lord Onslow. He'd last seen him, armed and in the Onslow livery, holding back the crowds around the King.

'James Copper' strode on, though his feet seemed more to glide over the ground than 'walk'. His face was set and angry. Adam had heard that the dead did not take kindly to reminders of life. The streams of blessed water were now surging and choppy.

Copper came through the 'door' like a rocket and then stopped abruptly, absolutely still, as though he'd hit a wall. When alive, his body would not have been able to so defy the rules of momentum. Jaw dropping slackly open, he surveyed the reception party with fish-on-a-slab eyes.

Pelling's emotions were strong enough to make him forget his fear.

'Jimmy!' he gasped. 'The bastards! Did they kill you?'

'My throat was pierced,' he confirmed, his sullen voice sounding far away. 'My head was shot. I tired and died.'

'What shall I tell Rosey?' cried Pelling. 'What about the kids?'

Copper stretched his mouth to make a smile. 'Tell her I preferred her sister,' he said. 'Tell them I don't miss them.'

Fred was shocked to silence. His friend had been the kindest of men, a faithful husband and loving father.

Adam would have interrupted him anyway. There was no time for domestic chit-chat.

'Who took you?' he said, loud and clear and confident. 'Who killed you? Where did you go? Where is the King?'

'He . . .' said Copper – and then said no more. His body remained but *he* was gone, snatched back as though pulled on a rope to whence he came. A new voice spoke from his mouth. The water in the trenches began to boil.

'I did it,' said the voice, the sweet sound of a giggly young girl. 'It was me. What of it?'

'James Copper' exploded and the entire party was splattered with his component parts. One of the Archbishop's advisors allowed himself to scream. It was a measure of the fires in which the others had been forged that they found time, even then, to glance at him in scorn. When eyes and mouths had been wiped, they saw that someone else stood in Copper's place.

The same face and figure that had beguiled Jonah the clothier cast its spell on the assembled men and they too had to stand against the inner roar of the libido. Smiling shyly, she looked at each in turn and challenged them with her sparkling gaze. Some saw half-hearted resignation, others bold – but brittle – defiance. A few saw an entirely different type of girl – or boy – altogether; the appeal was tailored to the man. Many quite forgot they were covered in gore.

Swift reminder came when 'she' tired of them. One of the master magicians had recovered sufficiently to ask a question. Adam didn't catch the gist of its beginning and no one caught its end. Before he'd finished speaking, an invisible hand whisked him away and ... merged him with the statue of St Augustine. The dome of his head, an arm and a leg, protruded from the weathered stone. Mercifully they did not move. The woman, closer than anyone else, looked sullenly upon her handiwork.

A volley of shots rang out, impressive in their unison of action. The Papal troopers were proving their worth. Unharmed, the woman turned them into smears on the wall behind and the gunpowder clouds where they had stood were tinged with red. The two men detailed to Adam only escaped their fellows' fate by their devotion to duty. The minute that things turned nasty, they'd rallied to the Sicarii, holding their fire and shielding him with their bodies. On the lawn the pentagram was tearing itself free, grass, earth, cloth and paint spiralling and twisting like a snake into the air.

Adam did not waste bullets on the apparition. Even as

110

his colleagues brought doom upon themselves, he started for the exit. Whilst the muskets were vainly fired, Adam's pistol shot the ancient lock off the door and his boot cleared the way of wood. He was first through, followed hotly by Pelling, the two bodyguards, the Archbishop, his aides and a couple of the more sensible magicians. Back inside, wild anarchy was loosed upon the world.

Two rearward escapees, both 'advisors' out of practice at pushing and shoving, were sucked back into the square by unseen, scratching talons. Flailing wildly, they were held high off the ground, facing the demon. Simultaneously, Adam witnessed the last stand of the two magicians who remained. They rained their worst on the uninvited guest but she seemed not to notice. When pausing for breath, they, too, were placed inside the statue. It now bristled with rigid, extraneous limbs.

Pelling and the Archbishop and friends had kept on going but the surviving thaumaturgists stayed with the Sicarii at the doorway, looking in. Their vaunted skills being casually brushed aside, Adam noted new-born doubt and panic in previously hard eyes.

'We're safe here,' gasped one: Oakley, as best Adam could recall. 'As safe here as anywhere. It chooses not to pass the gate.'

This rang true, even to Adam's unattuned mind. The world here was not so charged with ... her as in the courtyard.

'Morris was tired and disgusted with life,' explained Oakley, rapidly regaining control. 'I don't know why Griffiths stayed.'

The demon now deigned to look at the prisoners dangling before her. All around and about them great gouts of soil and turf and less pleasant things were swirling round. The place smelt of lust and gunpowder.

She smiled. 'Tell me,' she said to one or both, in a little-girl voice, 'what is an "enclosure"?'

They didn't understand or were too frightened to say. She tired of waiting, and in two seconds flat had waved them into nothingness.

Then she grew, retaining proper proportion and all her beauty and allure; expanding by the sensuous development of curves. Adam had once seen a giant python shedding its skin, and there was something akin to that in the unfolding scene. Her body was being reinforced by exuberant, inexhaustible life from within.

When she was tall enough to see over the walls, she started to snigger, the sound of a malicious, irresponsible child. It was at that point Adam left. He had not been commissioned to stand and gawp, no matter how remarkable the sight. As far as he was concerned, this particular episode was effectively concluded. Now he had other business to attend to.

Accordingly, he wasn't privileged to see the five-minute show put on for tens of thousands of stunned and fearful Londoners. Because of his devotion to duty, Adam never observed the titanic figure that towered briefly over the city and the panic that followed. He wasn't witness to the monstrous yet elegant black-tipped finger which reached out to Lepanto Square, at the heart of the metropolis, and toppled the effigy atop St Peter's Column, to smash into ruins far below.

# Part the Second

*O clouds, unfold!*

# A THIRD BLAST ON THE TRUMPET TO THE PEOPLE OF ENGLAND-THAT-IS AND ENGLAND-THAT-IS-TO-BE

WE SAY TO THE RIGHTEOUS PORTION OF THE COMMON-WEALTH THAT THERE IS NO REASON FOR FEAR IN THE STRANGE AND WONDROUS SIGHTS RECENTLY SEEN. THE G*DLY SHALL LOOK FOR FORETOLD SIGNS AND REJOICE UPON BEHOLDING THEM. THE MAN WHO IS SHIELDED IN VIRTUE SHALL RISE IN RAPTURE AT THE TRUMPET CALL TO FINAL BATTLE. WHEREFORE THE LAST OF THE FOUR ANTI-CHRISTIAN MONARCHIES SHALL SOON FALL (ROME PERISHING IN THE SAME LIKE AS EGYPT, ASSYRIA AND BABYLON BEFORE THEM). WE HUNGER AND THIRST FOR THE THOUSAND-YEAR REIGN OF KING JESUS AND THE SAINT-KINGS HE SHALL RAISE FROM HUMBLE HOMES. WE SAY THAT THE UNG*DLY SHOULD NOT STAND AGAINST US IN OUR HEARTFELT AIM OR THEY SHALL PERISH, THERE BEING NO SIN IN THAT ACT. LIKEWISE WE PROCLAIM AS SIMPLE TRUTH THOSE SAME UNG*DLY HAVE NO TITLE TO THEIR LIVES OR PROPERTY AND IT IS NO WRONG TO DEPRIVE THEM.

ARISE! ARISE FROM YOUR KNEES WHERETO YOUR FORE-FATHERS WERE FORCED. SEE THE SIGNS OF ONCOMING SALVATION! WHAT WAS BEHELD OVER BABYLONDON, THOUGH CURIOUS IN FORM AND MANNER, IS A TOOL OF THE G*DLY PARTY. WHAT WAS TOPPLED IN EFFIGY BY OUR WILL IN LEPANTO SQUARE SHALL SOON LIKEWISE BE SHATTERED THROUGHOUT THE LAND BY G*D'S GOOD HAND DIRECTING OUR OWN.

ARISE! ARISE! ARISE! ARISE! ARISE! ARISE! ARISE! ARISE!

I have read the above and fully approve and concur with the sentiments within. Wherefore I set my seal, in the Year of our Lord, 1995.

Charles IV, King of England, Wales and Cornwall; Protector of Mannin and the Isles; Patron of the Jerusalem and Jaffa Citadels.

[Leaflet found scattered at St Guy's Station, London]

115

'No real reason,' said Adam. 'I just thought I'd give it a miss.'

He and Pelling hadn't spoken much on the journey down from London. Both, in their separate ways, had had much to think about. It was only now they were settled in warmth and comfort, Fred had dared to question their hasty departure from the capital.

'Give what a miss?'

Adam leaned on the balcony rail and took a sip of his coffee. 'The fuss, the riots, the explanations,' he said. 'None of them would further our purpose.'

Pelling said an inward 'amen' to that. His last recollection of London was the distant sound of the militia opening fire on the mob. It hadn't exactly been a heart-wrenching experience for him to leave. The temptation to wait for the twice-weekly Guildford train was readily resistible.

'The Archbishop won't like you disappearing,' he felt obliged to say. Pelling had discovered a certain niche for himself in the present situation. There was a role to play as the Sicarii's advisor on etiquette. Otherwise, Adam had a certain robustness with people that wasn't wise.

'Tough,' replied the soldier, confirming Fred's gravest doubts. 'He knows where I'm heading and that's sufficient. Anyway, he'll be too busy to care for a while. Even when they've regained control of the streets, cleared the bodies away and invented a lie about what was seen, there'll be other things to keep the pot boiling. You don't mean to tell me that people – even Londoners – run amok and burn churches because they see something in the sky? No chance! That panic was taken advantage of, take my word for it. It's what I'd do if I was in the Levellers' position. They want the authorities distracted.'

Fred frowned. 'Yeah, well, if you've only got seven days I suppose that's good reason to press on.'

Adam snorted dismissively. 'That's just for English consumption. It makes the ordeal of my company seem finite and tolerable – something people can sit out quietly. Don't worry, Fred, my real orders say otherwise. I've got as long as it takes.'

Whilst Pelling was reeling that happy news in, and dining on its implications, Adam went back into the room to help himself to some more material and wholesome rations. A minor feast had been laid on for their benefit.

Their hosts had asked no questions; they either knew Adam or knew of him. Likewise Adam, though in new territory, seemed to know the way to their isolated manor house. Wary of his companion's abstracted mood, Pelling hadn't questioned the wide berth they'd given Guildford, their supposed objective. At the end of a long day's ride, they'd swung south, round and past the town and out into the dark countryside beyond. Without once consulting a route map, the Sicarii had led them direct to Polsted Manor.

The briefest of conversations (which Pelling didn't catch) with the owners, a man and wife in their fifties, had secured them entry. Rooms and stabling were provided and then the couple withdrew, not to be seen again. After assessing the property's security aspects, the two troopers billeted themselves in the main entrance hall and taciturn servants thereafter attended to the party's every need. Fred Pelling, once again, had cause to be impressed. He'd been aware of this place since childhood and had spent his life working within a mile of it, but never once suspected it was a safe house for the Church.

Now he was looking out into the night from the balcony attached to the third-floor dining room. There wasn't much to be seen: the slightest signs of life from Compton and Binscombe, two nearby hamlets, and, a mile off, the bolder lights of Loseley House, ancestral home of the Weston-Onslows and, until recently, the centre of Fred's existence. Elsewhere everything was inky black, right out to the Hog's Back ridge. Even the revolutionary street lighting of Guildford failed to raise a glow on the horizon, though Pelling could illustrate the scene from memory. He didn't know whether to feel at home or not. Somehow it didn't seem advisable to relax yet.

Adam rejoined him bearing two grilled mutton chops and handed one over.

'You should eat more,' he said, smiling. 'There may come a time when you wish you had.'

Fred made the pretence of consumption, but his heart wasn't in it.

'What is this place then?' he asked, mid-mouthful.

'Just one of many,' Adam answered, staring into the distance. 'The secret fortresses of Christendom, if you're feeling poetic. They're activated as and when necessary. Oh, I forgot, this is your neck of the woods, isn't it?' That's why it all seems strange to you.'

Pelling could have remarked that everything had taken a turn for the weird since he first clapped eyes on Adam – but wisely forewent that luxury.

'Sort of,' he said.

'Ordinarily this is pretty quiet country, I should imagine.'

Fred, a fierce local patriot, a son-of-Surrey before he was Wessex-man, before he was English, sensed a mild slight in that (correct) judgement.

'We've made it so,' he said proudly. 'It isn't Northumbria or Cornwall where mankind's still contesting ownership, if that's what you mean.'

118

Adam, who'd actually meant nothing by his remark and who, spending his life defending it, preferred civilization to half-held territory, didn't pick up on the affront.

'Is there any pre-man stuff?' he enquired. 'Or is it dealt with?'

Pelling looked out across his homeland and, against his inclinations, struggled for a truthful answer.

'Pretty much,' he replied. 'The local Crusades "dealt" with them last century – and we lost heavily doing it, I might add. You hear tell of the odd nest or two out on the heathlands, maybe some *disva* and *padfoots* or *downs tigers* along the Hog's Back. There's talk of *Surrey pumas*, taking sheep and the occasional child. I've never come across anything, though. If they *are* still out there, they learned their lesson long ago.'

The two men studied the silent landscape, as though trying to judge the security of man's hold on it. The breeds that had preceded man, nature's blind alleys, the Church's 'demi-demons', did indeed seem absent. Nowadays, it was only in the remote north and west that the night was rent by strange cries and farmers ploughed the land with gun to hand. The more modern cottages hereabouts weren't even designed with defence in mind. Even so, Adam still didn't seem content.

'What about Beltane-Night?' he asked. 'What's it like at Samhain?'

Again, Pelling was reluctantly honest. 'There's a fair number of bonfires,' he admitted. 'But less and less each year, and only round the backward villages. I've never been, of course, but they say it's mostly oldsters. The young people want nothing to do with it, or with those stupid revivalists – and quite right too.'

Adam silently agreed. Less thoughtful minds in the Church would have sanctioned persecution of the rag-tag

119

remnants of earlier religions. Thankfully, the gentler and more subtle heads invariably in control were content to let reason and ridicule, and the mere passage of time, do the same job.

'So okay,' he said. 'You've convinced me. What shall we do next? Imagine we've really only got seven days to play with before your torment's over – one way or another.'

Pelling shrugged his shoulders. 'I don't know,' he replied, in all sincerity. 'I don't know why we're here instead of Guildford. I've no idea why you didn't make more of the thing over London. Your thoughts are a mystery to me.'

Adam pondered a while on this outbreak of candour. 'I judged the summoning debacle contained self-evident lessons,' he said, breaking the silence and sounding almost apologetic. 'I didn't think any commentary was necessary – but that's just me, I suppose. Okay, I'll expound on the subject. For one: if this "new thing" that people in the know are on about could sweep aside the best the Archbishop can gather together, there was little point in me hanging around. Two: whatever it is is undisciplined and let slip an interesting clue, so ditto about lingering on. Thirdly: I reckon the answer to our problems is here, so where else should I go?'

Pelling felt none the wiser. 'I know the King went from here,' he said in a puzzled tone, 'but that thing was in London and it—'

'You may think this area's settled,' Adam interrupted, 'and perhaps that was once so. But now I reckon your "thing" – and those who delude themselves they use it – has changed that. We've come here to visit it at home.'

'The town's under interdict,' said the soldier. 'No one goes in or out.'

Adam hadn't been paying attention up to that point. He turned his horse to face Pelling's opponent.

'Except us, of course,' he said casually.

The officer looked at Adam and the two brooding troopers behind him. Even presented with such compelling arguments, he still had to think about it.

'If you must, you must,' he conceded at last. 'I shall have to submit a report, but in the circumstances . . .'

Fred Pelling glanced nervously back at the rest of his party. He was between the devil and the deep blue sea here. On the one hand, a military roadblock was denying him entry to his home town. On the other, he knew that Adam's fuse had started its short countdown. He would be in the middle of any explosion.

'I should just do it,' he said to the officer in charge, giving his honest opinion. The man took it the wrong way.

'You come in as a concession, not as of right,' he said, not sounding quite as confident as he looked. 'But if you want the plague, then go get it.'

He signalled to the platoon of bluecoats behind that they should disengage trigger fingers and clear the way. They were only too pleased to comply, heaving the heavy wagon off the Portsmouth Road with a will. No one had ever heard of the army in a fire-fight with Papal forces, but at one point things had looked to be heading that way. They might have been simple men and ex-churls, but were wise enough to see that such a fracas could only end with a bullet or the gallows.

The party of visitors ambled their way through the gap made for them. Pelling's heels caused his mount to venture that little bit faster than ambling speed.

Halfway through Adam paused and stared down at the soldier. 'And another thing,' he said. 'You're getting above yourself, you are. Only the Church puts places under interdict. The state hasn't got sacraments to deprive people of.'

The man seemed to have several answers to that, but spoke them in the silence and privacy of his head.

'Fare ye well,' he said insincerely. Pelling sighed. Another enemy.

In strict terms Adam had been correct. Only a bishop, or those in the dizzy heights above, had the power to exclude persons from the community of faith, rendering them solitary and helpless in this world and the next. However, the English Crown had seen fit to impose a passable secular equivalent on Guildford. The place was ringed with troops, all the roads blocked off. On their way in from Polsted, they'd even seen patrols crossing the outlying fields and farms, deterring more adventurous attempts to gain entrance or exit. The last time Adam had witnessed anything so ambitious and thorough was round a Gnostic settlement in the Holy Land – and that had been scheduled for destruction.

A plague outbreak was the official explanation and maybe some of the peripheral military even believed it. Certainly, it would serve to scare off the casual visitor. No one in their right mind would court the risk of groin and armpit bumps just to trade or socialize. Close to, though, it could hardly convince. Since when did anyone place a garrison actually *in* a plague town? Where was the drifting stench of the death pits? The great proclamations on the borough boundaries (bearing the Archbishop's seal, not the missing Royal version, Adam noted) wouldn't satisfy the more thinking types. The muskets of the soldiers, though – they might.

The Sicarii didn't make a show of turning round, but all the same he noted the flash of the soldiers' hurried heliograph signals to the town. He hadn't entertained hope of an unheralded arrival. A short-notice entry from an unexpected direction was the best that might be reasonably expected. In fact, there wasn't much point at all in such stratagems, other than they were second nature to him. Their arrival was expected, sooner or later, and if anything untoward wasn't concealed by now it never would be. The whole mission had been dogged with fig leaves of deception and omission, placed by those who should be revealing all. Doubtless Guildford, in its humble, provincial way, would be the same.

They passed by Loseley's gatehouse and the armed Onslow retainers there saluted and called out encouragement to Fred Pelling. Adam's eyebrow was caused to rise and he noted that someone, at least, thought highly of the man for what he was rather than what he knew. Closer examination revealed that Pelling, now he was back on home ground, had gained in confidence and stature. Adam smiled to himself. It was nice, he thought, that every fish should have its own pond to swim in, no matter how minuscule.

The soldiers above the road on St Catherine's Mount didn't smile or cheer. They'd clearly heard of the party's arrival but had nothing to say on the matter. Staring shamelessly back, Adam counted the unfriendly faces on the walls of the ancient priory and wondered where the nuns had gone. All of the group were glad to be past that section where the road narrowed and bored through the red and crumbly sides of the hill. The guardians of St Catherine's Priory hadn't looked to be ordinary soldiers, but bearers of some grim mission. Turning your back on their gaze made one's shoulder blades want to clench.

After that they were apparently past the rings of defence and it was a short way to the town proper. They clattered and splashed across the ford over the Wey and presented themselves at the gates. A local militia man made show of asking their business, but it was clear that he was under the tutelage of the bluecoat beside him.

'You know me full well, Tom Champion,' said Pelling, pushing past to cross the bridge over the dry moat. 'So don't ask such damn-fool questions. We went to school together and if you don't remember my name now it's too late to ask.'

The Royal soldier looked as though he might have some comment to make but, after reflection, thought better of it. The four men rode in.

Pelling wondered who on earth owned such a loud time piece and then realized it was Adam tutting.

'Look at the walls,' he said bitterly. 'Not repaired since my biblical namesake was a boy! And the ditch! It's full of cack and refuse and dead things. You could take this place with a determined charge of mop ladies.'

Fred happened to agree, but wouldn't admit it.

'There's never the money for repairs,' he explained. 'Besides, there's been no fighting here since the Cornish invasion – unless you count the Gladstone Rising and—'

Adam waved him to silence. The less said about either. . . miscalculation the better. 'Who's this?'

A slim young man in Onslow livery was racing down the slope of the High Street, giving every indication of wanting to meet them. Up to that point, the few Guildfordians around had carefully kept their eyes to themselves. It wasn't every day – or, indeed, ever – that Papal redcoats came to town, but prudence suggested it was best to see what they wanted before gawping. In vindication of this instinctive wisdom, the soldiers tensed and shifted stance. They were averse to people rushing at them.

'It's okay,' said Pelling, dismounting and smiling in welcome. 'I know him. He works for me.'

The young man arrived, similarly wreathed in smiles, and pumped Fred's hand. Adam and his assistants looked coolly on.

'I'm sorry,' the young man wheezed. 'There should have been someone to meet you but, well, you know, when you didn't turn up yesterday . . .'

'No problem, Jacko. We made a detour. These men are with me.'

'Nice to meet you,' said the pleasant fellow. 'I'm—'

'No time for that,' interrupted Pelling. 'We're on a tight schedule. What's been arranged?'

The man straightened and assumed a more serious face. He hadn't expected such haste to get to business.

'Not much, really,' he admitted reluctantly. 'You're Head of the Cabinet now, and we were waiting on you. We've moved your stuff into the big office at Loseley, so that's ready for you and—'

'Too far away,' said Pelling, who had already learned something from his brief association with Adam. 'We'd always be toing and froing to town and getting mucked about by the soldiers. Book us into the Spread if there's room, or somewhere else handy.'

'Righto, and I'll—'

'And take this. I want to know the whereabouts of all, *all* mark you, the names on this list.'

Adam, a great one for lists and inventories, hadn't been aware that Pelling had been busy putting his suspicions on paper. He was impressed.

Jacko scanned the sheet handed him and nodded. Its contents seemed to make good sense to him.

'Same old faces,' he commented with a grin. 'Want us to round them up?'

Pelling was looking at the town as though he owned it. 'Nope,' he said. 'Just do as you're asked. Accommodation and whereabouts, that's all that's required for the moment. When you've done that, go to Loseley and present my respects and apologies to Her Ladyship. Say I'll attend on her as soon as possible and kindly forgive our impoliteness.'

'Consider it done,' said the young man. He made a perfunctory bow to Adam (Another bloody Albionite, thought the Sicarii) and then sped away.

'My assistant,' explained Fred to his companions. 'A foreigner from Arundel: still young, but keen. He helps organize the local Churchales and other beery festivals. I may make him number two in His Lordship's Cabinet if he acquits himself well in this.'

'Wonderful,' said Adam, not really interested. 'Is he also a magician?'

'No,' Pelling said, surprised. 'Whatever gave you that idea?'

Adam shrugged. 'Well, *someone's* hit you with an efficiency spell, Fred Pelling. Or maybe the Guildford air agrees with you. Either way, I like it.'

Pelling laughed, none too mirthfully, and, remounting, spurred his horse forward. Adam and his men were happy to accept Fred's leadership and duly followed.

Watched by myriad covert eyes concealed behind first-floor window lattices and curtains, the party clattered their way up the steep stone setts of the High Street. On the ground they were studiously ignored. Fred saw many familiar faces but in present company they chose not to greet him.

It was a busy working day and the streets were quite

crowded with men and beasts. Nevertheless they made rapid progress. Like the waters of the Red Sea before the children of Israel, the people parted and made way for them.

~

Jacko's keen ears caught the 'foreigner' reference, but it wasn't that that made him frown as he left to do Fred's bidding. He was well aware that his exotic Sussex provenance made him a newcomer here for decades to come, perhaps for the rest of his days. Jacko could live with it – in fact it made him more interesting to the ladies and he was all for that. True acceptance would come in its own good time, when he married 'local' and showed he'd put down roots. Meanwhile, occasional good-natured gibes he could put up with. No, it was thoughts of his birthplace rather than present home which cast a shadow today.

Arundel was the home and possession of the mighty Howard family, joint Dukes of Norfolk and Earls of Sussex. Their rock-solid loyalty in the dark 'protestant' days, albeit centuries ago, earned them a pre-eminent place amidst the nobility of England. Kings and cardinals listened to them with respect. Almost alone they were allowed to retain their castle unaltered when the Church returned triumphant and the stone strongholds of other less faithful lords were felled. Improved and strengthened in succeeding generations, its gargoyle-festooned bulk dominated the town and that entire part of the world. It even loomed over the nearby romanesque cathedral. First-born sons inherited the castle whilst younger offspring often became bishop alongside. In enforcing their will, or in the wars of the King, their black-armoured Sussex cavalry rode together. The Howards of Arundel were openly blessed with exceptional favour which continued to this day.

In his childhood, Jacko's intelligence and sunny disposition had brought him the heavy hand of Howard patronage. His father, a mere crossbowman in their service, had dared to push him forward into the light of their gaze. He dared because he did not wish his beloved son to spend his life as he would, trapped in a limited, illiterate span, bound by a few miles and housed in dwellings of plank.

That wild daring had not earned rebuke, but quite the contrary. He still spent hours on his knees in the echoing, candle blaze of the cathedral, giving thanks for the unbelievable success granted him. Jacko's childhood was sacrificed to hard years of both learning and forgetting. Relations with his family remained warm, but a certain distance entered in. From the battlements of Arundel Castle Jacko glimpsed a wider world. He could never retrace his steps.

Some idle talk at court, of which he'd never know the details, and some minor exchange of favours saw him then transferred to Onslow service in the strange land of Surrey. His agreement was kindly sought but never for a moment doubted. In fact he accepted with alacrity.

For, as has been said, the Howards had the ears of the mighty. Certain such whispers echoed as far down as Jacko. He heard talk of conspiracies and plots, of whose stock rode high and who plummeted to ruin and the executioner's axe. What he heard worried him. Friendship and loyalty, kindness and charity, these seemed just ... words in the snake pit that was statecraft. The aspiring struggled and strove, writhing about for favour and trampling each other in the process. He knew he would never be more than a pawn in the game, but noticed that

128

nemesis falls as readily on them as on more exalted pieces – though with less justification. So when the chance came to steer himself to some sleepy backwater he grabbed it with both hands. Far better, he reasoned, to have an insignificant quiet time, even amongst strangers, arranging their little festivals and importuning their daughters, than to dance upon the precipice of politics.

Jacko was not an Albionite nationalist as Adam presumed. He was true-Church through and through – though prone to fleshly lapses. Given his origin he could hardly be otherwise. His present melancholy stemmed instead from having seen all this before. He had observed the arrival of Crown men and Papal lackeys at Arundel and it'd never boded well. If he'd but known it, Adam would not have expected a warm welcome from Jacko. The Sicarii was part of the storm that had found out his safe harbour.

The 'Spread' proved to be the Spread Eagle, a cut-above-the-rest alehouse and hostelry slightly off the town centre. It was walled round to a height of eight feet, with one way out and in, and so Adam immediately approved. By way of a bonus the hospitality and accommodation were also good. Preceded by Jacko's presence and the 'open sesame' of the Onslow name, the fatted calf was straight away dispatched for their benefit. Whilst it was dying (in a nearby butchers), Adam and the two troopers assessed the place's defensive potential and Pelling made himself comfortable. It was only after the Sicarii had checked the horses were well cared for and stabled close by that he joined Fred in their allotted rooms.

'Who's on that list?' he asked, without preamble.

Pelling was reading his traveller's Bible and seemed

loathe to leave it. 'Naughty folk,' he answered. 'People I've been on a collision course with for years. I want to know where they are. It might be a good time to deal with them. Some might be involved.'

He was talking Adam's language and the soldier was glad of it.

'So bring them in,' he said. 'Apply flames to their feet and make them sing.'

Pelling shook his head, self-assurance growing by the minute. 'That's not our way,' he replied, as though that concluded the matter. 'They're people with families and occupations – positions in the town. It would cause too much upset. Best leave it to me, I know what I'm doing.'

'It's your world,' conceded Adam, only slightly dubious. 'Take it at your own pace. Don't be too long about it, though.'

Pelling put down his book and crossed to the window. 'I know your thoughts,' he said quietly. 'You think we're in search of something bigger than a few rural malcontents.'

'Yes, those are my thoughts,' agreed Adam.

'But if this place is the seat of our troubles, as you surmise, then my local knowledge may be the key to detecting . . . Hang on.'

'I wasn't going to interrupt,' said the Sicarii, looking with distaste on the discarded Scripture. Translations out of the Latin, into English and every other hoi-polloi tongue, were a recent concession and jarred with the traditionally minded.

'No, no, I didn't mean—' Pelling was staring raptly out of the window, surveying the town spread out before him. He was practically forcing his head through the frame in his zeal to see something. 'It can't have—'

Adam realized that something had happened to whip the rug from under Fred Pelling's new-found firm footing. He allowed the tone of authority, temporarily put to slumber, to re-enter his voice.

'What? Spit it out.'

Pelling looked round, eyes wide, seeking but finding no alternative to the words which came to him.

'The castle's gone,' he said blankly.

Adam was at the window in two swift paces and shouldered him aside. A one-second traverse of the town revealed an absence of fortified places.

'Explain.'

Pelling made some space at the window and pointed. 'You wouldn't notice, not the way we came in,' he said, still only partly there as he thought through the implications. 'You wouldn't see it at the bottom of the High Street behind the houses.'

'But now you would?'

Pelling nodded vehemently. 'Of course. It's mostly ruins and only the keep's left, but you'd see it from here. I didn't think to look – you don't expect ... it's just gone.' Fred stepped back into the room, shaking his head in sad puzzlement. 'A huge thing like that ... doesn't ... We'd better go and—'

The window pane smashed and showered them both with glass.

An arrow had entered the room. Breaking the glass had not slowed it or altered its trajectory straight towards Adam's head. Its speed was such that it would have done its job before either man had seen the thing for what it was. The only way they even knew that they played host to a missile was because it paused short of consummation. Entirely unlike arrows do, it hung stock still in the air, almost as though scenting it, a mere inch from Adam's unflinching face.

Pelling's nerves hadn't finished formulating possible responses before the Sicarii acted. He trod furiously backward, not so much away from the arrow but towards his companion. Cannoning into him, he rammed Fred into a corner of the room and pressed him into it, covering the man with his greater bulk.

Thunderous steps up the stairs were followed by the crash of the door being booted open. Pelling recognized the voice and methods of the Papal bodyguards, drawn by the sounds of chaos. The Swiss identified himself by one questioning guttural word before Adam interrupted.

'Wait!' Fred heard him command. '*Sagittari!* Substitution – no other way.'

They seemed content with that, saying nothing more, awaiting developments in the doorway.

Threatened suffocation gave Pelling the wild strength to free his face and peer round his protector. The arrow had remained where it was, suspended six feet above the sundered splinters of glass. A gust of fresh air entered through the gap it had made.

Then, to his speechless horror, it began slowly to turn, shifting on its axis to face them. In its unhurried motion there seemed to be an element of horrible confidence.

'Ready to die?' asked Adam, his voice inappropriately level. It appeared to be a real, as opposed to a rhetorical, question.

'No,' whispered Pelling. He'd no time for thought or repentance, let alone proper last rites. He was unprepared and therefore fearful of eternity.

'Then stay behind me,' said the Sicarii. 'Hide yourself. This is for you.'

So saying he spread out his coat, an inadequate conceal-

132

ing veil. Fred's last sight of the room was of the arrow pointed straight at him and starting to quiver, as if building up vigour for a new assault. He felt Adam lurch back, compressing him into an even smaller space.

'That was another go,' Adam said. 'It's in front of my nose. I'm not the one it wants, or else I'd be dead by now. Do you understand what we must do?'

'Of course I don't!' wailed Fred.

'Then I'll explain. Stay completely out of view or it'll have you. This isn't clean magic so death might not be the end of your suffering. Undress yourself.'

'What?'

'Shortly it'll decide to get to you *through* me and I won't permit that. Do as I say and don't question. Every single stitch – off!'

It wasn't easy in such a confined space, but Pelling found his hands possessed new reserves of power. What didn't come away easily was torn off.

'Give me your jacket. Don't make it visible, just pass it me.'

Fred managed this and felt a surge of movement, as though Adam had hurled the jacket across the room. The door slammed shut. It must have been a close run thing, since Adam let out a rare exclamation.

'Right,' he then said. 'Now wait. Pray if you like – but silently.'

Pelling crouched down, naked, fearful and racked with cramp. Then, just when he thought he'd be willing to exchange life for a second of stretching, he heard a tentative knock at the door.

'Come in,' said Adam.

The door creaked open and a youthful voice said, 'I've come to thank you for the—'

The sentence was cut off with a hollow sound, like that

133

of a cricket bat making contact. At the same moment, Adam stood aside, freeing Pelling from his tiny prison and revealing him in all his naked glory. The Swiss laughed uproariously at the sight.

On the floor, an expression of gratitude still occupying his freckled face, was the Spread Eagle's taproom boy, with whom Fred had been on 'good morning' terms for years past. He was wearing Fred's jacket and the arrow through his head. From the exit wound made by a wicked flint tip, the stuff that had kept the youth alive the short span of his life was spreading out to form a pool.

Fred Pelling groaned and placed his face in his hands.

'It fed on your scent,' said Adam, his voice devoid of sympathy, 'and ditching your togs could only cause temporary delay. You should be grateful it accepted the false trail. Nothing else would have sufficed. The Arrow of the *Sagittari* is implacable and someone had to die.'

Pelling was not consoled. He knew the boy's widowed mother. He had been her only son.

'So much,' said the Sicarii witheringly, 'for the outbreak of confidence. Fred Pelling, you should have *known* this was no mere Guildford matter.'

Jonah wasn't a stupid man; he instantly discerned the purpose of the High Council's request. Even so he prayerfully reflected on the matter, as bidden, and then gave his consent. Adherence to the 'democratic centralism' of the Levellers was a hard habit to shake and besides, if they did succeed in displacing him, that would be an end to his ordeal.

Whereas the summonings of the council's best magicians went unanswered, the 'woman' came to Jonah's merest call. She just ... appeared in the chosen barn and smiled upon him.

The others present were survivors of harsh personal histories. They had emerged from decades of bloody conspiracy and persecution with steel edges welded upon them. Nevertheless, they flinched before the sight of this diminutive maiden – or however they perceived 'her' – and avoided her eyes. Each had made the traditional final examination of conscience before arriving.

There hadn't been full agreement in the council about the wisdom or probity of this move. Several dissenting members were obliged to partake in a 're-evaluation' retreat in a distant safe house, from which they might – or might not – emerge duly chastened. One stubborn and principled white-beard even needed to be 'cast out', and would turn up in the Thames at Gravesend, a few days hence, to puzzle the overstretched authorities. Misgivings about the ethics of this commerce were growing in the secret hearts of some and a firm, correcting hand was required.

'After last time,' she giggled, not actually looking at anyone bar Jonah, but addressing the council all the same, 'I hope no one else is entertaining wicked, lustful thoughts.'

No one was. In view of the experience of the previous encounter, and the shaming deaths by intercourse, those present had reluctantly submitted to a programme of 'erotic expenditure' with self-sacrificing younger cadre members. Sore and tired, they were, for a while, proof against the banshee shriek of the flesh.

'Madam,' said the most exalted elder of the movement, fixing his fiery gaze just above her head, 'you have granted all that we have asked – and we are grateful—'

'All that *Jonah* asked,' she corrected, still not bothering to look at him. 'I don't listen to *your* prayers.'

'We are grateful, as I say,' the old man persevered. He had fifty years of coarsening activist involvement behind him, three major assassinations to his credit and, at the age of sixty, had cut his way out of the Reading bloodbath with a sabre. Fear was a distant, childhood memory to the man. Yet at that moment he felt it calling to him across the gulf of years.

She might not care if they were grateful or not. Exhaustive discussions hadn't agreed whether she ever really *noticed* their presence as separate entities. Everything she'd said and done had always been focused through the inadequate medium of Jonah Ransom, clothier of Guildford Town. This was the problem they sought to address.

'We wish to make our gratitude manifest,' he went on, 'if you will permit it . . .'

For a long, long while she stared up at a cross-beam in the barn roof. There was no reason to find it so utterly fascinating. It made her seem even more chillingly *alien* to them.

'Jonah?' she asked eventually. 'What do you think?'

He shrugged. Adrift in a mental and emotional tornado, he'd not much time for reasoning and decisions any more.

'Very well,' she said, and gave a curious little smirk and a twist of the shoulders like a society flirt.

The elder commended himself to Almighty God and then signalled that the door be opened.

In stepped the very finest specimen of young manhood – as conceived of by an unworldly, European terrorist movement. His hair was blond and thick, the eyes as blue and steely as could be reasonably wished. The fashionable claret frock-coat and silk breeches, the cravat and buckled shoes enhanced his soldierly frame as far as decency would permit. No expense had been spared on his clothes or on a crash course in the arts of love, courtesy of the Church-supervised brothels of Southwark. More importantly, the Leveller's ideologues had honed the hitherto serious and virginal youth to a high appreciation of his great mission. He knew precisely what he had to do and why. Their channel to the demon via Jonah wasn't good enough. The Levellers wanted to get a firmer grip on this sword they were wielding.

In view of the sad, known facts, wilder spirits in the council had suggested also providing a comparable female specimen for the monster to choose between, but the outrageous suggestion had been howled down. They hadn't gone *that* far down the road – not yet. With such thoughts of the indignities inflicted by cruel necessity, they awaited the crucial moment of decision.

Concealing the roar of his nerves, the youth flashed a perfect white smile at her.

There was a second or two of silence, then she smiled back and drew him to her side. This wasn't achieved in any normal way – nor performed with any affection. A huge invisible hand swept him up, wiping the smile from his face, and hurled him at the woman like a toy. Once there, she embraced him and an opaque haze surrounded the two. He began to scream.

No one moved to help. Jonah, the one man with any influence, thought she could do no wrong and the Levellers did not dare intervene. When they forced themselves, periodically, to watch, they could see glimpses of naked skin and entwined limbs and modesty was a welcome excuse to look away.

It was plain, though, that the youth was . . . diminishing. His shrill keening of distress was altering in tone, becoming thinner and less lusty. It began to be interspersed with great wrenching sobs.

After five minutes she simply expelled him from her

presence and he staggered back. The finery that had so stretched the Levellers' tithing of its members was as splendid as ever – but not so the man within. She had taken the years from him and the frock-coat which recently hugged his barrel chest now flapped loose over a withered frame. Its rich colour and newness of cut served only to contrast with the grey strands of hair and lined face above. The old-young man raised his creaking matchstick arms in horror and began to scream again.

The woman licked her lips.

'No,' she said. 'Very succulent, but, thank you all the same, I prefer Jonah.'

~

'What – more?' said Adam. 'You'll be drunk. I'm not having that.'

Nevertheless, the landlord of the Spread Eagle, who stoutly deluded himself he was still monarch of his own house, brought his townsman another sloe gin. Like its predecessors, it was downed in one.

'There's need of it,' gasped Pelling. 'I almost died, and the boy—'

'Rather him than you, that's what you should be saying.' Adam shrugged. 'Society hasn't the same need of him as it has of you – at the moment,' he added tactlessly.

The inn had swarmed with town constables before Adam's exchange of messages with Loseley brought their amateur investigations to an abrupt halt. Both the body and the cause of its demise were now taken away and given into the custody of the Church; each to be made safe – in their separate ways – in consecrated ground. Skivvies were cleaning up the blood and mending the window, and soon all visible signs of the incident would be gone. The gap left in Guildford life by the pot-boy's passing on was negligible. Within the hour his sole memorials would be an inconsolable woman and a freshly cast adrift Fred Pelling.

Even Adam saw the need for a degree of humouring the survivor. He nobly ignored the lack of thanks and coined the notion that Fred should be honoured by events.

'It's a weapon to take out kings and cardinals,' he'd said. 'An Arrow of the *Sagittari* isn't used on any old Tom, Dick or Pius. Someone thinks you're very important.'

Pelling wasn't comforted by the accolade. The reorientation he'd felt on reaching home ground had flooded away. The maelstrom of events had reached in and playfully rendered 'home' unrecognizable. If Adam would only permit it, he'd have sought oblivion in alcohol.

'Have you lost something recently?' the Sicarii asked, stretching out his legs in acceptance that they'd be in this corner seat for some time yet.

Fred could have answered in metaphysical terms about peace of mind but chose not.

'How do you mean?' he croaked, gazing into his empty glass.

'Some personal item. Clothing or something like that.'

Material possessions were the last considerations riding his thoughts at the moment. Pelling shook his head.

'Well you must have done,' said Adam. 'That's what they would have used to prime the arrow.'

'Most of my gear is at Loseley. I haven't checked.'

'There you are then. What they do is get some item intimately connected with the target and use magic to make the link. After that, it'll find you wherever you go. It's a terrible weapon, the *Sagittari*.'

Fred Pelling wasn't going to argue with that. 'I'm not worth one of those,' he complained.

'No, you wouldn't think so,' agreed Adam, unkindly.

'It's a question of the expense and the consequences of manufacture. I doubt any king in Christendom has more than a couple in his arsenal. You have to get Church licence for every one, of course, and there's so much blood and months of magic that has to go into the making. It puts years on the thaumaturgist and imperils his soul.'

'Will there be another?' said Pelling.

The Sicarii stared abstractedly at the other people in the bar. Without exception, the assembled yeomanry pretended there weren't Papal soldiers in their midst.

'I'd be very surprised,' he said. 'You've already bankrupted some great man or organization. I can't conceive of anyone rich enough to have two goes.' He at last condescended to take a drink from the mug of bitter beer provided him. The two troopers, ever on duty, continued to ignore theirs. 'Mind you,' he added, his face wrapped in puzzlement as the long-forgotten taste lingered pleasurably on his palate, 'don't listen to me. I didn't expect the first try.'

Pelling called for more gin.

~

'Bugger off! Oh . . .'

'Sorry?' said Adam. 'I didn't quite catch that.'

The bluecoat hadn't realized there was anyone standing behind Fred Pelling. The revised greeting came out impressively pat, in broad Norfolk.

'I said good morning, sir. Is there anything I can do for you?'

'Yes, there is actually. Bugger off,' said the Sicarii, strolling past him. Pelling hurriedly followed.

The little incident at the security cordon hadn't gone unnoticed. Already reinforcements were rushing up from the centre of the site. The way forward was blocked.

'Good day to you, Sicarii,' said the officer at their head. He was still buckling on his sword belt. 'How may I be of service?'

To a certain extent he already had been. The speed of the response, the way his men unobtrusively spread out into a semicircle round the visitors, spoke volumes. These weren't recent recruits or easily intimidated.

'I'm not altogether sure,' answered Adam. 'How do you think you may be of service?'

The officer was young but hardened. His faculty for easy amusement had been wrung out of him. 'I could introduce you to my commander,' he said, smiling. 'I think that would be a helpful move.'

Adam looked above and behind the man to where Guildford Castle had, he was reliably informed, once been. The jumble of rubble told him nothing.

'I concur,' he said, after a long and – to Pelling – fraught silence. 'Lead on.'

Predictably, that involved moving them off-site, and while most of the soldiers went ahead to show the way a few held back to deter loitering. Adam continued to be instructed.

The bluecoats had quite taken over Sydenham Road, a line of beam-and-daub artisans' cottages and alehouses which ran directly parallel to the High Street without actually joining it and thus letting the side down. Contrary to good military practice, a whole regiment had been jammed into the confined space, billeted in all the houses and spilling out, in tents, on to the road. Someone was evidently keen to pack a lot of force into a small place, ready for instant action. Adam noted that also and wondered who the 'someone' was.

That last question barely had time to make itself at home in the Sicarii's cold thoughts before it was answered.

Colonel Longstaff emerged from the gaudy command pavilion as Adam and Pelling and their escort approached. He didn't bother to hide his lack of joy at renewing their acquaintance.

'I heard you'd made it,' he said resignedly, signing papers for a military aide hovering by his side. 'Give me a few seconds to finish this, and then you can start bossing us around.'

~

'It fell down,' said Longstaff. 'Of old age. Even castles don't live for ever.'

Adam looked at Father Bancroft and Assistant Grandmaster Hillaire, but read nothing of value in either face. Grown old in the service of hard vocations, both had long since self-severed the connections between thought and expression.

'I recall,' said the Sicarii, 'a fortification in Lebanon-Philistia that was Crusader upon Roman upon Greek work. Yet, despite their antiquity, those walls served its Maronite defenders most well. We fought for two days to get in there. Afterwards, our legion had to be reformed.'

Longstaff twirled his inkstick around on the desk blotter.

'Perhaps the English climate is less kind to elderly structures,' he speculated. 'And it wasn't very well maintained, I'm told. The keep dated from King John's time, so you can hardly say it owed us money ... Is any of this at all important?'

Bancroft, his two magicians and the gaunt Hillaire had been 'at home' in the Angel coaching inn, more or less awaiting Adam's arrival. Once gathered together by Longstaff, they'd repaired to an upper room to confer.

From the very start it was clear that, for all that their

surroundings were comfort itself, despite the deep arm-chairs and blazing apple-log fire of the cigar-lounge the meeting would be less than convivial. Adam was plainly a loose cannon hurtling across the deck of other people's plans and he got the appropriate welcome. Loose cannons were usually tied down or pitched overboard and the Sicarii couldn't yet discern which was the favoured option.

'It might be important,' he replied to Longstaff. 'It might not be. Have you such a richness of leads that you can afford to dismiss anything?'

Father Bancroft steepled his fingers and appeared some-what fatigued. 'I do take your point, Sicarii,' he said, 'but I think we might risk excluding the collapse of aged structures from our foremost thoughts. I can't see that it betokens much of relevance to us. Are we to be so universally suspicious as to ponder on every little hap-penstance? Events urge us on at a more spritely pace, surely.'

Hillaire looked at Adam, thinking his own thoughts. The Sicarii noted that and was advised.

'You've got seven days, we know that,' said Longstaff, as blunt as you like. 'Six now. Shouldn't you be out and about concerning yourself with better things than dead monuments?'

Events could have taken a lively turn then, had not Hillaire intervened.

'We heard of the events in London, Sicarii,' he said. 'The disastrous summoning and ensuing unrest. You were an eyewitness. I should like to speak to you about it.'

The others paused, waiting for him to continue, but the magician leant back in his chair, content with silent listening once again. Adam found cheerful confirmation of factionalism within the English contingent. At least one representative would rather confer in private. That was heartening.

Bancroft allowed only a surface ripple of his displeasure to show. He stirred restlessly in his seat to occupy the awkward moment, frowning at the upholstery's noisy protests.

'An inquest has been convened,' he said, tacking something of his own on to Hillaire's words to give the impression of continuity. 'Two grandmasters are analysing the demonic intrusion which you saw – and happily survived. I'll make their report available to you, of course. Meanwhile, all major summonings are under a ban, for fear of permitting the abomination entrance again.'

'From what I hear,' commented Hillaire, 'she'll come, should she so want, whether we call or not. What say you, Sicarii?'

'I agree,' replied Adam. 'She wasn't too troubled by mere human magic last time.'

'All the more reason,' snapped Bancroft, 'to strive against there ever being a next time. We seem to be in an age of black miracles, gentlemen: Kings disappear whilst the excrements of Satan come unbidden. Am I alone in seeking the most direct route back to blessed normality?'

'One does wonder ...' mused Longstaff, looking at no one in particular.

Adam stared into the crackling heart of the fire and smiled as though at some private witticism.

'Very well,' he said. 'I'll be as direct as you could wish. One: are you the slightest step nearer to His Majesty the King?'

Bancroft opened his mouth to speak but Hillaire was quicker.

'No,' he said.

'Right. Two: who owns the soldiers?'

'Me,' said Longstaff. 'I've been given temporary colonelcy of the Wisbech Regiment.'

'How curious *they* should turn up in Guildford,' observed Adam. 'How nice, how ... unprecedented. Three: who'd shoot a *Sagittari* at my good friend Fred Pelling?'

There was no surprise in the room; half the town had heard of the incident and the other half soon would.

'No one in their right mind,' answered Father Bancroft. 'It must have been meant for you.'

'No,' said Adam. 'It had its chance with me and didn't take it.'

'Then someone out of their mind,' Bancroft shot back. 'I suppose that could, by definition, include those who hold His Majesty. Up to now, though, one hasn't despised their judgement and strategy ...'

Adam got up, the rapid movement taking the others present by surprise.

'I shouldn't start, then,' he said to the priest-turned-spy. 'They've made monkeys of us so far. Keep up the good work. Let me know if you do anything useful.'

He was away out of the room before a suitable farewell could be composed. In the hallway outside, Pelling was waiting and wilting under the gaze of Father Bancroft's two magicians. Only too happy to be swept along and away in the wake of the Sicarii, he fled the hotel which, like so much else, was once familiar but now under strange occupation. Neither spoke until they were out of earshot, in the neutral bustle of the High Street.

'So?' enquired Pelling, who'd had enough of tense silence and muffled, raised voices from behind closed doors.

'Nothing but bad news,' said Adam as they walked on side by side.

Pelling's steps faltered.

They passed under the great gilded projection of the town clock and it struck a stately quarter-chime.

'We're on our own,' Adam said. 'Those who are meant to help us won't. For some reason, we're about the only ones who want to see the King again.'

Pelling constructed a weak smile. 'Yes, you could call that bad news,' he said.

'It makes my job a bit harder. We have to watch our backs. By the way, that wasn't Guildford Castle, was it?'

'No,' said Pelling. 'It's builder's rubble brought in from somewhere. The castle was built of different stuff. It's gone.'

'I thought so. Well, now Guildford may go the same way.'

Pelling's head swivelled round in dismay. 'What?'

'That's the really bad news – as far as you're concerned. The Tigers are here.'

Access to a 'can-do' mentality and unlimited slave labour enabled the Romans to make something of the Fens. At Britannia's height of achievement huge Imperial farming estates wrenched prosperity from land that rightly belonged to Neptune. As the Imperium then faded gradually away, so the water made a slow return and the 'Great Drownings' came back into being.

Other civilizations took up the struggle in turn. The labour of monks held the line for some centuries before their works were brought to nothing in the calamitous Wars of Religion. Their successors, the secular 'protestant' lords who appropriated the monastic holdings, then kept up the work for the few brief decades granted them as a class.

When it arrived and secured mastery, the resurgent Church had better things to do than worry over the estates of its enemies. There were more worthy recipients for its charity. Those same lords had enclosed the land and dispossessed its people. In their hour of need, there was no honest peasantry left to proxy-plead their cause and touch the Church's heart. The dykes and ditches were permitted to clog and, one winter, a storm carried the roaring sea into the heart of East Anglia. Water, in either fresh or salt form, was there to stay.

'Protector' Cromwell had wrought his will upon the waters, using prisoners from his Scottish wars. Then he thought better of it, hearing the petitions of the Fen fish and reed men, who liked things as they were. The revival of the Drownings had made them masterless and brought a fair living in its wake. When the drainage systems were left unfinished, they hailed him 'Lord of the Fens' and he, bar holy Mother Church, was the last ruler they ever acknowledged.

In the infancy of the twentieth century, when a later, proper King of England revived the project, people had forgotten the Fens had ever been anything other than what they were now. Just because there was a sudden surplus of labour, captives from yet another northern border war, the Fenfolk saw no reason why their world should be destroyed. They fought the labourers (descendants of those who'd laboured in vain before) and the Dutch and English engineers, bizarrely re-fighting His Majesty's Caledonian campaign in miniature two hundred miles further south.

In the day they would snipe at the operations, bringing down the supervisors with their long-barrelled fowling pieces. At night they glided in on low black punts to kill the workers and burn the works. Pursuing troops perished in the trackless wastes, victims of treacherous tides or ambushed by shot-filled punt-cannons. His Majesty became angry, but the grim Fenmen were not impressed or persuaded by the ring of gibbets round their watery homes. They didn't take prisoners either.

The Church patched things up when they heard the King planned genocide. He was brought to wiser counsel by a no-nonsense talk with a Papal Legate, but his face was saved by the savage penance imposed on the rebels. The hate-filled eyes of the surrounding Royal troops beheld great numbers of the short, dark Fenfolk emerge from the reeds to make expiation and peace with Mitre and Crown.

The Drownings remained, the Fen's inhabitants stayed a people apart. Hard things were said of them: that they worked their children and that sister was the same as wife amongst them. It was whispered that they revered a watery Fengod in the privacy of their land and made sacrifice to it, seizing upon hapless lost travellers. What was indisputable was that malaria made their lives hard and short, and between that and childbirth women didn't last long there. The richer Fenmen bought new wives from greedy flatland farmers and ferried them back to an unenviable life. A few years later, the same men would be back for a replacement. It was said that they didn't bother to give their females names.

Then there were the 'Fen Tigers', rarely seen but often heard; blood-freezing howls coming from the marshland fringe at night. Occasionally, in hard years, sheep and children were taken from the flatlands, leaving only a smear of blood. Nature's first-born, its experiments from before man, found it easy to hang on in the water wastes of the Fens when their brethren were expelled from more settled lands. The Fen dwellers said the tigers were man-shaped but 'all hair and teeth' and they waged a bloody, endless war against them. Their elders were content with that ceaseless struggle. It made them watchful, they said, and weeded out the weaklings.

When, as part of that Church-arranged apology to His Majesty, they agreed, for the first time, to send young men to serve in his forces, the new-raised regiment needed to be named. Officially it received the prosaic title of Wisbech, the nearest town, where Fenmen rarely went and were never welcome. Unofficially they were called the 'Fen Tigers', initially from the creatures they first fought and then, when that war was as won as it'd ever be, from their manner in the outside world. For the Fenmen had no love for the soft, easy-living 'drylanders' and didn't bother to hide their disdain. The Crown soon learned to be careful where it posted the regiment, and it required harsher handling than most. Slit throats and the gibbet seemed to follow it around.

On the plus side, though, the Tigers – or even the threat of them – were found to be very good at extracting back taxes from recalcitrant areas. When Cornwall (or 'Kernow' as was) was absorbed on this pretext in the 'twenties, the Wisbech Regiment did the job almost single-handed. True, the strict need for the Sack of Truro was, at best, debatable, but the Crown made swift amends by posting the regiment abroad. Based in the Jaffa Citadel, and then in the endless wheat plains of the Ukraine, the Tigers learned new tricks from pagan enemies and honed their low opinion of the world. At home His Majesty's generals remained proud of their fierce and expendable English-yet-foreigners and brought them back as soon as the Cornish scandal died down.

Now, in Adam's day, the unwelcome gift of Father

Bancroft's 'age of black miracles', someone had seen fit for the Tigers to pay their respects to Fred Pelling's homeland.

~

The Church had accepted the development of railways, albeit with a show of ill grace. Even today the ultra-pious declined to venture on them, eschewing the 'presumption' of transport quicker than that provided by nature. Nevertheless the Church Universal, in its great wisdom, had seen that steam power could not be uninvented. Nor could the restless minds of men be persuaded, save by shameful force, from toying with the benefits following in its noisy wake. Besides, even the most regretful of 'advances' could prove of legitimate use . . .

In Italy and the Empire – and even, to a lesser extent, in sleepy United England – the nineteenth century became remembered as the age of the railway. Each successive Holy Father had watched benignly on, reconciled that life should become a little faster and more frantic. If ever that pace of change became excessive, they stepped in to calm the fevered developers and curb their infinite greed. In the end it worked rather well. The fabric of society was gently stretched rather than torn asunder. The town walls were breached – by track – but not burst. Increased trade benefited all, and easier, more frequent travel amongst the rich (who alone could afford the Church-determined fares) suited the Vatican's cosmopolitan integrationist aims. The firm prohibition against kings and princes travelling thus similarly served to hobble the Church's rivals. It was thought appropriate that the heads of mere nations should shift themselves about at a more . . . stately pace.

Best of all, the heir of St Peter found that the new invention was the means of making his will the more quickly known. Instead of relying on slow and all-too-fallible relays of horse-borne messengers, letters, Bulls and proclamations could now be in the furthest reaches of Christendom within days of their conception. It was likewise by means of the steam locomotive that Adam was rushed to do his master's will from the Land of the Mameluke-Caliph to London in such very short order.

The radical, unsettling implications of the invention of rail were thus felt everywhere by high and low alike, even down to Adam's day in provincial Guildford.

~

'I'll need to know soon,' grunted the bluecoat. 'He's travelling some.'

His officer, standing behind him, frowned in indecision. 'Keep your aim,' he said. 'I'm thinking.'

The soldier obediently continued to train his long-barrelled fowling rifle on the target below. He was confident of a hit for a good few seconds yet. Red-coated horsemen, even galloping ones, were easy meat compared to the wary birds and beasts he'd been trained on.

The Papal courier had been tracked ever since he disembarked at Dover. Observant eyes had followed him first to London and then into Surrey. It had been done efficiently enough and no one could complain. At the same time, though, there'd been a pitiful failure of will. No decision had been made; no one wanted to be the one to act. Now, at the last possible moment, it was left for a junior officer of the Tigers to make a move – or not – as he thought best. Not for the first time recently, that man wished birth and chance had put him on the side with bit of *backbone* to it. If he truly understood the way things were going, they'd need a command made of sterner stuff in days to come.

And talking of days, the officer cursed the damned

railways and the way they speeded things up. They'd not be tolerated around the edge of the Drownings, he mused, that's for sure. His people might well be as rough as coal-bunkers in many respects, but they kept to the faith – as best they could. But for those dirty, blasphemous machines, the courier would still be on his way to London. But for them, the officer wouldn't need to decide whether to silence the Pope.

Rail-hastened and cosseted for most of his way, the courier was blissfully unaware that on the walls of St Catherine's Priory the grim reaper was peering down a barrel at him. As far as he was concerned, Guildford and his mission's end were in sight. It was quite unthinkable that anyone should seek to hinder him in his task, let alone abort it. No one ever attacked a Papal courier for fear of overwhelming reprisals – in this world and the next. It had never happened, not in living memory. His uniform was far better protection than the sword and pistol he also happened to carry.

In the pouch bouncing against the horse's lathered side were vellum scripts, sealed with dark red wax and the cross-keys imprint. The pouch itself bore a similar closure. Five days before they'd rested on a most exalted desk in Rome for perusal and approval. A secretary's hand had addressed them to Adam. Now a Fenland captain stood in judgement as to whether the ruler of half the world should be heard. He'd never thought to achieve such 'promotion'.

When it was almost now-or-never, his net-and-gun-calloused hand gently pressed the rifle down off-target. Both men sighed their quiet relief. In the chilly privacy of his thoughts and prayers, the officer of the Tigers had found guidance, and the strength to refrain from action.

'Let His Holiness speak to the Sicarii monster,' he

muttered. 'That way, whatever happens, it's plainly God's own will.'

The common soldier, who had a hearty fear of God's will – and an even greater terror of events outside it – uncocked his gun and crossed himself.

~

'Aren't we lucky people,' said Adam. 'Letters in the post and all of them good news, no doubt.'

'No doubt,' echoed Fred Pelling in ironic tone, looking dubiously at the courier's deliveries spread out on the table. The giant, unpromising red seals didn't have the air of concealing glad tidings.

'Right,' the Sicarii continued, 'a spot of paperwork and then we can move to settle this nonsense.'

The Pelling eyebrows were raised. 'As simple as that?' he asked, not knowing whether to be relieved or fearful.

Adam looked at him with the innocent eyes of the fearless. 'Everything's simple if you're *direct* enough,' he said, as though stating the obvious, and returned to sorting his correspondence.

Pelling was still chewing on that one when the door of their room was knocked upon. Adam consulted his pocket chronometer.

'It should be that army chap,' he said, louder than was normal for him, loud enough to be heard outside. 'Let him in, will you? And don't worry: *Sagittari* arrows never knock before entering.'

That might have passed for humour in Sicarii circles, but the fun was lost on Fred. He gingerly eased the door open to find it was indeed Colonel Longstaff. Two men of the Wisbechs accompanied him.

'You summoned me?' he said drily, addressing Adam.

153

'I did. Come in. No, don't sit down, this won't take long. Are you free later this afternoon?'

The soldier was studying the various exalted communications on the table, extracting what information he could from the sight.

'I'm at your disposal,' he answered, deadpan. 'As you well know. For the moment, that is.'

'Oh, good,' said Adam, sounding like a little lad given a new toy to play with. 'Perhaps you'd be kind enough to meet me at about five by the far end of the castle remnant – across from the bear garden.'

'Very well,' said Longstaff. 'Why?'

'Just a chat and consultation. We stand in need of your expert opinion. Now, if you'll excuse us . . .'

The Colonel was keen to delay compliance with his rough dismissal.

'By the way,' he said, 'the wizard Hillaire's gone – been called elsewhere. Thought you might like to know.'

Adam disobligingly failed to react. 'I was all too aware he'd not called on me as promised. Goodbye then, Assistant Grandmaster Hillaire. And likewise goodbye, Colonel Longstaff.'

Longstaff pursed his lips in some sort of farewell and about turned. All too predictably, the door was slammed.

Pelling allowed time for three sets of boots to clump their way down the Spread Eagle stairs before speaking.

'What for?' he asked. 'He's no help. You've so determinedly insulted him that all he wants to do is kill us. Why are we going to meet him?'

'We're not,' answered Adam, somewhat abstracted as he slit the first of the vellum packages with a slim knife that, worryingly for Pelling, had seemed to come from nowhere. 'I want him out of the way at a certain time, just like they wanted Hillaire out of the way. The colonel

can wait in limbo while we have our town tour undisturbed. It's all right, there's a nice view for him to look
at.'

'But—'

'And speaking of disturbances, I've told the landlord no
more visitors after Longstaff, not until I say so. The
troopers will enforce it. Were you expecting anyone?'

'No.'

'And he's to bring us some spiced beer and food at
about three. There's pease pudding on the menu. That
suit you?'

'Yeah, I suppose so, though—'

'We should be through by then. I hope he serves it with
bacon fat and pepper. Do you think he will?'

'Well, probably. That's the traditional—'

'*So* then, this one's from the Archbishop of London.'

Pelling looked out of the window. He could see the
High Street and all the normal life therein. Fred studied
it as a drowning man would dry land.

'Hmm, interesting,' said Adam, recalling his companion's attention. 'There are extracts from the official
report about what he calls "The London Incursion".' He
unfolded the large sheet and smoothed it down with his
hand. It was covered from top to toe in copperplate
Church Latin.

'The what?' queried Fred, resignedly sitting himself
down across from the Sicarii. This cup clearly wasn't
going to 'pass from his lips'.

'You know,' said Adam, looking up. 'The summoning
at the citadel. Surely you haven't—'

'No, I haven't forgotten,' said Pelling, enunciating the
words very clearly. 'There's precious little danger of that.
It was the terminology that—'

'Let me see ...' Adam scanned the document. 'There

155

are casualty figures – goodness me – and stuff like that. And what's the point of all this thaumaturgic algebra? I can't read that; someone's just trying to fill a page. Ah, but here we are: "Preliminary Speculations". Demon lords ... intrusive ravishment of laws of summoning ... penetrative breach of divinely ordained separation of worlds ... tentative identifications – see separate sheet ...'

Adam delved into the covering wrapper and extracted a smaller leaf of vellum.

'"Abigor: a demon of high degree, the Grand Duke of Hell. Sixty legions are under his command. He reveals himself as a handsome rider bearing a mace, standard or sceptre; or else a lithesome maid flaunting her private parts. He knows all the secrets of war, foresees the future and can tell kings the way to win the love of their soldiers.

'"Adrammelech: Grand Chancellor of Hell, Superintendent of the Wardrobe of the ruler of demons and President of the High Council of Devils. He has the face of an ugly hag and is seen riding on an infernal dragon, holding a viper in his left hand. He was worshipped at Sepharvahim, an Assyrian city, where children were burned on altars of bronze. He sports a fan of peacock feathers from his fundament and commands ninety legions ..."

'There are a few more. Do you want me to read them, Fred?'

'No,' said Pelling. 'Those'll do to be going on with.'

'I agree. They've no idea really. The gist of it seems to be that something new and huge came through, and at its own behest. "This contradicts all precedent and understanding of the rules of demonic interaction. Accordingly, all future summonings, until further notice, require licensing at episcopal level for fear of re-contact." Basically, we're dealing with an unknown and we're on our own.

156

Best of luck, boys. That seems a fair summary, wouldn't you say?'

'I'd question the "fair" bit,' said Pelling.

'Me too. Open the other one, would you? I'll check there's nothing else relevant here.'

Fred Pelling had never thought to see the day when he'd open a letter from His Holiness. There was no sense to his reluctance, but he hardly dared to break a seal that bore the mark of Rome. What proper connection could there be between a Pelling and a man who was ruler of this world and had contacts in the next? His hands fumbled over the task. Adam noted it.

'He's a mortal man the same as us,' he said. 'Besides, it was probably only a cardinal. Get on with it.'

Pelling broke the great red disc in two and opened the stiff covering sheet. A number of pages tumbled on to the table and to the floor. Fred hastened to recover these errant leaves, so disrespectfully scattered at his feet, and made to hand them to Adam.

'No, you look,' he said. 'I'm still reading this.'

Fred warily addressed his eyes to the missive and began to scan. Within minutes his sense of wonder started to dissipate. As Adam had said, it was just plain handwriting, the script of a mere man – and none too neat at that. Once that was accepted his brain could start to look for meaning in the words.

'It's notes,' he said eventually. 'Random notes.'

Adam looked up, patently bored with his own letter. 'Show,' he said.

Pelling obliged.

'These are the Legate's notes,' explained the Sicarii. 'His research for the trip here. There'll be nothing random about them. Leastways, someone thought them worth passing on. Give me a précis.'

Pelling refocused on the red-ink scrawl.

'Well . . .' he read, 'the first lot's about olden times: the Wessex Riots in the 'twenties, my dad told me about them. A load of stuff about hayrick burning and hangings. There's a bit about some peasants transported to the Med-galleys in 'forty-five. He's cross-referenced that to a load of figures about the Church-dole take-up and . . . enforce-ment of those minimum wage Bulls Pope Cornelius proclaimed in—'

'Skip it,' interrupted Adam, his full interest obviously awakened. 'Numbers only ever tell half a story.'

'Suits me, I never got round to numeracy studies. They cost extra and the family couldn't—'

'Just read, will you?' snapped the Sicarii with rare impatience.

'Okay, okay. Then there's a fair bit about the Thames Valley Crusade in 1990 – you know the song "Reading's Burning" and all that – but he's crossed it out for some reason. The next part's rather dull.'

'It's probably important then,' commented Adam, making it as good as an order.

'All right. It seems to be a list of Parliament Bills – the Westminster talking shop. They're land-improvement leg-islation "for the more efficient usage of agriculture". It starts in 1931 and goes up to a few years back – though there's less detail about the recent ones. He's got the area affected, the bill's sponsor, the acreage . . . Are you sure this is relevant?'

'Desperately,' mused the Sicarii, his eyes glazed by contemplation.

'If you say so. After that he's back to his "rural unrest" theme, revolting peasants here and there, troublemakers going for the "long drop" . . . stuff about average churl remuneration in returns to the Vatican College of "Temporal Welfare". He doesn't draw any conclusions.'

'I shouldn't be so sure of that,' said Adam, with a smug smile. 'I hear his footsteps keeping pace with my inmost thoughts.'

'Well, anyway it ends there, except someone else has put a single note at the bottom – the hand and the ink are different.'

Adam peered at the section Pelling indicated. 'I recognize it,' he said evenly. 'The general of my order wrote that. I'm honoured.'

Fred looked again at the confident script. It seemed imbued with new authority.

'Couldn't he have written you a letter? Wouldn't that be plainer?'

Adam shook his head. 'Not necessary. We think alike. If he searched the Legate's papers and made this selection, that should suffice.'

'It's nothing new,' said Pelling, reading on, 'only an update. Apparently there are land-improvement bills going through regarding Hampshire and Wiltshire, and there was a tithe riot in Basingstoke last year. So what? They're half mad there anyway.'

'They are now,' sighed Adam. 'Is that it?'

'That's it.'

'What's that other loose sheet attached?'

Pelling unfolded it and gave the contents a distrustful look.

'I'm not a dab hand at neo-Latin. I can make myself understood, like, but—'

Adam reached lazily over and took it. '"Diatribe De Mille Annis Apocalypticis",' he read. 'It's a heading sheet from a Papal Encyclical, a warning issued before you were born.'

'Against what?' asked Pelling. He was very attentive as regards warnings – particularly so of late.

'Against lots of things, Fred.' Adam's face was a mask of cold disdain. 'Against trying to bring on Doomsday. Against thinking enough blood will summon "King Jesus" to rule on earth. Against a monarchy of "saints" ruling a world of "unsanctified" human cattle. Minor stuff like that.'

Sensing all too well which side of the fence he'd find himself on that day, Pelling could heartily share the Sicarii's disapproval. He looked at the Latin text as though it described the programme for tomorrow.

Adam snapped him out of it by smiling broadly. 'So that's that then, Fred Pelling.' He beamed. 'We've got it now. You and I have saved the King and rescued England from itself.'

'We have?' said Pelling warily.

'Well ... in principle anyway,' Adam conceded. 'We'd better round things off and actually *do* it ...'

Reviewing their long and hazardous years of training, every newly qualified thaumaturgist gives thanks for mere survival and considers himself Lord of All Creation. He then turns his attention to the field of demonology and finds that he teeters on the edge of uncharted seas, a hapless, ignorant and frightened student once again.

Most – and there is great wisdom in this – turn back inshore and lead lives of usefulness and contentment in the 'ordinary' practice of their art. The courage (and folly) of illustrious predecessors have given them the ten major and ninety-seven minor summonings and that suffices. A very few, however, slaves to dangerous compulsions, cannot let matters rest. They are driven (for there can surely be no other reason) to venture out on that sea of unknowing, in far from serviceable craft. Of those few explorers and fishermen – to labour the maritime metaphor – a tiny number come back with a worthwhile catch. No one seems to dwell overmuch on those who fail to return.

In the thirteenth century, the Spaniard Ibarra told us of the powers in the darkness. The Church resisted the news and then, capitulating, called them 'demons'. Four centuries on, the English Arch-mage Robin Corbishly stared them in the face and wrote down their names. They regarded us with new respect. Two centuries later still, Liguori rewrote the 'Corbishly Codex' and dispensed with the division into 'good' and 'evil'. I, in my own day, allowed man to know them better, the easier to prostitute them to our wishes. The Church, my profession, my peers, they all honoured me for this. They were mistaken.

Here at the end of my life, I look out from my palace at Pevensey Bay and watch the sea. The sea does not alarm me; it might be stormy and full of peril, but I know it will ultimately respect the land and not venture in. Moreover, I know it is not infinite. There is an end to the sea and then

*there is France. The same cannot be said of the demonological
ocean.*

*Another, younger I sailed far out into that expanse and saw
that there was no end to it. There is nothing wholesome
beyond its furthest limit. Behind the mere 'demons' we scarce
dare to summon stand their still stronger masters, ascending in
power; beyond our comprehension, in unceasing array. Mankind ought not to bring himself to their attention. Should that
tide ever sweep in, I misdoubt they would even sense our
species' demise.*

*But I am old and tired and all that I have learned in my
life leads me not to care . . .*

(Suppressed) Introduction to fifth, revised edition of
*Demonology – an Over-elaborate Art* by Grandmaster of Magic
(South-East) Tobias Oakley B.A., M.A., Ph.D. (Thau).
Published Eastbourne, Auto-da-fé Press. The Year of Our
Salvation 2027.

'"Arrival at borough boundary, after night spent at Loseley House as guest of Lady Onslow, approx nine a.m. Civic reception."'

'They were running late,' Pelling informed Adam. 'His Majesty wanted second helpings of breakfast – or another wench, I dunno. Anyway, it were nearer ten o'clock.'

The Sicarii looked up from the printed itinerary he had been reading from.

'Well,' he observed drily, 'that may have screwed up (if you'll excuse the phrase) some people's plans, but not everyone's. The trap still worked.'

Pelling could hardly deny it. He shrugged.

'I can't believe this was run off for public circulation!' Adam protested, shaking the itinerary in disgust. 'Civic crest and all! Do you know what this *is*? This is a fervent prayer for King Charles' assassination – or worse. Don't you like him here?'

Pelling bridled. 'We're loyal enough!' he said. '*Libera deinde Fidelis*. Faithful because Free. That's the town motto. Your standards aren't ours. This isn't Muscovy: we don't carry a stone in our sling every bloody minute of the day. There's no need ... not normally,' he concluded weakly.

Adam turned his glacial and humourless gaze full blast on to Fred Pelling. A silence fell between them that stretched abominably on. Pelling resigned himself to a blow of some sort.

'Fair enough,' snapped the Sicarii, apparently accepting the argument and resuming his study of the itinerary. 'I still maintain it's bad security, though.'

'As you say,' said Pelling, wildly happy to have something to agree with and amazed by Adam's strange, new liberality. 'Look, why don't we move out of the road and discuss this somewhere safe?'

The Sicarii had insisted on occupying the centre of the High Street to make his considered analysis. He wanted to see *precisely* what the King might have seen just before he ascended the cathedral steps and stepped out of history. More to the point, he wished to note who might have seen the Monarch of United England at that exact moment. He'd made an inventory of the relevant windows and vantage spots.

That was all very well but they were holding up the traffic. Ordinarily, the carters and coachmen weaving around them might have had choice words to say. However, in deference to the uniform of red, they'd so far restricted themselves to grim glances at Fred.

'Safe?' asked Adam. 'Where's safe here?'

Pelling deftly indicated the raised pavement – and a particularly large public-hire cab and four bearing down on them.

Adam looked at it without concern, but moved all the same. 'Okay,' he said. 'I've seen what I want to.'

Off the steeply pitched setts of the High Street, Pelling could relax a little, though he was conscious that across the town the fiery Colonel Longstaff was, at that very moment, keeping a solitary appointment.

'Then they processed to here,' he explained to Adam, keen to divert his nervousness, 'so as to meet the Bishop. He was waiting at the cathedral door at the top of the steps. If things had gone on he would have delivered a collective blessing and conditional indulgence. You see, if you've got a king nearby—'

'Yes, yes,' interrupted the Sicarii, '"King David's Blessing" – proximate sanctification via the Royal and Anointed. We get to see a fair few kings in Rome, you know.'

'I dare say you do,' said Pelling. It was a sore point with

patriots everywhere that no monarch could be crowned in his own land. His Holiness alone was able to confer a throne.

Adam reconsulted the itinerary. 'Then there was to be High Mass – concelebration with full thaumaturgic auxiliaries: say an hour and a quarter. What about the Bishop's sermon, though?'

'Short and sweet. His Majesty's well known for that preference.'

Adam looked up at the bargate and flint crenelated tower of Holy Trinity Cathedral that soared above the town. He followed its 'broach' spire's trajectory into the heavens seeking inspiration or, perhaps, patience.

'No,' he commented without inflection. 'Charles is not the most pious of men, is he? But perhaps recent events will refresh his wells of wisdom. There is that good to be hoped for from all this, if nothing else.'

Pelling nodded dubiously.

'And after that,' Adam went on, 'there should have been the "Popular Address" from the cathedral gate.'

'Five minutes, maximum,' said Pelling.

'A jest, stock flattery of the town, an admonition to duty and prompt payment of tax,' agreed the Sicarii. 'Then the blessing of the Guildhall by the Legate.'

As though answering its name, the clock projecting from that structure called out the hour. They would soon be late for Colonel Longstaff.

'"A Progress from the town to the Challonor Shrine at Sutton Place." What's that?'

'It's where the Westons lived in the Days of Darkness – when they were recusants and persecuted. After the Church came back they were given Loseley House and their old place was sanctified. All the Guildford martyrs from them days are buried there.'

'Not the sort of venue his Regal and Holy Highness Charles would hang around at unduly, I shouldn't reckon,' ventured Adam.

'No,' conceded Pelling. 'We didn't think so either. Not his idea of fun.'

'So he'd be away within the hour and out of the area by one-ish. That's three hours total in Guildford proper. A narrow window of time for a big operation – not much leeway.'

'It was enough,' muttered Fred.

'Interesting,' mused Adam, more to himself than to his companion. 'The power they're wielding is controllable to that extent anyway. It can be aimed. Let's go in.'

Pelling had noticed before the Sicarii's manner of closing down a line of thought with guillotine abruptness. He pondered, concluded – and moved straight on, regardless of whether others were keeping pace. Growing familiarity made it no less disconcerting.

'Where?' asked Fred – but Adam was already halfway across the street, ready to bound up the cathedral steps.

These were new and hurriedly constructed: untreated wooden replacements for the hallowed slabs of Horsham stone that had – along with Monarch, Legate and Bishop – been taken. Studying them properly for the first time, a new mood dawned unexpectedly upon Fred Pelling. He compared their transitory appearance to recollections of what had been before and at last perceived the vast ... slight upon his church and town and nation. Because of what had happened, the steps that his forefathers had trod, that had borne their brides and babies and, at the end, their box, were gone and lost. The source of salvation in Guildford had now to be approached by way of ... planks. Tacked on to the work of a thousand faithful years, they made everything seem shoddy.

166

The Pelling that followed Adam into Holy Trinity was freshly inspired. A moment's thought, and it had all become strangely personal.

He joined the Sicarii beyond the porch. Together they dipped fingertips in the water stoups and genuflected to the altar light. Neither was really aware of having made the sign of the cross, so instinctive had the act become. At the same time, the sights within reached out and touched their hearts. Separate, but equal, indoctrinations in youth made it almost inevitable.

The Commissioners of Mary III 'Restorationist' had brought Holy Trinity back into proper life and done so in glorious form. Money (courtesy of the 'Tudor nobility', church-land grabbers now dispossessed in turn) had been no object. The very best of everything, of skills and wealth, had been put to work in the ravished churches of England. Nor had the avenging Queen acted alone. As in most places, the laymen of Guildford had come forward, slowly at first and then more swiftly, confident that the 'Changes' were at an end, bringing images and relics long hidden from the 'protestant' iconoclasts. Carefully 'broken' rood screens and altar rails were reassembled and put back. The saints were recovered from obscure concealment and restored to places of honour.

In this atmosphere of fervour the tomb of Guildford's most famous son and generous benefactor, George Abbot, King James I's excommunicate Archbishop of Canterbury, had been smashed asunder. All memory of his 'negligent stewardship' was expelled from Holy Trinity. But then, when the great struggle was past question and heresy quashed, calmer minds prevailed. A wiser, more forgiving Prince of the Church had returned him to his first resting place.

Who, he had asked, could be sure that they would have

stood unbending before the winds that blew in that reign? Only the good that men did should be recalled; their wickedness should be left buried with them.

The tomb was reassembled as best it could be and Guildford's patron was brought back from the unhallowed pit to which he'd been confined. The townsfolk said little but, with this and other gestures, slowly grew to love Mother Church once again.

Whilst Pelling, the local patriot, rested his eyes on the famous 'Sundered Tomb', Adam, who was possessed of wider sympathies, checked that all was as it should be. Through training and experience he knew what to expect of every grade of church. Any manifestation of neglect or unorthodoxy would have screamed out at him. He could see none and was reassured.

As provincial cathedrals in second-rate nations went, this was, he felt sure, a living, thriving centre of worship. The banners of the trade guilds and religious confraternities, the pennants of the 'Knights', the Hospitalers and the Leagues of Mary were present and correct. He observed that the humbler classes had given freely of their time and coin to beautify this house with embroidery and carving and every sundry artisan skill. The metallic big toe of the St Peter of the Keys by the door was shiny through constant supplication by the faithful and the Lady Chapel was aglow with flowers.

For a moment Adam unclenched the fist that had been made of his heart. He permitted himself to realize the great ... joy he felt to be part of this civilization, this cosmic plan, and everything that really mattered. He could not recall the last time he had been so tempted to ... weaken. Proximity to Pelling and the soft Surrey life he represented seemed to have unlocked some doors in him.

For the briefest of intervals shafts of light fell in long-darkened rooms. Adam was shocked.

'Nice, innit?' whispered Pelling, snapping the Sicarii out of his rare holiday. Fred didn't understand why his question merited such a black look.

'It'll do,' Adam answered. 'Do you want to go?'

Pelling wasn't a great churchgoer. It felt slightly odd to be there outside holy or sabbath days.

'When you're ready.'

Adam was no thaumaturgist, but as far as reason could allow he felt sure that the enemy had not passed these doors. The power he was hunting therefore came solely from without. It was a relief to find that the foundations of all that was right and proper had not been undermined, however ropey the visible structure – mere kings and governments – might presently seem. That greatly simplified his job.

'Give me a minute.'

The Sicarii left Pelling and strode along the nave. In common with other Guildfordians, the few elderly folk and professional chantrists there pretended he was invisible. The priest attending the confessionals graciously overlooked the solecism of a sword borne near the body of the Living God.

Adam went down on one knee and bowed his head before the flare of candlelight atop the altar.

Pelling politely ignored Adam's devotions and idly browsed the gratis Auto-da-fé publications in the racks by the door. He'd read most of them already, though a new treatise on purgatory seemed worth pocketing (not to mention appropriate) for future study when – and if – life returned to normal.

It had never occurred to Fred that the Sicarii could *grow* in confidence. But when Adam returned Pelling saw that the trick was indeed possible. He had referred some decision to the Almighty and obtained approval. Fred didn't dare doubt the wisdom of the Lord but, for his part, he rather preferred the old, unjustified Adam.

Smiling, the Sicarii passed him by. He was saying something. Wrapped up in new concerns, Pelling missed it.

'Sorry?' He caught up.

'I *said*,' snapped Adam, 'is there someone who hears everything? Most small towns have one. Is there a person with his finger on Guildford's feeble pulse?'

Pelling let that pass – since he was in church. He thought on.

'Well ...' There was no great recommendation in his voice. 'There is the "Hermit with the Clock" ...'

'Couldn't be better,' purred Adam.

Fred Pelling didn't see what there was to approve of in the wreck of the Hermit's room. It was as plain as a pike to the eye that the occupant never left its confines from one year's end to the next.

The squat little hermit took the Sicarii's judgement at face value. Through the medium of pebble glasses he also surveyed his private world with pleasure.

'It suits me.' He beamed and fiddled with his frayed shirt-cuffs. 'We have grown attached, this room and I.'

Without invitation, Adam picked his way through the teetering piles of books and cleared a space to sit. He didn't mind signs of learning so long as they weren't attended by squalor. Unhappily, these were.

Pelling, for his part, believed that books should keep to their proper place – which was to say a bookcase – and breed in moderate numbers. Since Holy Writ contained

170

all wisdom in one compact volume, he didn't see the need to labour the point in additional volumes. The bibliomania of the hermit struck him as mere indulgence.

He didn't fancy joining Adam on the divan that was the only concession to visitors and so remained, 'on guard', at the door. The hermit expressed silent alarm at these signs of an extended invasion of his privacy and ruffled his shaggy hair.

'Gentlemen,' he said, 'I have no objection to brief consultations but . . .'

'Good,' said Adam. He looked askance at the vast clock of wood and brass whose thunderous tick was the dominant feature of the room, even more than the books. Alone amongst the inhabitants of Guildford, it had succeeded in putting him off his stride. 'We won't trouble you longer than necessary.'

The hermit wasn't so much troubled as pained. 'I should hope not,' he said, avoiding either of his visitor's eyes. 'I'm a busy man.'

This was entirely possible. Amidst the private universe he'd constructed in his room at Castle Arch, the 'Town Remembrancer' could impose such burdens upon himself as he saw fit. All the Corporation asked of him was that the town Year Book was annually compiled. How exhaustive or informative it might be was up to him. No one much cared. Save that civic pride and the Church demanded it, the chore would have been forgotten. Still, it was well known in the town how glad the hermit's despairing family had been to secure him the sinecure. There were precious few opportunities, and less sympathy, for agoraphobics in the world.

'I can let you browse through some previous volumes,' he suggested hopefully. 'In a neighbouring room . . .'

'No time,' said Adam – omitting, in deference to

Pelling's presence, 'or inclination'. 'You wrote them, you tell us.'

The remembrancer wasn't accustomed to pressing interest in his works. For the first time he wondered if he was fulfilling the wishes of Church and State as he really should. His solipsistic happiness was crumbling. Pelling noted it with sorrow.

'What my colleague wants,' he said (rather daringly – and Adam questioned the description with a look), 'is news of untoward events – anything from the last year or so.'

'Other than trifles like the disappearance of kings,' amplified the Sicarii.

'Inexplicable things and reported curiosities,' continued Fred. 'You're brought word of every new matter from birth to death. If you don't know the secret heart of Guildford, who does?'

As intended, that went down rather well. The remembrancer almost smiled.

'Perhaps I can recall some things,' he murmured to the floor.

Adam looked out of the ivy-obscured window down into the commerce of Quarry Street. The clock boomed away a few more seconds of precious time.

'Then recall, recall, *recall*,' he said as quietly as the clock would permit.

The hermit glanced conspiratorially at him. 'Some people have been seeing funny stuff.' He smirked.

Adam sighed. 'Well, thank you for being so frank with us, Remembrancer.'

The hermit didn't like to be hurried. He looked at Pelling in mute appeal. Fred shrugged helplessly.

'I refer to tales of apparitions!' the hermit protested.

'Grey Ladies and headless riders we can skip,' Adam said.

'And black monsters?' asked the remembrancer, with hollow defiance.

'No, those we'll have.'

The hermit leaned forward.

'I received two different accounts of phantasmagoria penetrating walls and frightening families with spectral scythes. Intrigued, I had my informants root out a further two incidents from more bashful householders. It seemed far from the usual run of otherworldly visitations.'

'If you say so. And where precisely *did* they "run"?'

'Where?' The remembrancer hadn't been expecting that particular question. He was looking forward to an embellished recounting of the gothic grisliness of the scenes. 'Along the High Street, through the courts and dwellings behind.'

'Upper or Lower High Street?'

The hermit considered. Despite his bumbling manner he retained the tidy mind that had first recommended him to this vocation.

'Middle,' he recalled. 'All of them, come to think of it. The same as the lady.'

'Not a grey one, I take it?' asked Pelling, before Adam could do so – and in less friendly tones.

'No,' giggled the hermit salaciously. 'A most real and ... mettlesome seeming variety – until she precipitously vanishes from view. Her pretty prying head has intruded on some townsfolk in their ... least guarded moments, the saucy thing. I rather wish' – he giggled again – 'that she would call on me!'

Adam looked at him with distaste. 'Sadly for you, she restricts her visits to the middle portions of the High Street, you say?'

The remembrancer picked up on the disapproval and became painfully shy once again.

'Yes,' he whispered, regretful of his sinful lubricity.

'You can see the entrance to the cathedral from the High Street,' stated Adam. 'I'm right, aren't I?'

'You can't see it from anywhere else,' answered Pelling for the saddened hermit. 'Not unless you're a bird.'

'The avian species are excluded from my suspicions,' said the Sicarii, refusing to relinquish his brow-beating advantage over the hermit. 'No other grouping is so favoured as yet. Tell me more stories about that part of town.'

The remembrancer had lost the vital sense of control over his one-room world and was visibly floundering.

'There aren't any!' he spluttered. All he wanted was for them to go.

'Well,' said Adam slowly. 'I don't doubt what you say but we must check. I'll peruse your last volume, tearing out each page as I go . . .'

'Maybe a few things, just a few,' pleaded the hermit, raising his voice above the timepiece which ruled his life.

'If you *can* save me the trouble,' said Adam, 'then we're all ears.'

'There was a pot-boy killed in the Spread Eagle.'

'We know about that,' said Pelling swiftly.

'And . . . and there was another odd death, not long ago.'

'Who? Where? How?' smiled the Sicarii.

'A clothier called Ransom. He's got a manufactory and shop in the High Street. His wife rotted away.'

'Plague?' suggested Adam. Even in hygiene-conscious Italy the 'Dark Visitor' was not a complete stranger.

'No, all in a night: really rotted away.'

Adam noted and considered the information in the

privacy of his head. No indication of any conclusion reached the outer world.

'And what about the castle?' he asked.

The remembrancer stopped his agitated writhings and was still. Slowly he placed both pale hands on the sides of his chair.

'I can tell you,' he said, 'the date that it fell down.'

Adam compressed his lips and studied the hermit with great sadness. 'Could you now?' he said mockingly. 'Well, whilst you're about that, tell me the date Colonel Longstaff came to see you about it. Did he bring a few Fen Tigers with him?'

Adam and Pelling went without saying goodbye, leaving the hermit to his floods of tears. For a while they almost missed the clock's stately marshalling of passing time.

Out in Quarry Street, the Sicarii turned back and looked up at the window that was the remembrancer's sole perspective on the wider world. He half expected to see a white and weeping face pressed against the panes, making sure they were gone. No one appeared. Through the ancient archway alongside could be seen the pile of builder's rubble masquerading as Guildford Castle.

'I expect you feel better for that,' he said to Pelling.

Fred considered saying the same to Adam – but thought better of it. Playing the bully made him feel sullied.

'No,' he said. 'Why should I?'

'*Because*,' explained Adam, as if to a slow schoolboy, 'you're safe now.'

'I am?' Pelling couldn't sense that much-missed quality.

'For sure. Our enemy wanted you dead because you had local knowledge. Thus, by implication, local knowledge was the crucial issue. Once we've consulted an

175

alternative source there's no more point in knocking you off.'

A flare of irrational joy lit briefly inside Fred Pelling but, learning fast, he didn't let it show.

'Why not knock you off instead?' he said. 'I'm nothing on my own.'

'True,' agreed the Sicarii ungraciously. 'But I'm just one of an array. Kill me and others, even more relentless, will follow. It would do them no good – quite the opposite, in fact. You should see some of the types we hold in reserve – real animals!'

Pelling didn't care to pursue the notion. They turned and walked in the direction of the High Street.

'Then why not kill the remembrancer?' Fred persisted. 'That's more certain than scaring him silent.' He was surprised and frightened to find how much his mind was being diverted along such wicked ways of thinking.

Adam tipped his hat to a pretty ladies' maid in black – who studiously looked through him.

'Again, no point. That would have answered my questions as good as seeing him. Likewise his "disappearance". No, they missed their chance with you. It's downhill from now on.'

You could take that both ways, and as they hit the bustle of the High Street Pelling did just that. But even so he could not but feel a little happier. There was no more need to search the skies for arrows with his name on.

~

'He didn't show,' said Colonel Longstaff. 'What a bloody insult!'

Father Brian Bancroft lit another cigarette. Things had got so that he was nigh-on chainsmoking nowadays.

'Off hand,' he replied comfortingly, 'I'd say it's all we

merit: nothing personal, just a correct assessment of our standing.'

The Colonel crossed to the Angel Hotel's new-fangled 'steam hot-plate' and helped himself to a mutton chop. It was just right: warm but not dried out. He reluctantly conceded that the invention had its uses, but couldn't wholly approve. The socially orthodox soldier was aware that such developments engendered unemployment and idleness amongst the servitor classes. The problem was that as soon as you banned one 'labour-saving' device, some artisan came up with another. There was no keeping pace with it. He likewise wished to dispute Bancroft's statement but couldn't muster sufficient good cause.

Longstaff felt ... rejected: discarded by events and unappreciated by that same stable order he strove might and main to preserve.

Father Bancroft poured him a measure from his silver coffee jug and passed the delicate porcelain cup. The Colonel accepted it with a grunt of acknowledgement. Suddenly the fight seemed to have gone out of him.

Bancroft noted that and saw an opportunity. His partner, hitherto bustling around with the martial fervour expected of him, had failed to see the way things were going. He still wanted to press on, taking more and more extreme measures, seeking to stem a tide that day by day grew unstoppable. The soldier was in danger of dragging them on into pointless wrongdoing – and appearing ridiculous in doing so. Enough was enough. At this rare low point in his spirits it was possible he would be open to accepting the inevitable.

'Let it go,' Bancroft said quietly.

Longstaff looked quizzically from the chop in one hand to the cup in the other.

'Why? They're fine.'

The priest smiled. 'No. I meant your present anger, your appalling drive. It's over.'

For a second the Colonel paused and then, understanding all too well, continued to affect puzzlement.

'What is?'

Bancroft was happy to humour his wounded honour. 'Our "mission", my friend, such as it was: over. The old order: over. Us – very probably: over.'

The soldier shook his long yellow locks. 'Not so, Father. So what if even the Arrow didn't work. It needn't matter. The Sicarii and his tame bumpkin, they're stumbling against the furniture in a darkened room. He's a sharp enough blade, I'll grant you, but we'll wear him down and blunt him. He won't be around for ever. Then, when he's gone, we can *sort* the Levellers and—'

'No,' said Bancroft, regretful but resolute. 'I don't think so. Better minds than ours don't think so. The Archbishop's communications grow ever more infrequent, more equivocal. There's little in his recent instructions to plainly justify *our* actions.'

The Colonel bit deep into the chop: a diversion for his lack of reply.

Father Bancroft lifted his scented kerchief to his aquiline nose and breathed deeply. For a glorious second he was away, free from the present ... nonsense. The perfume recalled simpler, more innocent times.

'I fear. . .' he said eventually. 'In fact, I just fear. But I also worry. I worry that our ship is sinking. The officers and first-class passengers are heading for the lifeboats. Strange to relate, however, they've neglected to alert the crew . . .'

Food and drink discarded, Longstaff sought to delay agreement.

'We acted under orders, with the best of intentions,' he

said, not protesting or whining, merely stating facts. 'We acted with honour, in accordance with duty.'

'That is true.' Bancroft settled relaxedly into the Angel's lounge armchair. 'But, in the words of the much maligned Pontius Pilate: "What is truth?"'

Longstaff waited for more, his corseted intellect not seeing that there was little more *to* say. The priest, against his will but impelled by charity, roused himself anew. He was so far resigned that the broad cockney tones of his youth rose, ghost-like, into his speech.

'What you say about orders, intentions, honour and duty,' he repeated, 'that's true. But don't dwell on it, Colonel, lest you come to bitter conclusions. We will make our peace with the Sicarii tomorrow.'

'He's not in,' said the youth.

Adam persevered. 'Where is he then?'

'Out.'

The apprentice realized he'd gone a league too far and stepped back into the undercroft. The Sicarii followed.

'Think of another answer,' he said softly. 'Before my patience likewise goes "out".'

The youth might have been feeling desperately truculent but he hadn't ditched all common sense. Everyone else in the shop was labouring away, leaving him to his fate.

'I don't know, sir. Really. Mr Ransom just comes and goes nowadays. There's no rhyme or reason to it.'

Adam glanced around. The apprentice's words could equally be applied to his place of work. It was going to ruin. Half the staff were only playing at work for the Sicarii's benefit, the stock was thinly spread and poor stuff even by English standards.

'Is he taking his wife's death badly?'

Several workers looked up at this. It seemed a personal question for a stranger, even such an exotic one.

'Hard to say, sir. He never mentions it. He started his wanderings before ... it happened.'

The skinny apprentice didn't feel 'it' needed defining.

'I'll return,' said Adam, and left.

He'd called at Jonah Ransom's shop as soon as the Guildhall bell was rung to signify six-thirty and the start of the working day. There was a crowded schedule to complete and he'd thought to fit this minor query in at its start. Now he wasn't so sure the bereaved clothier could be readily crossed off the list of loose ends. Instinct, which he trusted more than reason, told him there might be something here for him to bite on. He upgraded the matter in his private store of worries.

Back on his borrowed horse, Adam threaded a way down the High Street towards the Town Gate. The lower orders were out and about now, making the world ready for their later-rising betters and the Sicarii's progress slow. Outside Archbishop Abbot's almshouse a queue of the elderly indigent, patiently awaiting distribution of the Church-dole, almost brought him to a halt.

If he'd been a free man, Adam would have scowled at them: he had no time for such people. Backed by the Church, the monastic banks and religious confraternities arranged pensions for all out of modest, regular contributions during working life. It was even a point of piety and pride amongst the more secure that they didn't take up their entitlement, thus making more available to the less fortunate. Accordingly, under Mother Church's benign direction, no one should have been afflicted by want when work was done. Strangely enough, though, the founder of that same Church dictated sympathy to the poor, deserving or not, and so Adam kept his opinions to himself.

Once through the ragged mob the Sicarii was able to break into a trot, thus giving him the enormous pleasure of passing Father Bancroft and Colonel Longstaff at a pace too fast to allow speech. Adam would have laid money, judging by their expressions, that they'd been coming to see him. The Colonel in particular looked aggrieved about being stood up a second time. He wouldn't even find the Papal troopers 'at home' to take a message – lately they were often absent, pursuing their own discreet projects. With a spur of his horse and a cheery wave Adam was beyond the two men and gone.

Half an hour's riding took him beyond St Catherine's, the roadblocks and the surly cordon of the Fen-Tigers. He didn't doubt he remained under scrutiny, but that wasn't important. Let Bancroft be bored and troubled by a detailed account of his innocent day in the country.

'Country' was never far away. Prodded by the Church, the Crown Governments of Christendom made the towns keep to themselves. Fearful of hefty fines, they were obliged to maintain constricting protective walls and so could only expand upwards, not outwards. The teetering four-story tenements of parts of Guildford (and all of London) were evidence of the pressures this caused, and a town-status charter was both a blessing and a straitjacket. Green fields and signs of the works of God-in-nature extended to the very walls of every settlement. The evidence Adam had come to study was right before him.

Beyond the borough boundary the great landowners and the free yeomanry were keeping their fields in the approved manner. Neat strip cultivation and fallow land, interspersed by small villages, were everywhere. Adam peered over hedgerows and made an inventory of these

*Artingtons*, *Shalfords* and *Peasmarshes* but could see nothing wrong. The tormented land portrayed in the Legate's notes wasn't to be found. Likewise, his portrait of England, constructed from statistics in Rome, bore no relation to the reality Adam saw. The peasantry might never get rich out of their small, rotated fields, but neither would they starve. There was enough common grazing land and rough pasture, sufficient breeding 'improvements' in the stock he saw, to put all but the idle well beyond mere subsistence. True, few of the children who waved at him as he passed wore shoes – and that would have been commented on in Italy and the Empire – but they were stocky little offspring and full of spirit. Adam had seen the works of famine in Muscovy and New Hamburg and was glad not to find its white finger pointed anywhere here. He was also puzzled.

Why should England be a troublesome province? Starving and despairing men might throw everything away in hopeless rebellion, but not people with chickens for the pot and a harvest festival to look forward to. Nor was it that they had some grounds to hate the Church: only intellectuals could be that perverse. The cottages he passed each had their doortop crucifix and often a favourite saint's sign as well. The roadside shrines to Our Lady had fresh flowers or produce set before them.

The Sicarii paused at such a sign of faith to eat lunch. It was at the crossroads between three parishes and gave a good view of each. There was a bench on which to rest and from it Adam recited his midday devotions.

Alongside the normal effigy of Mary there was a figure of St Dismas, the 'good thief' of the Crucifixion story. His presence there was no mere chance. It was at such in-between places that were buried the hanged men, the suicides, the atheists and, in less enlightened times, the unchristened infants. The common people reckoned that respect paid to a saint of kindred spirit might appease the evil dead and persuade them not to walk. In practice it seemed to work rather well and Dismas was better served than many a more deserving saint. Even so, other than to bring their offerings and top up the level of prayer, men tended not to linger in such no-man's lands. If they didn't have one already, they soon acquired a forsaken feeling.

None of this concerned Adam. It wasn't that he disbelieved in possible ravening ghosts, but rather that he felt up to dealing with them. If he was obliged to tarry, then he'd do it somewhere useful, regardless of supernatural peril. The view around meant that even this surrender to the weak demands of the body might not be wasted time.

Because Adam was at a loss and hadn't found what he'd expected to, he continued to study and appraise as he ate the Spread Eagle's pork pie and drank its bottled Director's Ale. Because of *this* he forgot to enjoy them or notice they were good. Much of his life was like that.

Adam's afternoon was more of the same. In Godalming and Thursley and Farncombe and Binscombe, or in the lands between, he could find no cause for malignance. It was not until three in the afternoon that he drove his tiring mount up the scarp slope of Binscombe Ridge. From its high top, he could see down into the next valley and suddenly everything became clear.

~

Jonah buried his face deep into the demon's gown and drank in her glorious perfume. He had no idea why he was so well favoured and seized the moment lest it be snatched away.

She smelt like the best woman ever, but more torrid and perfect – and there were undertones of pepper and

183

spice. Animal heat was seething through the cool silk dress and Jonah's watering eyes were pressed against the yielding limbs beneath. Inflamed and made dizzy by intolerable pleasure he rained down kisses on her. Then suddenly she was gone.

Jonah Ransom was racked by deprivation. He'd wished for that brief moment never to end and his body shook with grief. The scent was ebbing away, its insufficient ghost lingering on his face to torment him.

He got up off his knees, graceless and stumbling, and looked for her. This was still his store cupboard but the walls now stretched out into infinity. Its furthest regions were beyond sight and he stood, alone, in the midst of a monstrous plain. Had she enlarged the room or diminished him? Jonah didn't care. Such miracles were minor considerations compared to his sense of loss. He called out for her.

'I'm here,' she whispered from behind him. 'I went to see another demon lord: we mated and had children. Then we ate them. Did you miss me?'

'Not long enough,' Jonah gasped. 'You didn't let me worship long enough . . .'

The girl struck a coquettish pose, one finger under her sharp chin.

'You can have too much of a good thing,' she lisped. 'I smiled upon your thinning pate and let you make free – for a little while. That is all modest lovers should do.'

The clothier's mouth gaped wide, closed and then, helpless, gaped again.

'*I* . . . cannot prevent myself,' he said. 'But do you say that *you* . . .?'

The girl's long gown flared with fresh rainbow swirls and tiny starbursts of white.

184

'I do,' she sang. 'We demons are capricious creatures. I've decided that I . . . what is that word?'

'Love!' Jonah said, his voice weird and piping from strain.

'Yes, *love*. I've decided to love you – like your God-thing is supposed to love all of you or the Christ-person loved John. It amuses me to "love" you. So I shall.'

Jonah felt like the sun was shining from inside his heart. The girl knew it and smiled on him.

'It is a time of novelties for me,' she explained. 'Suddenly I have access to your world and can walk free. What was forbidden me is now spread on a bed, ready to ravish. I'm not sure what I should do yet. It's very odd and inexplicable, but we're not the types to question unduly. Amidst such wonders why shouldn't a giant betroth a flea?'

She laughed, and the sound from her long white throat rose and rose until it passed beyond Jonah's mortal hearing. The flagstones beneath their feet heaved sensuously up, joining in their mistress's amusement, and unseen things below chattered and screamed.

With a tiny wave of her hand everything was abruptly restored to peace.

'Not everyone loves you, though,' she added sadly, more like a sulky girl again. 'I haven't fully awakened in your world so I don't understand that yet. Do you? There are two human creatures looking for you. I don't think I like that. You're mine.'

A window, a view of some other place appeared, hanging free in the air beside the demon and the clothier. A man in a scarlet cowl was seated at a desk, poring over a monstrous tome and making notes on a pad. The girl studied the scene no less intently, as though she were reading it.

'Here's one. He's a monk,' she recounted as the information came through to her. 'A sorcerer also. I sense a commission to seek us out. He ... knows about the "thaumaturgic intrusion" and he's looking for its "penetrative temporal nexus". That's me and you respectively.' She grinned at Jonah. 'I don't understand the technical terms; they're his, but I get the meaning. He's quite a clever boy, he'll get there soon. I'm seeing the name ... Hume.'

'The Abbot of Walsingham,' said Jonah dully. 'He's famous. The Government asks his advice. Spells he devised dispersed the Great Anglia Plague a few years back. They reckon he'll be a saint.'

The girl pursed her ebony lips.

'Sooner than he thinks.'

She frowned.

The man in the picture clapped his hands to his face. A sound of anguish emerged, muffled, from behind them. He rocketed to his feet, belying his age and toppling the desk and book. His notepad burst into flames and dwindled to cinders in a second.

'No, I *won't* go back,' she scolded him. 'Recognize your new god.' He seemed to hear and turned to face the sound. Jonah saw his head was melting.

For a few minutes more the monk-magician cannoned round his room, wrecking its fittings and upsetting all. No noise could escape his fused mouth, but they heard the splintering of wood and the protests of paper trod underfoot. At length he found what he sought and scrabbled at the crucifix above his bed. There he gave in and died, his combusted face adhering him upright to the wall. The scene faded.

Jonah looked within but found no protest forming. That saddened him.

'The second one's more interesting,' said the girl. 'Shall we go and see him?'

The world changed and Jonah wondered why they were in church.

~

'You may well ask.'

Adam reined in his temper as he had his horse. He needed the information held in this yokel's brain and it was best it be given freely.

'Well, I *did* ask. Any chance of an answer?'

'Maybe so, if you're civil. Mind you, my dogs want their walk and it's a grim old tale, I tell you.'

'I'm used to those. It won't affect me. Speak on.'

The tall thin man eyed him suspiciously from over the field fence. Down in the sunken lane below, Adam looked up and returned the gaze head on.

'I don't want to talk out of turn,' said the man.

The Sicarii revised his opinion; this was probably a yeoman, educated enough to appreciate discretion but proud enough to speak his mind. He'd struck lucky.

'You won't,' he assured him. 'You may even do some good.'

The man snorted. 'God knows it needs doing. If this weren't Onslow land we'd be in the same state. You hear of it happening everywhere.'

'Over the hill isn't Weston-Onslow fief, then?'

The man stooped down to quieten one of his lurcher dogs and temporarily disappeared from view. His reply could still be heard.

'Nope. That ends atop the ridge and then the devastation begins.'

'So I saw.'

The yeoman returned and leaned his arms on the fence.

'You could hardly miss it, could ye? I just hope I've laid my head in clay before it comes here. I couldn't abide seeing that.'

Adam considered dismounting, but didn't want to break the exchange. He prayed that no one else came along to disturb them.

'Do you think it might?'

The man pondered at length. 'Quite possible,' he said finally. 'Old man Onslow won't live for ever. There'll be some future agent or elder son who'll see the possibilities. They say even monastic tenants aren't safe nowadays – nowhere is, not unless you're beside some road or railway where *furriners* might see.'

Adam reflected that by doubling back down to this one-plough village, this Binscombe or whatever it was called, he had learned more than in all his consulting with the high and mighty. There was a lesson in that.

'You've got to have progress,' he ventured, playing devil's advocate. The yeoman, warming to the subject, rose to the bait.

'Depends what you call "progress", don't it? I don't call clearing out villages and tearing a man from his land progress. Not of any sort. Maybe they see things different where you come from.'

'No ... no,' said the Sicarii, as much to himself as anyone. 'Where I've come from they'll see things the same as you.'

'Don't get me wrong. I'm not anti-sheep: there's a powerful lot of employment that goes with flocks and the kersey trade – at certain times of year, that is. But men have to live all the year round, they don't just eat at lambing and shearing. They need their bit of land to call their own.'

Adam nodded: this was orthodox social theory. He

188

didn't expect to hear it even questioned, let alone spat upon over a swathe of countryside.

'What about my original question? When were those hamlets cleared? Who demolished the farmsteads?'

The yeoman pulled a face and made as if to go. His obedient dogs leapt to their feet.

'I've said enough. You find out the rest if you're so curious. Those as did such things have friends and retainers – and lawyers to turn black into white. I might have sons and guns but I can't fight "Acts of Parliament" or "Orders in Council". That's how the trick's done. My family's farmed these lands for four centuries but I can't *prove* I own the land – there's no legal document from way back then. Come the right Act of Parliament they'd have it off me.'

Adam was respectful of righteous anger; indeed, he harnessed its power himself.

'What would you do?'

The yeoman looked at the afternoon sun playing on the thatch of the village roofs, perhaps seeing less happy vistas.

'I'd maybe slit some exalted throat, go out guns blazing: burn the place down round me ears – some useless gesture like that. It happened that way once or twice over there.'

He indicated the ridge, meaning the depopulated, ruin-dotted prairies Adam had sighted earlier.

'Ah hell!' the yeoman spat, all pretence of cool detachment hurled aside. Adam was dismissed with a wave. 'It makes me angry. The world falls to pieces and the Church looks on with a smile. I know I've no title in what I hold – not if some fat cat wants it. I've ceased to worry. With luck I'll die before it happens; worse comes to worse, I'll die during: it makes no odds. Go and tell your masters

189

that if you want. Go tell 'em what yeoman Whitbourn thinks, for all I care!'

The man strode off with his dogs and Adam silently thanked him. He had at last learned why England was a troublesome province.

~

The Sicarii took this fresh supply of information back on to the ridge, to work it into shape and compare it to the evidence on the ground. Those erased villages, those shells of farmsteads took on fresh significance; the innocent sheep and fields sang a much clearer song. It all held true. Now he had eyes to see it, the contrast between the paternalist Weston-Onslow estate and those adjoining screamed out to be noticed. That was just as well. The people who'd lived in the latter were no longer around to scream anything.

In the distance Adam saw the little village of Compton. It fell the right side of the great divide and thus remained alive. He beheld the spire of its church and suddenly felt compelled to go to it.

~

Adam knew the compulsion was not natural. In normal circumstances, he would never have attacked a church in his mad haste to be within. If the idea had come from his own thoughts, he would have paused and delayed to see the villagers of Compton miraculously frozen in time.

Instead, he ignored the display of living statuary and took no note of the sunbeams caught in flight. He nigh-on suffered injury throwing himself off his horse at the lych gate and bruised his shoulder against the Norman metalwork of the church door. At first it resisted his best efforts but then surrendered with a groan of wood and hinges that sounded like a maiden's permission. The Sicarii, with that part of his mind still answering the helm, recognized that the invading erotic notions were not of his own creation. He felt angry, used and helpless.

The demon and Jonah Ransom were standing in Compton church's unique upper sanctuary, right above the chancel. Only the 'girl' smiled to see Adam burst in.

To left and right, around the aisle pillars of white 'clunch' chalk, the Sicarii glimpsed half-formed shadows that moved to a music they alone heard. He paid no heed to the phantom congregation; his attention was given, willing or not, to the girl. He had control enough to think the final words of contrition. Adam realized they'd met before, in London, when she was in more monstrous, boisterous form. The demon showed no sign of recognition.

'Hmmm,' she purred, staring down at him. 'You're choice. Where are your softer inclinations?'

Adam was granted his mind back. A yoke was lifted and he could speak.

'Cut out,' he said. 'Gone.'

She nodded agreement and extended one slim arm to lightly stroke the sullen Jonah's head.

'Will you hurt him?' she asked.

Adam looked at the clothier, trembling under her black-painted fingertips. He liked, if possible, to feel compassion for the abject, so the wise answer was also truthful.

'No, not unless I'm ordered.'

He felt something akin to those same fingers slip invisibly into his head. They probed and withdrew.

'So . . . rigid,' she whispered. The words echoed around the church. 'So unbending. You're interesting. I think I'll spare you for a while.'

Jonah showed dissent but was ignored.

'As you wish, lady,' said Adam and bowed his head.

The submission made her gleefully clench her hands. 'Play with me,' she laughed. 'Unfold and indulge.'

The shadows to either side took on flesh. They became numberless facsimiles of the girl, all black hair and flashing eyes in second skins of ebon velvet. Packed together like snakes in a pit, they moved lithely in complicated dance, brushing past each other with expressions of delight. Great thudding music filled the House of God and they undulated to its beat, parting black lips to sing soaringly along. Adam thought to have conquered the beast of desire long ago, but he was overwhelmed. He could not understand how they might be clothed, but naked and perfect at the same time. Each mocking smile washed over his barriers of denial.

Adam had ripped off half his clothes when he saw that the images and effigies themselves were joining in the dance. The stone and plaster saints were jigging on their pedestals to the music, their blank faces comically uninvolved. It took the Sicarii's remaining will to avert his eyes from the Lady Chapel and the figure within. That he could not bear to see. The demon had overreached herself.

'No!'

Adam's cry killed the scene. Instantly the sounds and sights were gone. The echoes of his anguish were all that remained.

The girl looked surprised. 'No? Something more to your tastes then?'

Once again those sensual 'fingers' penetrated Adam's brain. They made rearrangements and inserted new information. Enlightenment, a jigsaw landing complete, fell on him like ecstasy.

'I don't see it myself,' said the girl, 'not yet. But you might comprehend.'

Adam did – and it felt better than the sea of writhing velvet. Fulfilment of his mission tasted sweeter than personal pleasure.

'Fancy preferring that!' she mused, and glanced across at the sheep-eyed Jonah. '*You* wouldn't, would you?'

He nodded agreement, not understanding; just desperate to please.

The girl appeared to arrive at some decision.

'I'm not going to squash you,' she told Adam. 'Go and see Jonah's home. Then, if he agrees, you can come and see mine.'

Jonah regarded him with hatred.

'I'll be there,' said Adam.

The demon and the clothier vanished.

Adam was left alone in the still and silent House of God. From outside the sounds of normal life resumed. Only a faint scent of spice remained to remind him that the church required reblessing.

*Your sheepe that were wont to be so meke and tame, and so small eaters, now, as I hear say, be become so great devourers and so wylde that they eat up, and swallow downe the very men themselves . . . Noblemen and gentlemen: yea and certain Abbottes, holy men no doubt . . . leave no ground for tillers, thei enclose al into pastures: they throw downe houses: they plucke downe townes and leave nothing standynge but only the churche to be made a sheephowse . . . The husbandman be thruste owte of their owne, or else either by coveyne and fraude, or by violent oppression they are put besides it, or by wronges and injuries they be so weried that they be compelled to sell all: by one means or by other either by hook or by crook they must needs depart awaye, poore selye, wretched soules, men, women, husbands, wives, fatherless children, widows, woful mothers with their yonge babes, and their whole household small in substance and much in number . . . And when they have wandered abrode tyll that be spent, what can they else do but steale and then justly pardy be hanged, or else go about a begging?*

From *Utopia* by St Thomas More (1477–1535), martyred by King Henry 'Abomination VIII-and-last'. Feast Day 9 September.

Taken as the preface to: '*An Admonition against the Arrogance of Wealth*. Final report of the all-Christendom restorationist Papal Commission on the Agrarian Question, 1888–1893.

*ENCYCLOPEDIA BRITANNICA 2020 EDITION*

CRUSADES: this term was originally applied to the great movements of Christian arms against the heathen in the Holy Land which occurred between the eleventh and seventeenth centuries prior to the great and abiding success of the so-called 'Enterprise of Richlieu' in 1635. [*See index for individual expeditions.*] In modern parlance, however, a crusade has come to mean a course of action, problem or area for concern declared to be a particularly valuable opportunity for the earning of grace. Such a crusade may be declared by a pope, a Church council speaking ex cathedra or, in certain circumstances, a 'provisional crusade' may be declared by an individual archbishop where a situation of emergency precludes times for contact with proper higher authorities.

In essence the defined doctrine on the modern crusade states that any effort made by one of the faithful to aid the said course of action or solve said problem earns grace and indulgences at a rate equal to that gained in a freely undertaken and sinless pilgrimage to the Holy Sepulchre. It can readily be appreciated, therefore, that participation in a modern crusade is of inestimable value to the soul's salvation. [*See: PILGRIMAGES; ACTS OF FAITH; HOLY LAND; HOLY LAND, MILITARY ORDERS OF. See also: ARMIES – SERVICE IN: BOSPHORUS, CRETE, MALTA, NEW MEXICO, THE PAPAL STATES, RHODES.*]

The present doctrine on crusading was first laid down by the Council of ABERLEMNO in 1848 . . . which stated that . . .

. . . therefore it comes as no surprise to see that most causes declared to be of crusade status have been able to call upon the services of myriad volunteers from all over

Christendom. It is because of this phenomenon that it is said of the Holy Father: 'His conquering armies are raised from empty air', and, 'He topples empires by proclamations'.

Anyone who wilfully opposes or hinders a matter of crusade status is deemed excommunicated.

By far the most common use of the crusading phenomenon has been either in the defeat of heresy or in the alleviation of suffering caused by famine or natural disaster.

One may convey some idea of the power implicit in the crusading ideal by quoting the example of the great Phillemian heresy current in the 1930s. In this case over 100,000 volunteer troops assisted the King of France's armed forces in stamping out the dangerous dualist heresy which had been declared by Pope Constantine III as 'the secret army of satan in Europe' (1939). [See: COMPIEGNE, BATTLE OF.]

Even in Britain, a nation not known for producing heresiarchs [But see: PELAGIUS], 40,000 volunteers flocked to the joint Papal-Royal banner to suppress the Levellers of the Thames Valley in the summer of 1990 . . .

. . . and responded with no less commitment to the joint thaumaturgic and agrarian scandals attendant to the 'Commotion Times' of the reign of Charles IV. The English Crusaders were inspired by the thundering words of Pope Simon Dismas:

Twenty centuries ago, God walked on Earth and, of his goodness, informed us how to live. Upon his death and resurrection he established an institution, the Church, to embody his very self, until he should come again. This is the truth of our holy charge and stewardship. How, then, could heretics delude themselves that we would stand idly by when the Cosmic Order is subjected to unnatural rape?

196

Likewise, a slur upon our good name, and that of Mother Church, is the same as to its founder, our Saviour. That slur shall be expunged most thoroughly and its authors vomited forth to their reward.

Some historians, in the pay of vested interests, have greatly exaggerated the ensuing 'massacres' . . .

When he returned to the Spread Eagle Adam wrote a letter. It took him most of the night. He refused to see Pelling or hear his 'pressing news', pleading excessive fatigue. It was only part way a lie.

In the early hours he hid the thick envelope in a prearranged drop point by the Town Wall. In a few hours at most a Papal agent, long concealed, unsuspected, in an obscure Guildford life, would collect it. Soon after it would grace the tables and thoughts of the mighty. Meanwhile, the Sicarii could at last surrender to shock and sleep.

A crusade was born.

'We broke them yesterday,' said Pelling, 'whilst you'd disappeared. It went very smoothly.'

'Congratulations,' said Adam, fetching his boots from under the bed and pulling them on. He tried to sound sincere.

'Jacko, my lieutenant, sorted out the names and I led the operation. We got the lot – took them out of their beds, still half asleep.'

'That's the way to do it!' said Adam, trying to join in the celebratory mood even though he had greater things on his mind. He scanned the list before him.

> Samuel Hammond, carpenter, Milk House Gate.
>   Malignant.
> Joseph Bush, drayman, Stoke-in-the-fields.
>   Absentee from Divine service and malignant.
> James Bexley, night watchman, Friary Lane.
>   Malignant.
> Abraham Padfield, bookbinder, Rat's Gate. 'Free-
>   thinker' and keeper of a concubine.

and so on through a page full of plain English names and minor delinquencies.

'So these are the Levellers in Guildford, are they?'

Pelling smiled and nodded. 'Activists *and* sympathizers. London proved very cooperative in supplying back-up information.'

'And what's this nonsense?' Adam sifted his hand through a pile of prints and bills on the table in front of him.

'We got their printing press as well, buried in a cellar workshop near the Royal Grammar School, if you please! They'd sound-proofed the walls with woolpacks.'

The Sicarii studied a few items at random: *Fox's Book of Martyrs – being the true history of Christians through the ages in struggle with the beast and antiChrist of Rome*; *Lions and Lambs – patterns for daily life in the reign of King Jesus*; *Zion's Joy and the Agreement of the People – the happy sack of Rome in the year 1527, together with a particular study of Psalm 149 and the text Isaiah 49:23 . . .*

Adam overcame his angry nausea and enquired within the latter. It began with a homespun verse:

> *Crownes, sceptres, jewells, ear-rings,*
> *golde, riche robes and costly things,*
> *thou gavest thy soldiers to despoil,*
> *and from the treasuries of Pope and preest*
> *their women weake, with little toil*
> *went well laden home.*
>
> *What once was, shall bee again,*
> *And all Rome's works bee in vain . . .*

He put it aside like something soiled. 'What will you do with them?'

'Due process of law, I'm afraid,' Pelling said. 'Jacko's team's pressing them for confessions, but without the rough stuff.'

The abolition of torture, save for highest heresy and treason, still rankled with some rigorists.

'There are names crossed off here. Who's Grimmond, for instance?'

Pelling's air of a job well done remained undiminished. 'London supplied those. Those are Leveller high-ups and murder men. I've heard Grimmond's supposed to be head of the Gideon military arm. They're people who've gone missing from Church and State surveillance, but that doesn't mean they're here.'

Adam shrugged. 'No, it doesn't – but I should imagine they are. This is the Levellers' last throw, their final chance to bring on the Apocalypse. It's doubtful their chieftains could keep away.'

'You're very dismissive. I haven't said how we got a score of muskets and a wagon's-worth of sidearms as well. I tell you, the Levellers are finished in Guildford!'

Adam felt sorry for spoiling Pelling's great day. As far as it went – which sadly wasn't very far – Fred was probably right. The larger events had allowed him to rise and purge his little world once and for all. The Sicarii tried to scale down his thoughts.

'No, it's highly commendable,' he assured him. 'Now we needn't worry about some miserable "protestant"' – he looked at the list again – 'bookbinder taking a rooftop potshot at us whilst we're about more important business. You've done well. Don't think we're not grateful.'

'But . . .' said Pelling resignedly.

'*But* I think there might be just *one* nest of them left. That's what I need to talk to you about before I go away and put you in charge. There's also some explaining to do.'

Pelling was aghast. He'd come to depend on the Sicarii

like a parent — a sometimes resented one, perhaps, but even so . . .

*'Away? Charge?'*

'To the bar,' said Adam, pointing in the direction of the stairs. 'You'll need a drink.'

~

'Demon lord? What's a demon lord when it's at home?'

At first Fred was more frightened of the *way* in which Adam was talking. He no longer seemed to care who overheard. The gentlemen and yeomen in the Spread Eagle saloon, catching words like 'demon', 'King' and 'death', were hard put to pretend they didn't hear. But then, as the conversation wore on, Pelling joined in with the same disregard for privacy. His voice could be heard, raised and sometimes tremulous, disbelieving Adam's previous remark.

'I've already gone through that,' said the Sicarii patiently. 'They exceed the common demonic type in power as a demon does a human. Do try and keep up.'

'I know, but . . .' Pelling mopped his brow and took another tot of sloe gin. 'I mean, what's it doing—'

'Whatever it likes, to an ever-increasing degree,' interrupted Adam.

'No, I mean, why . . .' he was going to say 'here', but that was too disturbing . . . 'in our world?'

'She doesn't know herself; that came through clearly amidst the information she gave me. It's some great . . . accident. From creation until now her type come to earth just by invitation, in highly restricted form. To date, what our magicians summoned was an infinitely tiny part of their whole. Such was the convenient cosmic status quo. Now, for some reason, "she" finds the way unbarred. She comes and goes as she pleases, in full manifestation. When she "wakes" fully . . .'

Pelling looked around the public house, noting the convivial normality he could never regain.

'Then it's the end,' he said in a monotone. 'It's finished with us.'

Adam wondered if he was right in detecting the merest hint of relief in Fred's voice.

'Possibly,' he agreed. 'I've alerted the people who matter, who might be able to do something about it. And since I'm no longer of any account, I intend to seek a solution myself. It doesn't matter if I fail.'

'Have you noticed,' asked Pelling, staring into his empty glass, 'how we're not talking much about His Majesty any more?'

'Side-show,' agreed Adam. 'Two evil tides converge by chance and make each other worse. The Levellers hope to ride the whirlwind and serve their own ends. They don't – or won't – understand. Underground life and pernicious tenets have sickened their brains. They amuse her – for the moment; she cooperates. It won't last.'

'It all seems a bit pointless,' said Pelling.

'Oh, no,' said Adam, trying to cheer him, 'we ought to continue. His Majesty deserves rescuing.'

'You think so?'

Adam played with the edges of the brawn and mustard sandwich he'd ordered. 'Certainly, even if he has colluded in the dispossession of his people. I don't see why he should escape punishment with the grandees who bought his blind eye. It looks like high elements of the English Church stayed significantly silent too. They'll need to answer—'

'I think you're overstating this "enclosure" thing, Sicarii.'

Adam shook his head. 'You're relatively unaffected here, though it's still bad enough. Onslow's too decent, you're too close to foreigners. But elsewhere, out of sight, they're slow-killing the peasantry. It's a great big corrupt circle. The demon explained it to me. The rich go to Parliament, Parliament provides the "law", the "law" takes the land and gives it to the rich. It's very neat – like a man-trap's "neat". The rich make "loans" to a weak and feckless King and he signs the laws. A certain Archbishop chooses not to report, to seal his ears against the cry of the poor, chooses not to enforce the agrarian statutes. The King and the rich love him for it; they'll gladly support his ... wider ambitions. It's been a while since there's been an English Pope. And if the King doesn't return, there's always the question of an Archbishop's regency.'

'I've noticed there's a lot more beggars around,' conceded Pelling. 'Able-bodied ones ... families. I've not had much sympathy with them.'

'That's right. The Legate was asked to query your savage property laws – the brandings and clipping of noses. Rome might move slowly, it might think in centuries, but it was on to you.'

'What's all this "you"?' protested Pelling. 'Leave me out!'

'Don't worry,' said Adam, placating him. 'It's not the English, we see that now. Just something rotten in the English state. It's a smallish cancer: easily burnt out.'

'If ... she permits you.'

'There is that, Fred. Still, you never know, the demon could be doing you a favour. Your upper echelons might have got away with their tricks for ever if she'd not come along. Her powers enabled the Levellers to strike a proper blow for once, instead of printing pitiful leaflets and knocking off priests. You should almost be grateful to

203

them. We could hardly fail to notice a vanished King and Legate. The authorities left behind must have been tearing their hair out. Lots of attention was the last thing they wanted. Hence the pathetic attempts to counterfeit normality: pretending the castle fell down and such. Actually, I suspect the more perceptive oppressors know the game's up. All we're facing are the skivvies of a regime on the run: people like Bancroft and Longstaff. Headless chickens. They might have pulled wool over the Legate's eyes, but—'

'I didn't say . . .' Pelling thought, and then called for more mother's ruin. 'It's not only the castle. We suspect some other places "went". A couple of out-of-town houses aren't there any more.'

'Wouldn't surprise me at all. Don't waste too much time on that now, though. Wait for the changes to begin.'

'Changes?'

'There'll be no shortage of them. I've set a juggernaut in motion; it starts off slowly but you'll see it soon enough. There's a letter in my room giving you full powers under martial law for the administration of the town. If I'm not back, show it to those who'll be arriving.'

Pelling was dumbfounded; a mere constable's son, he'd never thought to be uncrowned king of Guildford.

'Begin harshly, become more liberal,' Adam advised him. 'Frighten people and then slacken off. That way they'll love you. The other way round breeds hatred. Hang one of your Leveller wretches in the High Street.'

The prospect of power, momentarily sweet, turned sour in Pelling's mouth.

'Which one?' he asked drily. The intonation bounced harmlessly off Adam.

'Doesn't matter,' he said, scanning the list again. 'Do it to Padfield.'

'Why him?'

Adam shrugged. 'It's the least pleasant name,' he said innocently.

The Sicarii ventured out to buy a sleeping draught from an apothecary's shop near the top of the High Street. Guarded by the two Papal troopers, he would sleep the clock round in drugged oblivion. There was no knowing when he would find time to rest again.

He studied the life of the town, the black-clad businessmen, the ladies in crinolines, the cocky little artisan kids, and reflected that this was what he fought to protect. People might not thank him or his masters for it, but his many sacrifices were made so that normal Christians might work and shop and play, living out their lives in a benevolent civilization. They didn't know what forces and ideas ranged outside to threaten them. Adam had never known the comfort of such ignorance. Now he had to leave the only world he knew on their behalf. He looked within and found he did not begrudge them.

A few yards down the street on the left was Jonah Ransom's establishment. He could see its canopy and the stairs leading down to its undercroft shop. Soon enough he'd be calling there but beyond that a veil fell. There might not *be* any beyond that.

Death held no terror for him. He was confident of his reward for so distorting his life in the service of good. There was also the appealing prospect of ... liberation from being Adam the Sicarii. And yet ... He'd heard that even ordinary demons could suspend the laws of Heaven in their own realms. In their grasp, on home ground, pain and suffering could be drawn out for ever ...

It was a consideration, that was all. He'd be more

cautious than usual. There was no question of drawing back. Oppression of the helpless, that could be accepted, albeit reluctantly. Even the Levellers' 'revolution' might be lived with if there were no alternative. But far better to tear the world apart, and himself with it, than tolerate more than one God on earth.

~

'I'm dead. I don't care.'

The Archbishop of London eyed the captive Leveller with equal bafflement and distaste.

'Well, you *should*, you silly man,' he said. 'I've told you time and time again we won't harm you.'

Actually, the young terrorist looked as though he'd had a rough ride on his way to the Westminster Citadel. One eye was puffed and closed and his clothes were torn. Feelings against his type were running high after the recent wave of bombings and assassinations. Even so, what the Archbishop had said was broadly true. There were corrective institutions more appropriate for deluded individuals such as this. With an immortal soul at stake the Church was reluctant to despair of reform. Only the most depraved and deserving forced their way on to the auto-da-fé.

'I don't believe you,' said the Leveller, glaring at the little Archbishop as best his one eye and chains would permit. 'You serve the Prince of Lies.'

'Manners,' said the seen-it-all-before custodian, cuffing the man with his elbow. The Archbishop frowned and indicated he should desist.

'You are not being incited to betrayal,' the prelate persevered. 'All I ask is some *guidance*; mere assistance in a matter of universal concern.'

'The only "guidance" I have for *you*,' spluttered the

prisoner, 'is to repent! Quit the service of Babylon. Even for you it might not be too late. Some souls are numbered among the elect with their last breath.'

'Yes, yes, thank you,' said the Archbishop wearily. 'I've studied your . . . theology. What I *need* to hear about is the demon you've raised: its provenance and powers, the bargain you struck. You are a high Gideon. We know you were present at one summoning; don't seek to deny it.'

'I deny *nothing*,' answered the Leveller quietly, and for a moment the Archbishop's hopes rose anew – only to fall all the further.

'I don't deny our hand is strengthened by the Lord,' the Leveller went on. 'I don't deny we wield a new weapon that strikes fear into your black heart. I don't deny we strive and suffer to erect God's kingdom in this England . . .'

'"This blessed plot, this earth, this realm, this England,"' quoted the Archbishop, gesturing theatrically with one slim hand.

The old-young man was taken aback at this evidence of culture amongst Satan's viceroys. 'Do not speak his words,' he said with passion. 'Shakespeare didn't write for you. He is the inheritance of the humble, the lowly, the hard-working. The high and mighty know him not—'

'And you do, I suppose,' snapped the Archbishop, touched upon a sore point.

'Anything that is the common man's is ours,' came the confident reply. 'And we are the commonality's spirit and soul and hope. We lead him where, in his heart, he wants to go. We are the vanguard party. God is on our side: you cannot win. Meanwhile, I'm dead. Be kind – don't prolong this limbo. Kill me now.'

'No,' said the Archbishop, relishing the last word in

this fruitless conversation. 'I won't. Lock him up safe, gaoler.'

He turned on his heels and left behind the ensuing muffled abuse. The Archbishop truly hated to hear the misguided so resolute and rational. It made him long to prise them open and pour in the calm of truth – and that was giving way to sinful anger.

Out in the corridor he was beyond the sound of the Leveller's tirade but felt little better for it. Apart from the mighty problems entrusted to him, he was troubled within. Never mind the realm of England or Mother Church, all was not well with himself. He recognized, once again, the pressing need to seek comfort in prayer.

This was an increasingly frequent occurrence lately, quite aside from his normal devotions, and, whilst laudable enough in itself, becoming rather ... noticeable. Not only that, but his private chapel lay on the other side of the citadel's central lawn from his rooms. It was, he supposed, a suitable penance for him to tread that route.

Ever since 'The London Incursion' the lawn had been out of bounds to almost everyone. Two Grandmasters of Magic had gingerly probed around it as part of their inquest and some condemned criminals had gone in to deal with the gore. The recoverable bodies were retrieved and that was all. Even the surrounding windows had been left boarded since that eventful night. Some lingering taint was perceived by the wizards, something bad enough for the haunt of centuries of archbishops to be sealed off. The present unhappy holder of that office admitted himself by the one remaining key and looked about.

There was still a pervading scent of musk and fear. He didn't think it was his imagination that made him detect that: the creature had left behind some part of itself. And it was here that their certainties had been blown apart. The magic they'd thought a tamed and useful beast had turned on them. It could never again be trusted.

The Archbishop forced himself to observe the statue of Augustine. Its myriad extra limbs, now beginning to decay, made it resemble some pagan idol. He had been unable to decide whether to destroy it or let nature take its course. Relatives were agitating for decent burial of the deceased – but how to sort and separate them? For the hundredth time the Archbishop postponed the decision.

The little chapel was blessedly cool and quiet. Its altar light and shrine to Our Lady re-anchored him to reality and faith. Tucked inside the cover of his personal breviary was a copy of the thrice daily prayer recently enjoined by Pope Simon Dismas on all the senior clergy of the Universal Church. The Archbishop hastened to his knees to recite it.

> Lord God, creator of the Universe,
> whose thought alone from second to second
> upholds all that we know and perceive,
> heal the wound in the world and bring us, we
>     beseech You,
> victorious to the end of this time of trial.
> Expel the spawn of Satan from this earth You gave
>     to Adam and his line.
> Return it to the pool of lead and fire that is its
>     proper abode.
> You do not test us beyond our strength but we are
>     weak.
> Smite Satan and his brood lest we falter.
> The enemy is strong and the shepherds stumble.
> Deliver us from the fury of the fiend.
> We ask this through Jesus Christ Our Lord. Amen

The Archbishop looked up at the altar. He knew he was joining his prayer to those of numberless others. These words were being repeated, day and night, by cardinals, bishops, abbots and renowned holy men and women. Their author, the Holy Father, said them. From the Basilica in St Peter's to the timber cathedrals of Greenland; from the Holy Sepulchre in the Jerusalem Citadel to the secret Jesuit utopias in Inca country, the Almighty was being beseeched in identical terms. He wondered what infinitesimal addition his own efforts made – and was not optimistic.

In here he could believe in the efficacy of his petition. Outside, beside the cursed lawn, he was less sanguine. Besides, why should God listen to him? The Archbishop knew in his heart of hearts he was compromised.

Little by little the years had worn him down. Heavy cares and futile ambitions had deafened his ears and deadened his charity. He had listened to those he should not and pretended not to hear the bleating of other, stricken sheep. Worst of all, he had convinced himself he was acting in good faith. Now this was his reward and quite proper punishment.

He turned to what was recently his favourite Biblical passage: Matthew 16:18. That particular page was well thumbed and worn.

. . . Thou art Peter, and upon this rock I will build my church; and the gates of hell shall not prevail against it.'

Well, that was plain enough, surely. Even if *he* was finished there were good grounds for wider hope.

Freshly confident, although not for himself, the Archbishop made his way back round the lawn and returned to the business of running the country.

~

'I expected you sooner.'

'There were things to do. Does she mind delay?'

Jonah shrugged. 'Who knows? Time's not the same to her as us. There's no saying.'

Adam had sensed the air of waiting the minute he descended the steps off the High Street down into the clothier's shop. Now that the business took a back seat in the establishment, the whole undercroft had a brooding air about it. The medieval walls and vaulted chalk ceiling gave the impression of there being more pressing things to think about. Few of the workers and apprentices he'd seen before were still there. Those left looked very much like the rearguard of a shattered army. There was precious little stock.

'Even so,' said the Sicarii, 'let's not prevaricate further and give offence. Take me to her.'

Jonah pondered the request as though he hadn't spent a desolate day and night awaiting it.

'The Brethren have left you be,' he said, 'up to now. They've not served justice on you for fear of who would follow in your steps.'

'Even Levellers can think straight sometimes.'

'That'll change when they hear you've beheld the portal. Come what may, the reward attending a servant of Babylon will be meted out to you.'

Adam smiled politely. 'I'm obliged for the warning. So, if you'd kindly lead on.'

'Don't get me wrong,' said Jonah, almost in a snarl. 'I half hope you die, at our hands or by hers. I don't want you intruding on the only thing that matters to me – the only thing that's ever *happened* to me. But ... I'm still Christian enough to foretell you.'

'Like I said, thanks, Leveller. Now *where*?'

Jonah gestured to a side door. 'If she wants you to

go, it'll be there. Otherwise there's only baulks of cloth.'

Adam didn't query the absurdity of visiting demons via cupboards. He'd been trained beyond surprise. Likewise, he remained alert to more plain and simple ambush. At the door, Jonah called him back.

'At the other end,' he said, 'there's a guard.'

Ever after Adam hoped that one selfless impulse would save the clothier from Hell.

~

For a second it was just a storeroom; his eyes had time to register the shapes and colours of Jonah's stock in trade. Then he was falling into a new world.

He landed like a cat, appraised the situation and then rolled. The musket ball passed through the air where he'd stood.

Adam was well armed, with various blades and a brace of pistols, but these were stowed away, out of sight as Guildford life required. It was simpler for him to rush the Leveller guard and part him from life with bare hands. The man wouldn't cooperate, plainly being a soldier of some experience, and the Sicarii was delayed several seconds.

Before the corpse fell from his grasp, another sentinel emerged from the long, lank grass where he'd evidently been resting. Adam wasn't too alarmed: there was time and distance enough for him to retrieve his guns and finish the job that way. The fresh nuisance had no weapons to hand. Then he made gestures which proved he'd no need of them. With a chill Adam recognized the arrival of a wizard – his last sensation for some time.

The spell held him fast, binding him in his pose like a statue. He'd had lessons in resisting the suggestions of

212

thaumaturgy. He understood that it was 'only' the struggle of one will against another, but that was no comfort or assistance. Wizards had will enough to shape and mould reality – that was their mark. Adam's mind was gripped by someone who genuinely believed his thoughts could be made fact.

The man came closer, still wary, careful to remain at the edge of Adam's vision. He was dressed in the black frock-coat favoured by the middle classes and had a pinched and embittered face.

'Well, hello,' he said, mock-friendly. 'And who might you be? Eh? Strong silent type, are you?'

More confident now, he came round to face the Sicarii and size him up.

'Well, you'll talk long enough back at base, never fear. There are tools to persuade you there. We've had ample opportunity to learn *their* use at the hands of your Church – 'cos that's who sends you, I'll be bound.'

An interesting thought seemed to come to him.

'Though seeing how' – he looked at the dead man's twisted head – 'I wonder if you might be . . .' He stepped back a few paces and stood in silent contemplation of his prisoner. A decision was eventually reached. He came right up to Adam and retrieved his dead colleague's musket and equipment. The wizard then positioned himself twenty yards or so away. He sat down cross-legged and began to reload the gun.

'We hear there's a Sicarii put on our tracks,' he said cheerfully as he worked. 'It occurs to me that you have the honour to be he. Certainly you polished off my brother handily enough. You have that inhuman look about you, too, for all your angelic features.'

Adam couldn't reply. He'd said the words of contrition. There was nothing more to do or think about.

213

'My spell lasts about five minutes,' the wizard went on. 'I *could* have you trussed up and bound in that time, I reckon. But I'm a modest man; aware of my limitations. I don't fancy my chances of shipping a Sicarii, however constrained, right the way home. You people *know* things: you'd slip out somehow and cause me trouble. Far better to blow a hole in your head here and now. Don't you agree?'

The wizard stood up and hefted the gun. 'There we are, all done – and so are you. Stoke high the fires of Hell!'

Adam stared along the barrel of the gun at the man's one open eye. He waited. A cruel and unnecessary second passed. He looked again – and was pleased to see something cause that eye to dim. A great blade had traversed his view and cut the wizard asunder at the waist. The body's last message of puzzlement reached his face and then he tumbled into ruin.

Adam was freed from bondage and hit the ground running. There was no real cover visible but he had hopes of gaining time to draw his firepower. He need not have worried or expended effort. The beast with the scythe did not follow.

Pistols to hand, Adam stood a way off and glanced back. Putting further distance between himself and the creature was pointless. He could never outrun its long spindly legs. This spot was as good as any for a last stand.

The monstrous insect was tipped forward, its muzzle dipped into the wizard's body, feeding noisily. From time to time the scythe blade flashed down to open new avenues of approach.

Adam studied its swarming limbs and shiny shell, wrapped in rags of black. He'd not seen its like in any of the catalogues of demi-demons, not even those applying to the wildest lands. He presumed it to be one of the demon's personal creations.

'That's right.' The monster jerked upright and spoke with the voice of its mistress. She sounded very sulky. 'You've kept me waiting. I have my *doubts* about you. I'm not sure why I bothered to save you. I shan't do it again. You should love me better.'

Adam bowed in greeting and prepared some disarming quip – but too late. She was gone.

Alarmed by the brief possession, the insect thing left its meal and scuttled off, chittering in distress. In the sudden silence Adam was free, for the first time since his arrival, to give proper attention to this new universe.

It was nice to know that the door back to Jonah's storeroom was still there, hanging implausibly free of support a few feet from the ground, but he ignored its temptations. Likewise he paid no attention to the incongruous presence of a flight of stone steps leading nowhere mere feet away. There were more pressing matters to consider.

It didn't take a Sicarii's experience of carnage to judge that some minor battle had swept over this place. The unburied dead lay in ones and twos all about. Interspersed with the human fallen were a few insectoids, punctured by gunfire and still intertwined with their final victims. Casualty-wise, mankind had suffered much the worst of the encounter.

A swift wander round, and Adam had reconstructed the story: an unexpected collision; a swirling fire-fight moving rapidly to close combat. There'd been no time for forming lines and mutual assistance. It had been every man for himself. Next he studied the bodies. The dead were dressed like civilians but didn't otherwise resemble them. Some soldiers in disguise had fought, prevailed and then moved on in a terrible hurry.

When fighting men don't bury fallen comrades Adam knew it was usually for one of two reasons: fanaticism or fear. He suspected both applied here.

They'd made time enough for some favoured tasks, however, though perhaps that was before they'd been attacked. Certainly, the circle of heads on spearpoints wasn't the work of five minutes. Ever conscientious, Adam went to check each.

Their carefully replaced *birettas* and clerical collars identified them. The priests of the King's and Legate's parties were there. So was the Legate himself, a mocking 666 daubed in red on his forehead. Beside him was the Bishop of Guildford, his mitre sewed securely on to his scalp. Adam prayed that had been done post mortem.

A new version of events presented itself. The King and Legate and their entourages had come through here. Overwhelming force had been waiting for them. Summary 'justice' had been served on servants of the Church. Soon after, the ambushers were themselves surprised. The survivors made off at speed, bearing with them the captive King.

A cold wind blew up, causing the endless sea of grass to wave and flow. There was nothing more to Adam's purpose in this place of death. He looked carefully around a full 360 degrees. Each direction promised as little as the others. This world was flat and green and featureless.

Adam sat down on the stolen steps of Guildford Cathedral and awaited inspiration or guidance. When 'night' came, he was still waiting. Only chance and boredom caused him to turn about and see behind him the distant lights.

~

It took Adam two full 'days' to reach the light source. He took bearings from it at 'dusk' and then rested in the long grass for the 'night'. Come morning, with the eye of faith, he could glimpse a shape on the horizon and the direction of the 'day's' march. Along the way he made an interesting discovery.

The mystery of Pelling's missing houses was solved. Adam came upon a fine, three-storey detached dwelling at the end of the first day. In its Guildford context it would have attracted no more than mild envy. Here, its red-brick normality seemed bizarre and threatening.

Adam stalked the house, approaching it upon his belly. He wasted an hour patiently watching for signs of life within. There were none. Then 'night' fell and he could see no more. No light flared within the house – apart from the persistent pinpoints on the horizon everything was dark. Adam lay on his back and looked for stars. He could not find any and the cloudless 'sky' was inky black.

When 'morning' came (from no direction in particular) he approached the front of the house and met its owners. They, their family, their servants, the entire household down to dogs and cats, had been sacrificed one by one. Their grand oak dining table, now stained blackish-red, had been pressed into service as a temporary altar. Adam said prayers for the souls of those in the heap of bodies, and then pressed hurriedly on.

On the 'morning' of the third 'day' he arrived at Guildford Castle.

~

He recognized the place from prints he'd seen, though it had undergone alterations since its change of worlds. The insulting flag of Leveller Green flying from the keep was the least of them.

217

A new defensive wall of earth had been thrown up around the castle. This was surmounted by a tangle of thorn and stakes, and faced with a ditch similarly lined as a welcome. The one gap through was turned into a strongpoint with a plank-built tower reinforced with huge wicker baskets of packed soil. An amateur student of siegecraft himself, Adam looked for weak spots and detected none. Clearly, the apostates were able to call on men of all the talents.

For this visit, however, Adam was more interested in the castle's new owners and inhabitants. All visible aspects of the defences were committed to memory and could be analysed later. The people inside required more immediate assessment. The Sicarii didn't want just any old prisoner to put his questions to.

There was a fair amount of activity in the 'courtyard' behind the earthen wall. Some menials were involved in the usual chopping and hewing activities whilst armed men patrolled the perimeter. Gun crews stood attentively by two cannon – little drakes or falcons by the looks of them, mounted on bastions atop the wall. It was a high level of alertness for a stronghold supposedly stranded in a world unknown to men. Adam wondered about that.

The answer to his puzzlement was supplied a few hours later. Adam's roving eyes caught a wave movement in the long grass. It came closer and closer to the castle, getting to within a hundred paces before detection. Then as a bell was rung and men cried out in alarm, a dozen of the insect things abandoned their creeping concealment and scuttled for the rampart. The cannons spoke and tore three or four to pieces with grapeshot. Detached limbs and green ichor flew over a wide area. The survivors made it to the ditch and, ignoring impalement on spike

218

and thorn, struggled frantically, one atop the other, to ascend.

The Levellers, reinforced by the minute, poured down fire into the chaotic, heaving mass but the creatures took a lot of killing. A few incautious fighters leaned too close and came in scythe range of the beasts. Several fell victim to such appalling blows; another was caught and pulled over into the scrum. There was a momentary lull in the attack as they consumed him.

In time, the Leveller's firepower tore the stubborn beasts from life. They lay in a shattered mass in the ditch, still twitching, screeching a last message of pain and anger. The humans made no attempt to retrieve their fallen comrade – and that was as informative as the assault itself.

It was clear they would not leave the safety of the castle, except for the most compelling reasons. Given what he'd just seen, Adam quite understood why. The insects had fought and died for a futile cause: there'd not been the slightest chance of them prevailing. The garrison *had* been depleted, though. For all the Sicarii, or anyone, knew, the insect things might be numberless; whereas the Levellers were not. Perhaps this was a war of attrition. That would explain the drawn faces of the defenders.

However sensible it was, this cautious doctrine did not suit Adam. He needed a portion of the garrison to detach itself and make some individual available for capture. Hoping that he would not become insectoid food before then, he lay in wait and thought of ways and means.

His prayers were answered the following 'day'. Quite unannounced, two figures slipped over the rampart and scrambled up the ditch. Sprinting as though Hell was at their heels, the young men passed quite close to Adam. Survival through speed was their sole consideration at that moment and so they did not see him. Their carelessness was deplorable, but if they were favoured enough to be entrusted with a mission they would do. The Sicarii bided a while and then followed on.

In such flat bare country he knew a lengthy pursuit was out of the question. It would be enough to get out of earshot of the castle. In the event, luck and good practice kept him from their notice for some few miles. Each time they turned, Adam's streamlined responses had put him to the ground, hidden by the universal grass. The Sicarii took rest and answered the call of nature when the Levellers did, and they travelled on in unsuspected tandem.

It got to the point where Adam knew he was pushing his luck and was fully prepared for discovery. So when one of the two unexpectedly swivelled and saw him, it was no disaster. Adam dropped to one knee, a pistol levelled over his arm. At that extreme range it was a very far from certain shot, but he was relaxed, knowing that there could be two goes at it. He should make a kill or else his training was in vain. It was not. One of the men leapt backwards, a new crimson medal on his breast, to lie spreadeagled on the ground. The other was still fumbling with his musket when Adam closed to point-blank.

'Hello, it's over,' he said to the man, causing him to look up – and down the barrel of the pistol pointing to his face. It was an old tactic to utter an ambiguous first phrase to end a fight. The thought required to understand, let alone answer, served to distract and break the flow of struggle.

The Leveller understood well enough to relinquish his

musket and slowly raise his hands. Adam smiled comfortingly and beckoned him down.

'The ground, if you'd be so kind, arms and legs out. That's right: like your late friend, only face first.'

Adam made sure of the other man's *late*ness with an English *seax* knife and then settled, cross-legged, before his living prize.

'Now then,' he said quietly, 'who do you think I am?'

The man lifted his face from the grass. 'The Sicarii we've heard of?'

'Just so. And have you heard *about* us?'

'Yes.'

'And the terrible things we're capable of?'

'Yes.'

'So can we cut out the delay and unpleasantness before you tell me everything?'

'Yes.'

Adam leaned forward. 'You're a very polite and sensible young man. I applaud that. So why should you be involved with Hell-bound criminals?'

'Ideals,' came the muffled reply. Adam nodded his understanding, if not approval. Face thrust in the ground, the Leveller did not see it.

'You don't seem very aggrieved to be caught.'

'I'm half glad.'

Adam chewed on that and then, his objective now splendidly achieved, at last permitted himself some consideration of self.

'I've been on a water regime the last three days. Have you any food?'

The Leveller turned his head as best he could. 'Obediah was carrying some beef sticks.'

Adam searched and found that this was so. Vigilance

undiminished, he resumed his place and worked upon the dried strips of meat.

'That's better. Now, why might you be "half glad"?'

'She's asked for more . . . offerings. Our sorcerers have brought another house through. It'll be somewhere round the gate and we were to . . . well, you know, perform the ritual.'

'I've seen. Two's not many for the job.'

'They're lost and confused when they come through. They're glad to see us at first. One gun overawes 'em whilst the other sets to . . . It's what *she* wants, not me. I didn't join up for that.'

If the Leveller could have beheld Adam's eyes, he would have abandoned hope then.

'Tell me how it's done.'

'Well, you get a table and a blade and you call on her and—'

'No, I meant the houses, the castle – the King.'

'That's sorcery business, I'm no thaumaturge.'

'No, but prolong your life a little. Tell me what you know.'

The Leveller raised his head a fraction but then tired and let it fall. 'The gateway: it's portable. Most of the time it stays where it first appeared, in that clothier's shop. If you ask, though – or if *he* asks – she'll permit it to be moved about. Our wizards worked out a spell. I don't follow how it's done, but four of 'em can sort of "carry" its corners a little distance. People don't see anything till they're in position and, well, they say they "let go" of it. Then it laps up whatever's in its space and whiplashes back home. Getting the King was easy: we just put our men in the crowd. Likewise the castle: four wizards standing in a diamond shape and . . .'

Adam was scanning the area around, making sure his fascinating chat was not about to be interrupted.

'King Charles I understand; but why the castle?'

'Survival. We were getting pasted. Those bug things were waiting for us when we came through. We lost a fifth of our strength there and then and we couldn't shake 'em off. They always found us sooner or later. We were spending all hours marching in a ring of pikes, trailing dead along the way. She wouldn't rein them in, though Jonah begged her. She said it was funny. We needed the protection of walls. Eventually we got them, though it pleased her to place it far in and make us fight to get there.'

'Fair enough,' said Adam. 'It was a bit of a giveaway, though. In their desperation for normality, the authorities said it had fallen down – and turned into brick at the same time.'

'Aye, we laughed about that one, though humour is precious rare in here. We welcome all the drama we can make. We want the people to hear and see the troubles, and realize the latter days are here!'

'One small point: the King's still alive, is he?'

'He is, and put to honest work when not subject to re-education. Likewise his gilded courtiers and the gentlemen of the castle. They now know what a spadeful of dirt looks like.'

'Slaves.'

'If you like – until they find justification in the Lord. Some of them are halfway there: we strike off their physical chains when they lose their mental ones. A few help in the defence of the castle against the Satan bugs.'

Adam nodded. 'Right, that's about it: thank you.'

The man spoke hurriedly, freeing his face of the turf. 'I have one question myself.'

The Sicarii's silence signalled his willingness to hear it.

'Am I to die?'

Adam smiled. 'We all are – but you're more likely to go before me, yes.'

'May I have time to compose myself?'

'There may be a problem there. I'm in a hurry and your sins are infinite.'

'Please? It's important to me.'

Adam thought and then relented with a grimace. Surprising himself by his kindness, he allowed the Leveller a full five minutes before he broke his neck.

The 'gateway' was still there, masquerading as one side of a cupboard door. In an otherwise featureless landscape it wasn't hard to find. The bodies of its two guards were gone, perhaps recovered by their comrades but more likely dragged off as insectoid dinner. The remnants of the battle were more skeletal than hitherto. Disdained for some reason by the bugs, the circle of martyred heads continued their silent vigil over the door and cathedral steps.

It had been an uneventful journey back. Though he'd looked, he hadn't spotted the freshly arrived house. It was easy to guess its occupants' eventual fate but he had to leave them to it. Greater issues hung in the balance. Doubtless that would be explained to them in the afterlife.

Aware of being under scrutiny, Adam bowed his thanks to the demon and turned his back on her world. Then he ran, as best the grass would permit, and leapt through the glowing portal. His body penetrated the illusory wood, landing with a roll amongst bales of cloth.

Out in the shop, a hard-faced giant was deep in conversation with Jonah Ransom. No other customers or workers were present. Both men turned to study the unshaven stranger emerging from a cupboard. Adam tipped his hat to them but didn't stop.

'Good morning!'

They didn't reply. With absolute lack of amusement, Ernest Grimmond, 'Chief Gideon', 'Elect of God and the Lord's correcting Right Arm on Earth', to give but two of his titles, watched Adam mount the steps to the street and leave the shop. 'The Beast of Reading' and 'Murderer of Saints' (as the Church termed him) then turned back to ask the clothier some rather serious questions.

# Part the Third

*Nor shall my sword sleep
in my hand*

# A SCHEDULE OF CAPITAL ENEMIES OF HIS MAJESTY

For distribution to approved members of the quality, town governors, harbourmasters, justices of the peace, constables-comitatus and *vicarii* appointed by the Warden of the Cinque Ports.

Revised and updated this day of our Salvation, 23 March 1995.

——— who harbours Welsh brigands to the injury of her neighbours and the King's good order. Of irregular private life. Fifty years old.

EAGLETON, John. A practiser of black magics and consorter with succubi. Native of the Lakes country and much partial thereto. Forty years old. Flaxen.

ELLIOT, Lady Katherine. Enchantress and seducer. A pagan and elve friend. Thirty years old. Petite.

FALCONBRIDGE, Gregory. A tale-bearer and sodomite. Courier of deviant books. A 'protestant'. Operates out of Alexandria and Antwerp port. Possesses safe conduct from the Cairo Caliph. Fifty years old. Normally accompanied by a boy. Epicene. Swarthy.

FETHERSTON, Glynnis. A foreteller and writer of sooth books. Inventress of scandals and untruths for the confusion of the common people. Employed by druids, 'humanists' and other disbelievers. Seventy years or upwards. Gaunt and of embittered visage.

GIANNOTTI, Donato-Jesus. Also MAXIMILIANUS. Florentine wizard. Sorcerous mercenary and assassin. Reputed poisoner of the Cardinal-Archbishop of Naples and ravisher of Queen Bridget of Sicily. Last reported sighting in Dieppe, meeting with English exiles and malcontents. Thirty years old. Runtish. Apostate Hebrew.

GRIMMOND, Ernest. Leveller, heresiarch and insurrectionist. Subject to death-on-sight notices since 1976. Do *not* arrest. Military wing commander since '78 (?). Chief Gideon since '92. Architect of London civilian bombing campaign 1990-date. Murdered own wife and family for 'backsliding', Birkenhead, '93. Sponsor of systematic atrocities against 'ungodly' during Thames Valley Insurrection, 1990. Forty years old. Former blacksmith. Powerful build.

GURNEY, Obediah. Arsonist . . .

... though it was rare indeed, in modern times, for any nation to merit two crusades within one generation. The Church, which thinks in centuries and acts with appropriate and informed caution, is unhappy to discover its ministrations merit such swift repetition.

The realm of England had long troubled the prayers of successive Holy Fathers. A certain relief therefore attended the affliction's bursting forth into open fever with the Levellers' Thames Valley Insurrection of 1990. After Orthodoxy's stern admonition had been administered, it was believed sufficient poison had been drained from the body politic. The fair bloom of happy and pious health could now return to Albion's fair face. It proved not so.

That restless nation continued to turn a disfiguring scowl to the world and its proper ordering. Mother Church was puzzled and distressed — hurt, even, to find her benevolent guidance so ill-received. She was not, however, discouraged. What St Augustine had termed the 'island of Angels' was most surely not beyond redemption. Subtle minds sought the will of G*d in prayer.

It transpired that the Church's one blind spot, its Achilles' heel, had been sought out and a wound delivered. That weakness was well known but considered too unlikely to merit consideration. It required a conjoining of dual disastrous happenstance for the strong fortress of Godly rule to be undermined. A corrupt regime and a complacent clergy are, praise G*d, not often found as bedfellows. For decades, the Church's parental scrutiny was thus deceived ...

... and that the secular arm of government is prey to the temptations of power is a commonplace. That is why the prerogatives of princes, kings and republics are kept circumscribed. The Holy Father maintains his own armed servants in every land to limit the pretensions of mere worldly rulers. This wise system has worked well. Everywhere men are *governed moderately, with as much consent as is ever likely in this sinful world. They are restrained only in wreaking harm or exploiting their weaker brethren. Conversely, their talents are not hamstrung by the pride of kings and rapacious taxation. For its part, the Church is liberal and easy-going, seeking not to pry in men's minds, but rather to direct their feet and outward actions in the ways of righteousness. Its corrections are mild and broadly welcomed. Judgement of sincerity is left to Almighty G\*d and the tribunal of the afterlife. Moreover, the Church binds society with its liturgical echoing of the seasons, its festivals and pilgrimages. The holy sacraments give comfort and security, and lend the dignity of meaning to man's short life. May feasts, 'churchales' and other official festivals of 'misrule' bring needful joy and frivolity to often harsh existence. All, in short, is ordered for the best.*

*It is only when rare sons and daughters of Christ's Holy Church harken to the vain worldly wisdom of kings, when they block their ears to the sighs of the poor, that all may come to nought. When this happens, Satan laughs and a sickness torments the soul of a nation. Successive Archbishops of London since the 1940s had failed to . . .*

From *The Young Lady's Guide to Political Economy – and a Risposte to the So-Called 'Neo-Christians'*. Cardinal Dave-Pierre Fairfax, Archbishop of New Wessex, Australasia. Fiat Lux Worldwide Press Corporation, Rome, the Year of Our Salvation 2425 A.D.

By pure chance, Adam had guessed right. It *was* morning back in Guildford, though the time correlation between his world and the demon's was not exact. He had been away long enough for great changes to have taken place.

'Colonel Longstaff's under arrest,' said Fred Pelling, as he watched Adam shave. 'So's Father Bancroft. The Archbishop of London's going to Rome for something called "consultations".'

'He'll be back, I expect,' mused the Sicarii, 'after a suitably rough time. It doesn't do to actually *remove* archbishops.'

'Don't see why not.'

'He'll be a *relic*,' Adam reassured him. 'He and those who matter will know it. That'll be his punishment – along with no cardinal's hat and the eternal eye being trained upon him. And who's to say the end of ambition won't chasten and save him? I'd impose a savage penance, though. Deprive him of Shakespeare, maybe.'

Fred remained unconvinced but, amidst so many wonders, didn't press the point.

'Well, happen so, but Canterbury's in charge of both sees for the time being. Lady Onslow told me there are people being displaced all over the Kingdom: real high-ups!'

'Just the start,' smiled the Sicarii with grim satisfaction as he glided the blade over his throat. 'Pretty soon they'll declare a crusade. Then you'll see some real changes. There'll be another Papal Legate, someone with authority for social engineering.'

Pelling gazed into his breakfast cup of tea. 'I'm not so sure I like the sound of that.'

'It'll be rough for a while,' agreed Adam. 'But in the long term you'll see the benefits. There's some bad blood in the system, that's all. It needs letting out: standard

233

medical practice. Besides, you'll be all right. I hear you've covered yourself in glory.'

'I ran the town during the transition like you stipulated. Lady Onslow supported me. Legitimate authority soon arrived. It was no great thing.'

'Did you hang your Leveller?'

'No.'

'Didn't think you would. You're a fool, Fred Pelling.'

'But surer of Heaven than you, I think.'

Adam laughed – and nicked himself with the razor. He dabbed the wound with a towel.

'I'm hoping the Almighty's more understanding than you give him credit for. Anything else I should know?'

'D'you recall the magician Hillaire?'

'Assistant Grandmaster for the South-East: last-legs look to him. Bancroft and co edged him out. Yes, I recall.'

'He's here.'

'Free?'

'Exalted. He's in charge. They've given him the Tigers. He's keen to see you.'

'And me him. A magician in charge of soldiers! Whatever next?'

'I know,' said Fred. 'There's something to tell your grandchildren!'

For a mere second Adam was quiet and sad – and jealous, remembering that he would never have any.

~

'What you've said accords with our suppositions,' said Hillaire. 'It supplies the corroboration we require in order to proceed.'

Adam lolled at ease in the oak-panelled Guildhall Council Chamber. The magician, looking even more wan than before, sat stiff-backed at the head of the huge table.

'You see a way forward then?' asked the Sicarii, idly surveying the depictions in oils of mayors past.

'We know most of the whys – both temporal and spiritual. Of course, our main hope is in the Church's campaign of prayer, but I humbly submit to have come across a possible remedy for the most immediate ill. Yes, I feel we are justified in progressing from the realm of thought. The location of the nexus was the missing link and you have now provided that.'

'I intended to seize and hold it. At the very least I'd be depriving them of free access. Shall I still go ahead?'

Hillaire nodded the death's head atop his high collar. 'In conjunction with our efforts, I think that would be fruitful. Without them, your success would be dangerously dependent on the creature's whim.'

'Do you think you can get a hold on her?'

'In principle, the thaumaturgic geometry of the spells I have devised should suffice. They have been studied by greater practitioners than I and not been found wanting.'

Adam looked directly at the magician. 'You've not met her.'

'No,' agreed Hillaire gravely, 'that is true. Also I think it is important that we consistently refer to "her" as "it" rather than anthropomorphize the phenomenon. Not everyone sees "it" as you have. Some of the London witnesses report an entirely different figure: a comely youth, an elderly strumpet, even an ambulatory orifice. Bear this in mind: correct mental perceptions will be vital to our success.'

'You've not met her,' Adam repeated.

Hillaire wouldn't relent. 'I have met *it* in books and careful thought. *Its* type has been long known to us. The form *it* takes is merely contingent and designed to seduce.'

Adam smiled without humour. 'We'll see if you believe with such conviction when you look her in the eye.'

Hillaire fiddled with the black magician's clasp bag on the table in front of him. He seemed to want to either leave or start again.

'Don't feel, Sicarii,' he said quietly, 'that we are ungrateful for your strivings. I do not deprecate them. I have secluded myself in my master's palace at Pevensey Bay searching for a cure to this wound in our world. You have grappled with it direct, to your great peril. I have been attended by some small success. My colleagues who were in turn commissioned to seek the nexus were less happily rewarded. They found only death or madness. You alone have survived the demon's notice to report where *it* unnaturally penetrates the dimensions. Without that information other efforts were in vain.'

Adam conceded the issue, willing, for a while, to defer to expert opinion.

'Okay, I'll get the portal. What then?'

'We enter in force. You will kindly organize the non-magical personnel for that. A contingent of sorcerers will quell the demon. The King will be rescued and then we will return, sealing the portal for ever behind us.'

Adam sighed. 'That seems simple enough. How do you propose quelling her?'

'You would not understand, Sicarii.'

'Indulge me.'

'My findings are expressed in the geometry of magic.'

'Then translate.'

Magicians were accustomed to implacable forces – though rarely in human form. Hillaire knew some things were best gone round than through. He stared out of the bay window down at the High Street.

'You were aware of demons,' he said sadly, 'now, along

236

with the higher sort of my calling, you are aware of the melancholy fact of "demon lords". Behind each abomination, in unending succession, stands a chain of superior beings leading up – or down – to the satanic Eminence itself. The lower sort owe fealty to and draw power from each succeeding higher.'

'So I've come to learn.'

'I'd be obliged if you'd refrain from interruption. This creature is merely one stage up from the plain demon magicians commonly summon – and even those we can scarcely control. This thing stands in relation to them as does a stallion to a mule. In our world it is beyond restraint. What I propose is a multiplicity of sorcerers, coming close enough to it for each to slip a block, a wall of human will, between the creature and its source of being. Cut off from its lord and master, the beast will weaken and sleep. We will do this for long enough to achieve our aims. Does my explanation suffice?'

Adam expelled a breath. 'It does, though your spells may not. Meanwhile, what of the town? I hear you have powers of life and death within its boundaries.'

Hillaire again looked out of the chamber, this time somewhat disdainfully.

'Those are mere matters of the flesh,' he said, pained even to think of them. 'You may deal with those.'

'Have you come to gloat? "How are the mighty fallen" and all that?'

It wasn't so much hatred firing the light in ex-Colonel Longstaff's eyes, Adam decided, but guilt. His visit here might not be fruitless.

'No, it's not that.'

'Then what?' asked Father Bancroft. 'We've made our full confessions already, and you can't supply absolution.'

'I wouldn't even if I could,' replied the Sicarii bluntly.

'Well, that's honest at least,' said the soldier, rearranging the chains coiled by his feet. 'So to what do we owe this unalloyed pleasure?'

Adam smiled, though there was nothing in this noisome cell to merit it.

'I think you struck upon it yourself: it's honesty. Lack of it has brought you to this. I've come to offer you a way back.'

Both Bancroft and Longstaff looked up. This was the last thing they expected to hear.

'I hadn't heard,' said the priest cautiously, 'that the Sicarii practised unnecessary cruelties.'

'That's right,' said Adam. 'We don't. There has to be good reason.'

'Therefore . . . your offer might be kindly meant.'

Adam shrugged. 'The motive's immaterial. This realm is about to receive an injection of honesty. I'm saying that you can assist the treatment.'

Bancroft and Longstaff exchanged incredulous glances. In their respective professions they'd grown unaccustomed to mercy.

'I suppose,' hazarded the soldier, 'that continued life is out of the question?'

'Pretty much,' agreed Adam. 'I was thinking more in terms of an honourable death.'

'Fair enough,' said Longstaff, looking wistfully at the rents in his blue uniform where the marks of rank had been. Father Bancroft also swiftly nodded.

The Sicarii was pleased that his presumption of faith and dignity in them had not been misplaced.

'Right then,' he said, 'here are some ways to die . . .'

~

Ernest Grimmond was dreaming. His lips stirred restlessly as he rebuked the ghost of Oliver Cromwell for lack of zeal. The dead Lord Protector stood abashed whilst his fondness for family, song and wicked morris dancing was flung against him. Sadly, the ultimate abomination of Oliver's conversion was not even touched upon when the dream mutated him into something strange and curvaceously ... feminine. Grimmond chose to avert his eyes from that and instead beheld the imaginary landscape beyond. It was a second Eden, the very country that Cromwell could have constructed had he been a little less *weak*. The Leveller indicated its salient points to the cowering statesman-thing.

The numberless tiny village churches, he said, were each independent of the other and went their own sweet way under the guidance of the Lord. Those simple homes and fields around them were all jointly held and jointly worked, for there was no 'property' any more. Each – Godly – male might own a Bible and a sword but nothing else. The last rich man had ages before been deprived of life or title or both. Their descendants, branded with the mark of Cain, laboured in chains at the meanest and hardest tasks alongside adulterers, blasphemers and self-polluters. Common criminals were their hash overseers. God's Elect were thus left free for lives of devotion and prayer.

The Cromwell temptation gaped in wonder, his/her chin falling implausibly to the ground. It remarked on the lack of towns. Grimmond explained they were long destroyed and forgotten; their vile, vice-addicted populace dispersed to seemly rural occupations. The land now lay quiet and at peace. Rome-Babylon was fallen and foreigners were no more. Swords were beaten into ploughshares and the lion lay down with the lamb. Cromwell then spoilt everything by asking what all the gallows were for. Angered, Grimmond awoke.

Because of his history, he never rose gradually from sleep. That was one of the many luxuries he had foregone in the service of his fellow man. Once his troubled eyes flickered open he was instantly ready to fight or flee. Though no milksop herself, the bodyguard secretary who stood vigil over him never liked to receive her master's first glance of the day.

'Are you rested?' she asked, as she always did. The health and welfare of the movement's best man was her one preoccupation.

'It will suffice,' he muttered, raising his giant frame and putting on his boots. 'God sent me a dream of Paradise and the new Jerusalem. Speak.'

She did not resent his lack of soft conversation, knowing how very much he had sacrificed for the cause and how *strong* he had to be. According to his lights he had truly loved his little family. That had been a *sad* necessity ...

'The London two-barrel bombs are placed and fused. The ten-barrel construction is still en route.'

Grimmoned frowned, whether at his uncooperative left boot or at the reported fall from perfection she could not tell.

'Discipline the laggard operatives,' he ordered. 'Ignite what is ready at ... noon. The deluded will be streaming in to their "mass" then. Prepare breakfast whilst I seek guidance.'

She signalled that his will would be done and then passed him his dog-eared Bible.

240

'There's no immediate rush,' said Adam. 'They'll be waiting for us, so let them sweat a bit.'

'What you propose is good policy,' agreed the Palestinian trooper. 'Their vigilance will be tested and diminished.'

Adam enjoyed these chats: professionals and brethren talking together as temporary equals. The setting and the sunshine put the cap on it. Created for the pleasure of the garrison commander's family, this park in the castle grounds was quite charming. Less happily, Adam wondered about that family's present position. No carefree hours for them, or games with the children there.

'Do not be too optimistic,' countered the Swiss Papal soldier, stretching his huge arm out along the back of the wrought-iron bench. 'For this vital task they will use their best people.'

The Palestinian pondered gravely and then nodded his acceptance of the point.

'If the Sicarii is quite convinced of his detection, then what you say is true,' he conceded graciously.

'I'm sure,' said Adam. 'The man with Jonah was no customer. He saw me leave the room in which the portal is contained. I did not stop to deal with him since my news was so vital. He was an unknown quantity at that time. I considered it better to take advantage of his surprise in order to depart.'

'If it was Grimmond, as we now suspect,' said the Swiss, 'then you did right. He was a tiger at Reading.'

Use of that term caused Adam to glance up and behold the soldiers at drill a little way off. The Fen Tigers were his to play with now, but at present he had scant use for them. The tasks in hand were for small squads of fully informed men. It was sufficient that they just be around and bind Guildford in awe.

'We'll use a few of that lot,' he informed his companions. 'A platoon at most. Choose one that's best.'

'That'll be *fun*,' said the Swiss, smiling broadly. 'They hate the English foreigners, let alone foreign foreigners.'

'Be gentle with them,' Adam admonished him. 'They have short fuses and less understanding.'

The trooper pulled a good humoured 'of course I will' face.

Confident in his subordinates, Adam could have the rare satisfaction of considering the matter closed: something that could be ticked off the list.

'Our attention will be engaged for a while,' he said, pressing on. 'Can I be sure of the town?'

'No problems exist,' the Palestinian assured him. 'Your Pelling person has arrested the more harmless subversives. We have occupied our free days contacting the rest.'

'Were there many?'

'Minimal numbers,' replied the Swiss. 'This is a good country at heart. A few prominent citizens had been seduced by the whispers of the Devil. The Levellers had secreted one or two fighters here. They were not hard to sniff out.'

'Where are they now?'

The bearded trooper looked upward as he tried to recall. 'Quarries, lakes, lonely places,' he said blithely. 'You won't see *them* again.'

The Sicarii signalled his approval. 'Good. That's about it, then.'

'What about Bancroft's two wizards?' asked the Palestinian. 'Shall we use those?'

Adam searched for any sign of resistance but found none. 'I don't see why not. I'm told that the association with their previous master is not held against them.

242

They're here for us to use or send away. We know the enemy will field similar gentlemen.'

'So, we have the people,' said the Swiss. 'What else?'

'Nothing much,' answered Adam. 'All we need now is an ancient lady and a brewer's dray . . .'

~

They were observed by innocent eyes. A child out walking in Sydenham Road watched the distant conference. She saw the sunlight weaken where the three men sat, and cold-heartedness rising off them like steam. She found cause to shrink close in to her mother's skirt.

'*So sweet*,' thought the mother, pleased and deceived. '*How she loves me . . .*'

~

Adam woke and knew that he was not alone. He was not entirely unfamiliar with shared beds, being only human, after all. That was how he also knew his companion wasn't human.

Seconds before sense returned, horse doses of electricity and adrenalin tore him from sleep and impelled his limbs to action. Enough power remained over to stretch out his arm, heading towards the last object of his attention the night before. The pistol on the bedside chair was grasped by a pre-cupped hand, its autonomous thumb cocked the mechanism. Only then did laggard reason arrive, Adam's personality slipping in to occupy the independent body. For the briefest while they tussled for supremacy, each believing it knew best, until the meat recognized its master and surrendered control. Adam now understood the situation but kept hold of the gun – for comfort's sake alone.

'Hello,' purred the demon, close into his ear. The air

was charged and crackled at the slightest movement. Her normal perfume of lust and spice was overlaid by the scent of scorched sheets.

The Sicarii turned on to his back. The blankets subsided and floated down to rest. Apart from the glow of the street lights against the curtains, the room remained in absolute darkness.

His mouth was clogged with sleep; he had to work his jaw and splutter before his voice would obey orders.

'Why?' he asked. It seemed the best catch-all question.

She laughed, a liquid, trilling sound; enough to wake the entire Spread Eagle.

'Why not? I had some other people to see. I thought you'd be pleased.'

'And I *am*.'

'Good.' The laughter was followed by giggles. Some of her delectable heat ebbed over to his side of the bed and he was aroused.

A slim questing hand snaked under the covers towards his parts. He intercepted it. Where they touched, his palm was burnt.

'Why?' she asked in her turn, sounding genuinely curious.

'I would die. My frame is too weak.' He thought it pointless to mention the idea of chastity.

'I know,' she said, still puzzled. 'So?'

'Who else must you see?' Adam asked, desperate to distract her. She shifted the slightest bit away from him. Familiar tetchiness, crossed with boredom, entered her reply.

'I'm seeing them now. I can visit Jonah and Hillaire and enjoy you all at the same time, little man.'

'Of course. What are you saying to them?'

The previous rejection abruptly forgotten, she seemed

244

flattered by his interest. He felt her turn towards him, a fresh wave of body heat converting the bed into a tropical zone. Adam was sweating with desire, only just short of climax. Her unseen face was alongside his, her molten breath on his cheek.

'I'm toying with Jonah because he's my pet. The wizard Hillaire is under instruction.'

'Tell me more about that.' Adam was gasping. 'Any-thing – else I won't last.'

Her hand had returned, walking like a spider, leaving light burns over his inner thigh. Adam fought against the pain.

'I thought I'd wake him up to tell him his magic wouldn't work. I felt kind. He's inverted an order of magnitude two-thirds through the spell's geometry. It would glance off me. I'm not being nasty to him, I do understand. It's a very abstruse feature and it was late at night when he made the mistake. He was excited by the progress being made.'

Adam was cooled from within. Authority's great plan turned out to be as useless as a pagan's prayers. The chill horror of embracing that notion allowed him to think more clearly.

'So what shall we do with you?' He tried to make the question sound innocent.

'Worship and serve me – and stop these nasty petitions to your old god. That's what I'm suggesting to Hillaire. He's crying, poor man. He's upset. I'll free him from the wall soon, and take his spell book from in front of his eyes – in a while, when he's learned his lesson. The cancer I've put in him is a slow one. He may have ten of your years to ponder his error and come to love me. I've just told him that but he's still weeping.'

The temptation was worse than in Compton Church –

but coupling with demons was a damnation offence. Adam was half minded to use his pistol on himself and thereby end it. He doubted she'd allow that, though.

'You can come and see me – and try to get your King,' she went on, 'spell or no spell. Actually, I insist on it. I've told Hillaire the same. Bring the army you were going to gather: I'll permit you through the portal and see who wins. I *love* this – such delicious drama!'

Her hands left Adam and fled back in order to play with herself. As he sank into the bed in relief, the demon bucked and writhed in instant ecstasy.

'I've decided,' she whispered huskily. 'You must come – it's the trip of a lifetime.'

'How so?'

'Because you'll never go home. The second visit is permanent. You become mine. It's the rules: something to do with reorientation of molecular structure – but you'd not follow any of that.' She broke off to give a plaintive little yelp of pleasure. Her torrid breathing increased. Adam's room was like a jungle; in the morning he would find the wallpaper sodden and dripping – and himself in similar state.

'Come to me,' she said in a heaving voice. 'It will be kinder for your world if you come to me.'

Then, like an explosion, she came in another way and was gone.

'Tell her to concentrate. The picture is ill-defined.'

Adam knew full well the reason for that. The old widow woman was terrified of the enormous wizard enclosing her forehead in his paw. It was only her true faith and desire to serve the Church's purpose that had got her this far. Both puzzled and pleased by his new-found compassion, Adam decided to indulge it. The Sicarii knelt down to her level and smiled reassuringly.

'Take no notice of him,' he told her, patting the hand clasped, white-knuckled, on her lap. 'He's a misery because the girls won't have him – not at any price. And can you blame them?'

The old lady smiled weakly. She was lost amongst this sea of soldiers and magicians and guns. Even one friendly face made a difference.

Bancroft's wizard didn't rise to the taunt. He was looking blankly ahead into some other place; the lack of complaint suggested an improvement in picture.

Adam smirked conspiratorially at her, like a schoolboy getting away with something.

'Tell you what, my love, remind me what was in that bag you left in the shop.'

She was only too glad to. 'I put in all my favourite knick-knacks, like I was told. The best thing was a miniature we had done of my Jimmy.'

'Was he your husband?'

'Oh yes, a lovely man and so ... well, *kind*. I do hope you'll get it back for me. It's the only likeness I have of him.'

Adam felt a twinge of conscience. 'Naturally,' he lied. 'That'll be our first job.'

'And he wrote me a love poem when we were courting. I told him I chucked it away like he asked – but I didn't. I've always kept it; and that's in the bag too. They'll think me a forgetful old so-and-so to leave it behind, won't they?'

'Who cares? We know you're not.'

'It's coming through like crystal,' said Bancroft's giant. 'Keep it up a little longer.'

Adam nodded. The psychic link with the item left in

247

Jonah's shop needed to be fairly intense before magic could tap into it. Once done, however, the wizard could ride along the bond and see through eyes remote from his body.

'What else is there? What about jewellery? I bet young men used to shower you with presents.'

She shrugged coquettishly, the ghost of a stratagem recalled from half a century ago.

'They may have done. But my Jimmy lashed out and bought me a—'

The wizard broke the link and lifted his massive hand from her head. The slipstream of the spell's death made the old woman wince.

'Complete success.' He beamed. 'I've seen all that's needful.'

Adam wasn't interested. 'Aren't you going to say thank you?'

'Do what?' Bancroft's magician didn't like his moment of triumph interrupted – especially by the man who'd lost him a finger.

'Where are your manners? Say thanks to the lady who made everything possible.'

The giant turned and made a mocking, over-formal bow. The widow took it at face value and blushed. Adam signalled to one of the Tigers to escort her away. Suddenly he was all business again.

'Well?'

'Like we thought,' reported the wizard. 'It's a house of death.'

In order to keep some element of surprise, the surrounding houses hadn't been evacuated. Adam sent some Tigers to remedy this. Providing the inhabitants didn't stop to collect any possessions, they'd just about make it out through the back in time. If need be, the troops could encourage haste with the butt of a musket.

Adam reckoned it vital there be no more than five to ten minutes between the old lady's fake shopping trip to Jonah's shop and the assault. He didn't want any of the defenders smelling a rat and moving out. Unfortunately, that didn't give much time to clear the High Street.

If all went well, they would harvest a good crop of Levellers. He'd guessed correctly that Grimmond would foresee an attack and prepare a warm welcome. Doubtless the man himself was there, infiltrated in to oversee things. Adam had been happy to turn a blind eye to it. Let them come and labour to achieve their own destruction. There was a certain ... inelasticity in military men's thinking that could be relied upon.

The wizard had seen the preparations in detail. There were barricades of innocent-looking bales of cloth in rows – each hollowed out to admit a musket. The Levellers stood to, invisible behind the blank facade, ready to release a storm of fire that would sweep the shop clear of life. Adam wondered whether Longstaff, if still in charge, would have blundered into it.

Right now, that gentleman was waiting amongst the other chosen few selected for the assault. A common soldier once again, though granted 'advisor' status, he acted as if a great weight was off his shoulders. Adam was pleased to be the catalyst for his new happiness. Alongside him, out of sight of Jonah's shop, in the cathedral churchyard, were a few dozen Tigers, Bancroft's two wizards, the Sicarii's troopers and two of the Wisbech Regiment's smaller cannons, complete with crew to trundle them into use. Adam looked around at all he had prepared and saw that it was good. Indeed it *was* good to be busy. With the collapse of Hillaire's grand design, there was a danger of losing impetus. Lesser projects, like the King and the Levellers, could at least maintain the illusion of purpose and progress. He gave the order to proceed.

The Lascelles Tickner brewery dray trundled off down the street. It looked about halfway through its deliveries, only lightly burdened with barrels. It was the correct place and state for it to be in at that time, on that day. Pelling had researched this, in spite of his fervent disapproval of Adam's plan. The carter was the fly in the ointment. Still, even if they recognized him as not the usual man, they'd not have time to act upon it.

The dray got to Jonah Ransom's shop. It went past it a little. This was the most fraught stage of operations. Detection might cause things to go horribly awry. For all his years of experience, Adam found he was holding his breath. The excitement of the uncertain moment never got any less.

That time of peril passed. The carter halted his team and then expertly backed them up. The dray moved menacingly towards the head of the steps leading down to the clothier's. It would do them no good to fire now: the barrels at the back held only beer.

The metal-shod rear of the dray crashed through the rail round the shop. Shaken free of their binding cords by the impact, the barrels tumbled off the back to fill the stairwell.

By then the carter was away, haring off down the High Street as best his legs and the slope could propel him. Less well-informed, the dray horses pulled free of the collision and ambled leisurely forward, puzzled by the radical change in routine. They did not have long to wonder.

Two hissing grenadoes were amongst the piled-up barrels. The Tigers who'd thrown them withdrew into deep cover. A bewildered face was seen pressed to the ground-floor window of Jonah's shop.

The town shook – or so it seemed to those waiting in the churchyard. Pieces of horse and masonry passed them by, flying up the High Street. The explosion was like the voice of God. As with the real thing, no one cared to speak afterwards. The team moved forward in silence with Adam at their head.

Guildford's main thoroughfare was no longer so easy – or pleasant – to negotiate. The gun crews in particular had difficulty in getting past the aftermath of the Sicarii's drastic solution. Looked at either architecturally or anatomically, some of the remnants were distressing.

Where Jonah's house had been there was now a hole. Much the same could be said of his neighbours to either side. The opposite side of the street was far less affected: almost all the damage there was reparable. Adam was pleased. It wasn't always possible to calculate gunpowder loads so nicely. Some townsfolk staggered out willing to dispute this judgement, but the Tigers drove them back in.

The portal alone remained untouched. The walls which had once hidden it and formed Jonah Ransom's stock cupboard were mere memories. Open to view in all its glory, the gateway to another world shed a yellowish glow over the pit in which it sat. Pre-warned and informed, Adam's army paid it no great attention.

The Sicarii had given thought to Leveller reinforcements issuing forth from the gate: hence the show of force. The minutes ticked by, however, as the gun crews prepared and no one appeared. The Tigers and the wizards stood ready but remained unemployed. Evidently the Levellers were more discouraged by Adam's surprise delivery than he'd envisaged. Their reserves, assuming they existed, stayed stunned and indecisive beyond the divide.

Since they would not come to him, Adam was obliged to send a greeting. As soon as the cannons were ready, stationed either side of the portal, he gave the order to fire. It was odd to see the charges of grapeshot rip into the void to no visible effect – and ultimately rather disheartening for the crews. He had to repeat the order to secure constant firing. It was a fair while before some response came.

A ragged volley of musket rounds came out of the portal and buried itself harmlessly in the Angel Hotel across the street. Adam had taken care to place his troops away from the front of the gate, knowing that the enemy would be firing blind. He smiled to himself. The delay in retaliation was gratifying. He had hopes of great gaps torn in the heretic ranks supporting the ambush in the shop. Certainly, it had taken a time to rally them and organize some resistance. The Levellers were now cut off from reinforcement and every death amongst them made Adam's task that much easier.

With that in mind, he ordered the guns to continue to play without cease, leaving Longstaff to vary the angle and rate of fire and keep the unseen target on the hop. Some heavier brethren, the sakers and culverins, would join in due course to add more strident notes to the tune.

It was not in Adam's mind to seize the gate yet; that would be premature. It was enough at present to deny it to the party of Satan. All the same, he was grimly determined that those who lingered on its other side be given a foretaste of Hell.

The Sicarii left the scene to the accompaniment of cannon fire, happy with a small task well done.

~

'Forgive me or hate me, I don't care which – just *work* with me.'

Fred Pelling sighed as he looked out over the view from the town walls.

'There's no question of me hating you. I understand what you're trying to do.'

'Well, then . . .'

Adam couldn't see what was so absorbing about these plain old fields and woods. He was getting impatient.

'It's just that working with you . . .' Pelling searched for the safe and proper words. 'It's like watching someone do sabre drill in a nursery. Your heart's in your mouth the whole time.'

Adam was mollified – even amused. 'I rather like that,' he said. 'Very witty.'

'The gunpowder business shocked us. That's why you keep meeting this hostility. All those houses . . .'

The Sicarii had had some problems with the locals of late. This last week people wouldn't stand near him at mass. A very respectable merchant, freshly homeless, had threatened him with a crossbow. It was only a minor irritant: nothing he or the Tigers couldn't handle.

'It was the neatest way of doing it,' Adam explained for the umpteenth time, wondering why Guildfordians didn't listen. 'You should count yourself lucky. Other places are faring worse.'

'So we hear.' Pelling sounded more downcast than before. Even in this nominally 'interdicted' town, news had seeped in of the harrowing of England.

'In Birmingham and Stalybridge they're eating the recent dead apparently; having run out of dogs and rats.

253

Such are the blessings of Leveller rule. How would you like to be starving and under siege like they are?'

Pelling was intrigued to hear the rumours confirmed. Up to now, Adam had been close lipped about the changes taking place.

'It said in the *Albion* there's plague in them and they're fighting amongst themselves. I read that the neo-Druids have got Cardiff and they're making sacrifices!'

The Sicarii smiled. 'Well, you don't want to believe everything you read in the newsheet, Fred: it's Church controlled. Still, there'll be something to it, I dare say. The poison's coming out: you can't expect it to be a pretty sight. Cruel to be kind – that's what you say here, isn't it?'

'Like in Liverpool, I suppose . . .'

'A crusade's often over-enthusiastic at first, and the army was fresh from its Welsh triumphs. Besides, an example at a campaign's start is always a good idea. Towns surrender more easily if they can see the fate in store for them.'

'A flat field with salt ploughed into it?'

'Most times you need only be that severe once. Ultimately, you end up saving lives.'

'Oh, that's all right, then.'

For once Adam didn't miss the sarcasm. 'This evil comes from the deeds of others, Fred. Wounds cause pain when they're dressed.'

Despite himself, Pelling seemed to see some consoling truth in that – and that in turn worried him.

'They're only deluded people,' he said. 'Deluded by the Levellers, deluded by the King's forged proclamations, deluded into helping those lords who took their land off them.'

Adam was unimpressed. 'A deluded man with a gun is as dangerous as any other. And you've forgotten the ones "deluded" by the devil. Look, are you going to provide the town militia or aren't you? That's what this discussion was meant to be about.'

Pelling had been distracted by visions of Crusaders dealing out the Liverpool treatment to the homeland he saw spread before him. He wondered why he, a field-mouse, bothered to squeak his protests at the harvesters.

'I doubt you need our humble help. Look at the force you've assembled here. What good's an extra few hundred yokels with shotguns and bills?'

Adam steeled himself to explain. 'The second regiment I requested isn't coming. I heard today. They're bogged down in Wessex with lots of minor landlords' risings. Some of your "deluded" folk are keeping them busy, determined to stay poor by protecting their masters' enclosed lands. We don't know for sure how many Levellers are in Guildford Castle. I need every single man I can get. Is that clear enough for you?'

As far as Pelling was concerned more than enough Guildfordians had died already, and that was that.

'You could have gone over my head to Lady Onslow for this, and—'

Adam waved him to silence. He was staring intently out into the countryside which hadn't, up to now, so gripped his attention.

'Leastways,' he said slowly, 'I was *told* there's no regiment coming . . .'

~

'Look on the bright side,' said Adam. 'We've solved one mystery.'

The question of the two Leveller regiments of foot who, five years before, had fought their way clear of the Battle of Reading had taxed the mind of Church and State ever since. The thought of those stockpiled arms and soldiers-in-waiting was a barrier to sound sleep amongst the exalted.

Now they could rest easy, all doubt being resolved. The offending formations were out in the open. Less happily, they'd been recruited back up to strength and had Guildford under close siege.

'I'd quite overlooked that source of joy,' said Pelling drily.

'That's your trouble,' countered the Sicarii, entirely relaxed and willing to be playful. 'You see the bad side of everything.'

Pelling sought support amongst the others round the Guildhall Council Chamber table. There wasn't any. He could have done with a Weston-Onslow beside him to lend authority to the side of reason, but that reserved seat was empty. Lady Onslow and her family, together with their tenants and retainers, were likewise beleaguered at Loseley. A few hundred heretics had them bottled up beyond communication.

'I'm striving to be realistic,' protested Pelling. 'I know the situation's not irretrievable. With this force you've gathered here, we can hold the walls. Two to one against's not bad odds for a siege, so I've read. It's more the question of supplies holding out until . . .'

He trailed off, aware that the others present were looking one to another, as though they knew something he didn't. In fact they did. Pelling didn't understand the ways of the world as well as them.

'I'm afraid,' said Assistant Grandmaster Hillaire (who'd been strangely quiet and chastened of late), 'there's no question of holding the walls. We are ordered onwards. The strength we have assembled is intended for greater tasks than the salvation of a minor market town – however intrinsically charming.'

'The apostates want to delay and wear us down,' said Longstaff. 'That's why their last trump card is sitting outside here. We need all we've got – and more – to go in and get the King. If and when we come out, we can deal with these Reading leftovers then.'

'I agree,' said Father Bancroft succinctly. He turned grave but not unsympathetic eyes on the aghast Frederick Pelling.

Pelling glanced along the table and found they were each favouring him with that pitying look.

'But . . . but how the swiving bloody hell do we defend the town?'

Adam graciously overlooked the profanity. 'I suggest you don't. If you won't come with us – and the invitation stands – and you won't supply the militia, I'd recommend you run for it. I should do so before this evening. That's when they'll storm the walls.'

'How do you know?' gasped Fred.

'Because that's when we move off. They'll be informed by their agents in the town and will seek to stop us. If you'd be kind enough to throw your life away holding them up for a few minutes, we'd be terribly grateful.'

'You'd be rewarded in Heaven,' Bancroft confided.

Pelling rudely left the room without a word. He – and his people – had been condescended to once too often. Like a revelation exploding, he saw clearly now. It was better to die alone on the walls of the town he loved than survive in the company of its betrayers.

It was on the walls that Adam found him, towards the end of the afternoon. In the event, Pelling wasn't alone.

The intervening hours of frantic activity and argument had provided him with company. The militia had answered the muster call of cathedral bells. There were mere boys, men in their prime and ancients with little to lose. Anyone who could hold or reload a musket or wield something sharp was welcome. Even the help of the more mettlesome women was not refused. Those who failed to arrive, the faint-hearted and narrow-souled, were not mentioned, nor ever would be again.

Pelling planted the golden Lion and Mitre standard of the Weston-Onslows above the South Gate and took his station beside it. Jacko, his lieutenant, and a few other Onslow retainers stranded in town were with him as the pitiful elite corps of the resistance. Fully informed of the Guildhall discussions, they looked on the Sicarii's arrival with disdain.

'Cheerio, Fred.'

Pelling stared straight ahead to where the enemy were already standing hurriedly to arms. News of activity in the town had been spread fast by traitors.

'And goodbye to you too.'

'I misdoubt we'll meet again.'

'No, your plans have seen to that. You're not open to last-minute persuasion, I suppose?'

Adam was casting an appraising eye over the Leveller ranks. 'No more than you are,' he answered. 'Thanks for your help.'

For all his preoccupations, Pelling was intrigued by the finality in Adam's tone. He turned to face him.

'Don't mention it. What is it you're so sure of? My death? Yours? Both?'

The Sicarii smiled sadly. 'That's in the Lord's hands and I wouldn't presume. The odds aren't good, I grant you. Neither of us should start a long book. No, I meant about returning. A second trip to the demon's world is final. She told me.'

Burning questions like 'when?' and 'how?' only seemed mundane. Pelling simply accepted what was said.

'I should look your last, then,' he said, gesturing with his arm to encompass not only Surrey or England, but the world kindly given to man. There was the slightest shake in Fred's voice.

'I have been,' Adam replied briskly, refusing to go along with the incipient emotionalism. 'That's how I can leave you a present. Look.'

Pelling followed the line of Adam's gloved hand. The stunted trees atop St Catherine's Mount only partly hid a swarm of figures standing, once one considered it, unnaturally still.

'I'd seen those skirmishers. The Levellers . . .'

'No. Don't *just* look: study.'

Pelling did so.

'Oh . . . glory!'

'Too dark, too thin for humans.'

'*Disva!*' exclaimed Pelling, apparently in despair.

'Demi-demons,' corrected Adam, supplying the proper term.

Jacko, paper-white but resolute, said he'd fetch a perspective glass.

'Best not,' said Adam, stopping him. 'You'll upset yourself and others. I can tell you if you're curious. Seen close up they're browny-black and sort of leathery with nasty teeth and claws, but good with blades too. Also, there's worse up there: I think I saw a *padfoot* and some *downs tigers*.'

Pelling was still stunned; even his birthplace seemed to have turned against him.

'How . . .?'

259

'Leveller wizards have roused the local pre-man life and bound them. I *thought* I'd seen too many scarecrows around these last few days ... Yes, it *can* be done, albeit at great cost. The magicians haemorrhage, so I'm told. They must be desperate.'

Pelling continued to survey the hilltop and priory, both obscenely handed over to non-human control.

'Thank you,' he said, without inflection. 'I shall miss your "presents".'

'That's all right,' said Adam, blindly missing any irony. 'Bear in mind they use slashing swords. The swing leaves their armpit open to an up-thrust.'

'I shall tell my tailors and barmen and shop clerks that.'

'Also none of them likes fire.'

'Fine.'

At that point the dimly glimpsed army out in the fields began to sing. It was well known that the warriors of 'protestantism' prepared for battle with psalms. The sound was taken up around the town accompanied by kettle-drums, until the air seemed filled with bass rumbling. Less human howls and gibberings from one quarter enlivened the music and made it uncanny.

The Levellers' black-clad 'pastors' began striding up and down in front of the line, exhorting their flock and chanting from books of scripture. The armoured pikemen at the centre of each formation went to 'port your pike' and men with ladders came to the fore.

A cannon fired, and smoke and splinters flew out of the wall a few score yards along from where Adam and Pelling stood. Someone nearby screamed in pain. The sound of singing turned into an oncoming roar.

'Right,' said Adam, 'I think it's time for me to go.'

~

Much as he would have liked to, Adam couldn't hang around to see the fall of Guildford. On the other hand, neither could he be in the first group through the portal. There might well be a hot welcome waiting for them on the other side and Hillaire, the joint commander, agreed that the Sicarii must survive. Sad to say, as someone even vaguely favoured by the demon, he was their best and last hope, aside from prayer.

Eventually Adam crossed over in the middle ranks, alongside the artillery and siege equipment. He was weak enough to take one last look back. Behind him the little army's rearguard of dragoons followed into the yellow glow as a tide of man and monster hit Guildford's southern gate. One minute there was the sound of battle, the next the silence of a new world.

There was no one to meet them. Adam's week-long cannonade had churned the ground into a sea of mud and shot. The stakes and heads were gone, lost into it, along with the grass and any other living thing that might have stood there. Even the severed cathedral steps were shattered into rubble. The military had complained of the cost, but the blind barrage had worked. They'd gained the time to catch their breath and survey this fresh day.

Adam paraded the troops as though they were in barracks. He'd noticed even the most trusty men craning their necks around in amazement and concern. An injection of normality and the mundanity of drill would help them adjust.

The Fen Tigers, being 'useful', were kept pretty much up to full strength. They mustered over a thousand men, a mere two hundred short of an infantry regiment's full complement. Adam found grounds for satisfaction in this rare occurrence as he rode along their front. Likewise, he marvelled at the fullness of their equipment: a sword for each man and armour for the pikemen. They even had the correct complement of artillery. The Sicarii gave silent thanks to the unknown colonel who'd declined to enrich himself with absent men's wages and 'missing' weaponry. The belligerent stares coming from the blue-clad ranks were likewise gratifying. God had favoured this errand with the right tools for the job.

The bigger guns stood either side of the Tigers, the crews and their charges well acquainted by recent exertions. Adam had seen them at work in the High Street and had no complaints. The sappers beside them were known to be the lowest of the low, mere machines trained to move stubborn earth swiftly. He declined to distress himself by paying them attention.

A corps of cavalry had been raised, since no one could expect the double-troop of dragoons to ride into battle on their nags and ponies. Longstaff, a *de facto* colonel again, had scoured the countryside before they were placed under siege and stolen enough horses to mount two score intrepid types. There'd been sufficient pot-and-plate armour in the cathedral armoury to go round. Then, from somewhere, he'd unearthed his Norfolk family banner and mounted it on a lance. Adam had graciously given permission for it to be the unit's standard. Thus, though nowhere recorded in army records, and its battle honours not of this earth, *Longstaff's Horse* was born.

Adam returned to halfway along the line. The rest of the 'general staff', Hillaire, Bancroft, his two wizards and the Papal troopers, were waiting for him there. The standard of the Tigers, the red and white of England's St George edged with the green of the fens, was called forward. The Tigers' corps of boy drummers sounded the call to attention.

The Sicarii looked at the staring faces and they looked

at him. He had his 'fairly impressed but not yet convinced' expression on.

'Not much to say,' he shouted. 'Much to do. Your King is here. Heresy is here. Are you worthy of the one, and foe of the other?'

A growl of affirmation rippled along the line as the question was heard.

'Well, maybe you are. I don't know. The Levellers say you're servants of the devil – and gutless with it!'

The response noise grew an angry edge.

'I don't believe them. We've put our boot in their door easy enough, I reckon. Not bad for us "cowards" and eaters of babies, eh? What do you say?'

They agreed, approval taking the form of a roar.

'What *I* say is let's show 'em some more of the same. Let's *explain* to those soft, towny shit-a-beds what true-Church can do!'

The acclamation grew louder, almost drowning Adam's speech.

'We'll ask the last survivor – some London-bred crow-bait I 'spect – if he's revised his opinion!'

They couldn't hear him now, but he whipped them on, punching the innocent air with a gauntleted fist.

'For Christ and England and Good King Charles!'

The hair-trigger button marked 'blood lust' firmly pressed, hats were taking to the air along the line. Adam dismounted and turned to Hillaire and company.

'Sorry about that,' he said disarmingly.

Though they stood ready to welcome them, no pursuers issued through the portal. Duly grateful for, if puzzled by, their undisturbed 'night', Adam was able to place that particular concern into limbo. Meanwhile, the present enemy hadn't troubled to mask the lights of Guildford Castle and so the army's way was clear. At 'dawn' they formed into a line of march and set off on the path Adam had trod before. Within an hour they learned the mistake of thinking of an 'enemy' in the singular.

The scythe-bearing bugs, being ravenous or brave or stupid, attacked them head-on. The outer cordon of cavalry and dragoons paid the penalty of not clutching Adam's warnings to their hearts.

A couple of men and horses went down to slashing blows and the beasts who'd delivered them rocketed out of the grass to feed. The rest tunnelled on through the concealing sward, mere dark shapes of movement, coming faster than a horse could gallop.

The practised drill worked quite well. Nearly all the insectoids ran on to the waiting hedge of eighteen-foot pikes, impaling themselves, yet struggling on at enormous cost in squealing pain. They tried to push their punctured frames up the pikeshaft and it needed more than one point pressed home to pin them to the ground. Only then could the musketmen come up and dismantle the things with lead. Each one required a great deal of loving attention. It was discovered, at the cost of three lives, that they were clever enough to feign death.

One bug somehow threaded through the pikes and found itself in a well-stocked larder of living things. The sprawling close-quarters mêlée with it only ended when Bancroft's Turkish wizard hit home with an *anathema* spell and the thing expired noisily in cold blue flame. Sinking down to death, the bug found final rest on an altar of bodies.

Dealing with the remainder was comparatively simple. The smaller artillery, the falcons and leather guns, could be trundled up to interrupt their meals and blow them into tiny pieces.

The bloodied soldiers watched that particular entertainment with great satisfaction and Adam had to ride round reminding them to pay heed to other directions. The inoffensive-seeming grass might well conceal another clutch of bugs, poised for launch and lunch. They must always assume, he said (or words to that effect), that those silver, faceted eyes had them under perpetual study.

As if that were not chastening thought enough, they received further reminder of their immigration-status in that world. As the last echo of cannon fire died away and relative silence returned to the flat prairie, a warm breeze came out of nowhere, raising their hair and causing the standard to crack to attention. Only Adam paid it much attention to start with, since only he knew what it was.

The demon then followed her sigh with laughter, and the sound was like thunder filling the universe. The army left off cleaning their blades and reloading their guns and looked to the sky in terror. They'd been told something of the matter they were about, but by no means all.

The malicious humour turned into a long purr of pleasure as the dead were resurrected. The recently fallen men and bugs, parts and whole, rose again and made their way, stiff-legged, to stand together. The living shrank away from the sight, though few had the strength to avert their eyes.

Then, when the revenants could jam themselves no closer, some of them, the more complete specimens, began to climb. Slowly, a writhing pyramid was formed.

There was the compensation that they were not aware. The light had not returned to those dead eyes; they did not know what was being done with them. Fortunately their souls had moved on, as was proper. Even so, it was a mercy to see the thing completed when the ground crept up and covered the heap with masking soil. Only a few heads and limbs remained protruding. From nowhere, a stone figure appeared to crown the pile. It was a perfect likeness of the demon's favourite, most girlish incarnation.

Adam saved everyone's life by commanding them to kneel. The few who did not, the pious and the slow, joined the monument like the magicians at the London summoning. The false homage seemed acceptable: no one else died.

There was a last chuckle of amusement, and then she was gone.

The army's salvation had lain in keeping busy. The officers harried the men up and down, getting them to retrieve and clean weapons, dressing their ranks and generally restoring command. It being imperative that no one be granted leisure to think, they'd moved off within minutes. Nevertheless, it was a close run thing: no one had given voice to their feelings, but most eyes turned to the new 'monument' as they passed by. Adam realized he had only a short space in which to find them a fightable enemy.

Evidently the Leveller commander thought likewise. Their progress through the quiet green world was left unhindered. The Sicarii admired the subtlety and restraint of the policy. His troops were left prey to their own imaginations and could not relax or be at ease for fear of the bugs, but neither was there anything to lash out at. In addition, it required only one more manifestation of the demon's supreme authority in her world and morale would haemorrhage away. Doing nothing in order to win without a fight was most impressive. Adam was of the opinion that Grimmond had survived the Guildford gunpowder plot. He detected his blood-stained hand at play here.

Towards the 'afternoon', in the space of a second, the sky turned sickly orange. Bathed in that light, every man looked both alien and ill. The soldiery were forbidden to comment on it and, after the first hesitation, they marched sullenly on.

At the end of the 'day' they came to the kidnapped house. At the same time it began to rain. Torrential sheets of water poured down on them, though not a cloud could be seen. Adam looked up at the empty orange sky, his mouth and eyes filling with the sour rain. He noted the natural human reaction of the army to edge towards the only cover – and he was suspicious. In these unprecedented events he thought he heard the Levellers' answered prayers. Jonah had spoken to the demon and . . .

'We back off from it,' he told Hillaire and the other assembled staff. 'Two dragoons check it out first.'

Bancroft, his two magicians and a number of others who should have known better were more anxious to get under cover, but the Papal troopers and Longstaff moved directly to shepherd the army away.

Adam regarded those still round him with displeasure. 'Shame on you. Why rush? Can you get any wetter?'

Answerless, they watched the two deputed horsemen canter off to the dark and forlorn-looking house. They saw their distant signs of horror at the sacrifices in front, and they saw the house explode into red ruin when the two entered in.

'A stay-behind,' nodded Adam sadly as brick and tile showered around. 'A fanatic in a cellar sitting on barrels of gunpowder, waiting for some officers who don't like to get wet.'

The rain stopped – which was confirmation enough.

When Bancroft celebrated mass for the army that 'night', Adam prayed that he be spared to reply to Grimmond's personal message to him.

. . . to each Church, shrine and Chantry-Chapel in each of the places hereafter: Walsingham, Wells-next-the-sea, Warham, Blakeney, Thornage and Stiffkey, the sum of two shillings; and one shilling to each parish priest who will pray for me. There shall be one shilling to every unbeneficed cleric in the diocese of Norwich, save those in bad reputation with the poor, and one pound of English coin to each religious house, save that of Binham Priory which shall have two pounds. There shall be five shillings to the high altar of All Saints Church, Thornage, and a shilling to the side altars, as many as shall be there at the time of my death. This last is conditional on my name being entered in perpetuity, and until our Saviour cometh, on the bead-rolls of said high altar so that mass may be said in my name every year upon the date of my obit.

I hereby also bequeath two pounds of English coin to the repair and upkeep of the wooden scene of the death of our Blessed Lady, which I once saw in Llandaff Cathedral in the Welsh Country when I was a soldier in the days of my health. There will be ten shillings apiece to each of the lazar houses and Church hospitals in the diocese of Norwich, and fourpence each to those tenants such as have farmed land in my family's possession for upward of twenty years. To the poor fishermen of Blakeney Point I leave my four-oar schooner and ten shillings for its upkeep. Such of my coats and bed-linen as my surviving brothers and sisters do not require shall go to said fishermen for their relief from the evil North Sea winds. My weapons shall all be sold and the proceeds given to the Jerusalem and Jaffa Citadels, for their defence against the infidel.

Forasmuch as I have been negligent to visit holy places and to go on pilgrimage, I bequeath such as remains of my cash and bullion to the Shrine of our Lady at Walsingham, where my own dear mother was wont to take me when I was a boy.

May the prayers and intercessions of the two aforementioned

*women save the soul of a miserable sinner and ease the torments of purgatory.*

Extract from the Last Will and Testament of Colonel James Constantine Longstaff, late of Town Farm, Thornage, in the County of Norfolk.

'In the name of God, Mother Church and His Majesty the King, I call on you to surrender—'

The herald's summons was abruptly ended by musket fire. He was slammed to the ground, never to rise again.

Adam had thought that might happen. Heretics and apostates could not always be trusted to observe the rules of truce and the herald's white token gave him no special status in their eyes. If one of the godless should choose to come into range, well – the Lord had delivered him into their hands.

The professional soldiery were shocked, however – so the youth's death was not a total loss. Adam had been looking for a way to personalize the conflict for the rank and file and this murder served very nicely. The army prepared for an immediate assault.

An offer of bloodless resolution to their differences having been refused, the contemporary etiquette of war allowed that no prisoners need now be taken. In present circumstances though, that was rather obvious, but for form's sake, and so the crazy Levellers be under no illusions, the Sicarii ordered the appropriate drum signal be given. The distant enemy responded with jeers and gestures.

Adam looked along the line and allowed himself a certain portion of pride (or was it relief?) in having got this far. Only a day before he'd had fears of arriving at Guildford Castle in 'command' of a rabble. When they'd woken the previous 'morning' it was under a 'sky' that had suddenly reverted to its normal blue. Everyone was glad of some warmth, for Adam had forbidden the drying of their sodden uniforms by the heat of the burning building. He'd thought that an appropriate punishment for their earlier weakness, as well as proper caution in the face of the enemy's subtle tricks. It was not beyond

Grimmond, or whichever satanic lieutenant it might be, to rig up a second surprise around the house of death.

Then there's been another 'day's' march and a further bloody brush with the bug creatures before they drew near journey's end. All in all, a mite too much was being demanded of mere men in their trudge through this unnatural world. Adam sensed the resentment of his harsh discipline on top of their other troubles. The succeeding 'night' encamped before the castle lights was restless.

Now, in the light of 'day', he realized he need not have worried. After all they'd been through, the army of orthodoxy were buzzing to get to grips with those who'd made the ordeal necessary. It only remained to aim and fire them.

Adam had taken up station in the centre of the Tigers, armed with his pepper-box revolver and a borrowed half-pike. His dispositions being made and instructions disseminated, there was no reason why the general shouldn't go in with the rest and play a humbler part. Longstaff, likewise, should have been with his troopers and dragoons (dismounted for the purposes of scrambling up defended ramparts) and the Sicarii was therefore surprised to encounter him out of place and on horseback.

'It might as well be now,' he said to Adam.

For a few seconds Adam had to ponder what that might mean but enlightenment soon dawned.

'As good a time as any,' he agreed.

'You've no objection?'

'Quite the contrary.'

'Honour will be served?'

'I'll square that.'

Longstaff glanced back in the direction of the faraway portal and the world they'd left behind.

'I was . . . misled,' he concluded. 'False idols and so on.'

The Sicarii nodded understandingly. 'It's done. It's over. You can make amends.'

The Colonel shifted his gaze to the castle. 'Yes, I can: thanks for the option.'

Adam nobly waved the gratitude away.

'My will's in my cartridge case,' said Longstaff.

'I shall see to it.'

'Right then, if you'll excuse me . . .'

'Not at all, carry on.'

The Colonel crossed himself and wheeled about, raising aloft his family banner. Elsewhere there was not a breath of wind, but a highly suspicious local zephyr kept the emblem stiffly unfurled. Adam guessed that someone else approved of what was to come.

Gathering pace rapidly, Longstaff thundered towards the castle and the end of his life. The Levellers, perhaps envisaging some important message, held fire. It was only when the headlong charge didn't slacken that they took alarm and sought to bring him down.

Fate, or perhaps the demon, smiled on Longstaff's reparation. Ball and bolt and arrow scorched the air around man and beast but none sank home. The ground between him and the enemy was soon covered. Somehow he convinced his fear-crazed horse to leap the yawning ditch.

It was an impossible jump and the beast impaled itself noisily on the thorn and stakes atop the wall. The army held its breath as they saw Longstaff hurl his banner – and his unit's honour with it – into the unseen enemy's midst. They issued a collective groan as he was shot down. His pierced body swayed back limply in the saddle, and for a moment stirrups held him in place. Then a halberdier came on to finish the job and put him into the ditch.

A low rumble of anger and acclamation, all the worse

for its restraint, issued from the Tiger ranks. Personally they might not have time for grand gestures, but they respected such urges in others. Anyone with the nerve to outstare the grim reaper was at least an honorary comrade. Meanwhile Longstaff's cavalry champed at the bit, loudly vowing revenge and the recovery of their standard.

Hearing the hate, the wiser Levellers cursed and wished they'd left the fool unharmed. All in all – from Adam's point of view – it was a very useful death.

'Shall I do likewise?' called Bancroft, somewhat drily, from his place with the command echelons behind Adam's position.

The Sicarii considered. 'In your own time, Father,' he replied. 'There's no rush and many different ways to make amends.'

'Speaking of time, Sicarii ...' prompted Hillaire. He sounded uncharacteristically impatient. Adam couldn't credit that the man was actually eager for battle; magicians, though often functionally mad, were rarely like that in his experience. Perhaps it was the demon's injected cancer that made him sensitive to delay – or maybe a wizard's war spells were hard to keep on the boil.

'Bide a while, if you please,' said Adam. He had to tread carefully, recalling that the Assistant Grandmaster was in nominal command of the expedition. 'The apostates will be feeling unworthy about what they did to Longstaff. If we strike directly it'll pass.'

The waiting stretched horribly on until, to the Sicarii's delight, someone in the castle lost their nerve. A cannon spoke from that direction. They were at extreme range and the ball lacked power. It merely rolled into the Tiger's ranks, snapping a few legs. So, there *was* some indiscipline over there. That was *most* encouraging.

'We go.'

274

Adam stepped forward and the regiment moved with him. The whole army fell into step, adjusting to the pace of the drums. From the castle came the predictable sound of psalms but it met with no reply. The tradition of the English army was that they attacked in silence; a grim, confident advance being more intimidating than any song.

Both side's cannons now felt free to speak. There was only time for a brief exchange of words before close combat was joined but the Royal artillery plainly had the best of it. The Leveller's earthen ramparts were all very well against bugs and lone horsemen, but they exploded into ruin under any bombardment. Adam noted the dramatic effect of a few direct hits. Likewise, it didn't take long to unmount one of the Leveller guns and scatter its crew. It was some compensation for the damage wreaked by the surviving enemy piece's case-shot which tore linear gaps in the Tiger's ranks. The Sicarii swore vengeance against it.

When close enough for there to be point to the exercise, the snipers of both sides opened up. The attackers were disadvantaged here in that they were on the move, whilst the besieged were behind cover and could rest their long-barrelled fowling guns to take leisurely aim. On the other hand, heresy was mostly a town-dweller's vice and few Levellers had a countryman's eye. In the Fens that was a requirement of survival. By the time the ditch was reached, the marksmanship honours were equally shared.

Just prior to this stage in the proceedings, the sappers came to the fore, passing down gaps in the files bearing great sheets of joined timber. They sped in front and raised up these portable palisades, sheltering the troops behind from the worst fire of the final moments. The wood splintered and complained under the musketry storm but the sappers pressed grimly on. One section was reduced to its component parts, along with the men bearing it, by case shot. Another team fell, tripped by a bug body part from some previous skirmish, and were trampled by the Tigers following close on. Late twentieth-century warfare held it vital that close formation should be kept at all times. Nothing could be allowed to imperil those neat lines, not even one's own side.

At the ditch edge the sappers abandoned their charges and toppled them forward. The shields became bridges, lodging across the gap and spanning the thorn-filled depths. Deprived of their cover, the exposed sappers fell victim to the enemy's impatient lust for a target. Their last service to the army was to absorb a close-range volley.

The Tigers brushed the survivors aside and those trained for the job bounded on to the boards to lob hissing grenadoes over the rampart. In the temporary absence of the enemy caused by their delivery, attempts were made to resite some of the bridge palisades fended off by the defender's pikes. Adam likewise took advantage of the lull to take a wider view and judge how things were going.

Since the attack had unsportingly ignored its carefully prepared fire lines, the Levellers were abandoning the gatehouse strongpoint. Reinforcements from there reached the rampart in time to say hello to the grenadoes. The explosions were followed by a gratifying chorus of screams. Adam smiled and, aiming overarm, scored a fairly flukey hit on a heretic officer unwise enough to show his head.

Further along, the dragoons and cavalrymen had already gone in. The Sicarii had a distant sight, diffused through swirling powder smoke, of a serpent of struggling figures swaying back and forth over the rampart line.

Faint cries and the 'pop-pop-pop' of gunfire reached his ears. He was inspired to order the Tigers on.

To put the matter beyond question, their beloved standard went first, but there was no real doubt they'd follow. Myriad army boots thumped hollowly on the boards and scrambled up the steep-pitched barrier. Adam's better-made footwear joined them.

He was well aware that perception of a battle shrank to a circle three or so feet around once one was engaged. Adam rather savoured the holiday from care and planning that it represented. More strategic considerations were now in the hands and minds of Hillaire and Bancroft and, thus freed, the Sicarii allowed his childhood training out to play. He could relax for a while and do what came naturally.

There was someone to meet him at the top of his climb and, most ungratefully, Adam jabbed him with the half-pike. The man went away to think about his mortal injury and the Sicarii piled over the rampart edge, through the broken thorn guard and into the space so helpfully cleared. Someone else rushed up in greeting and was similarly rebuffed. In the interval of rest gained, Adam dropped the useful spear and drew his pepper-box. There were still five cartridges within and he disposed of them to left and right, twisting the barrel with his free hand. This procured him a degree of solitude and time to think besides. He took advantage of it.

The Levellers were good, no doubt about it. No Tiger would ever jest about the torrid time they were getting now. There were new causeways across the ditch made of blue-uniformed dead. Even so, numbers and simple practice were beginning to tell. The colour mix on the rampart walkway was getting bluer by the moment. In a few seconds they'd be able to press on, down into the courtyard and up to the castle keep. It didn't matter that the cavalry and dragoons were making heavier weather of things; they were occupying a creditable number of opponents. Adam saw victory in his grasp.

He also saw Grimmond. Grimmond seemed to have a different view of events. Adam didn't return the smile. He'd have rather sent something more dramatic but was out of range of the Leveller commander. Instead, he looked over to the keep where the man stood, surrounded by his 'pastors' and bodyguards, and pondered the cause of his cheerfulness.

Outside Royal or Papal occasions, or thaumaturgic conventions, it was rare for magicians to meet in number. Europe had been at peace for two centuries and the old military corps of wizards were just something in history books. The summoning at the Westminster Citadel had equalled anything Adam had encountered in a lifetime of periphery wars and consorting with popes. Imagine his surprise, therefore, to see it surpassed that day in the courtyard of a third-rate castle.

Somehow, with unguessable effort, the Levellers had amassed a full dozen wizards. These were people they'd raised from birth or first discovery, drawing out their talent, shielding it from the attention of the Church, clutching them close to their angry hearts. They were the movement's most precious treasures, as dear to them as salvation, and far from lightly deployed. Even the 1990 Thames Valley Insurrection hadn't enjoyed their open assistance. It was only now, seeing these men and women rush forth, that Adam fully appreciated the importance the enemy attached to this project.

They were preceded by a screen of expendables, protection against any yet unused firearm. Behind them followed a phalanx of pikemen. Adam had time to wonder what they might be for.

Then, along with every other living thing on the rampart, the Sicarii was forced to rest his weary limbs. More precisely, they were suddenly frozen into stiff immobility – but it amounted to the same thing. His eyes alone still answered instructions and Adam used that last remaining freedom to look about. In a long line, left and right of him, he was in the company of living statues. Men were caught in curiously violent poses or in the act of dying.

He knew the spell, he knew its effect, he knew everything about it save how to cast or escape it. What wizards called 'judgement' induced that extremity of fear which causes animals to freeze and meekly await death. Adam and his time might be ignorant of adrenalin's exact composition, but he recognized the racing pulse of his body's fight-or-flee mechanism. The agony lay in not being able to obey it. Already he saw that a few men's hearts had given up and let them depart from life. The one blessing was that he could not raise his face to see Grimmond.

Cast so abundantly, this assassin's spell became a battle winner. Those few lucky or 'psychically damp' enough to escape it were felled by targeted magic. They exploded in *anathema* flame, imploded in on themselves or were shrivelled up; removed from events by the grimmer sections of the standard spell book. For a brief interval all was quiet on the rampart. The smirking wizards made way and the pikemen moved up.

It was not pleasant to behold one's nemesis approach and be helpless before it. Adam had always hoped, when his time came, that he might think great thoughts or frame fervent prayers. Instead, the image of an abattoir he'd once seen took centre stage. The animals there had also been aware but impotent.

The pikemen were working their way along the rampart, finishing off the statues with great impaling thrusts to the chest. He watched his two Papal troopers dealt with in this way. There was no prospect of rescue: the Tigers on the outside had drawn back, unnerved by the wizardry. They were even prepared to let their banner fall to the enemy. Across the way, Adam saw that the dragoons and cavalry had been repelled. He was dying in failure and felt unhappy about that.

Behind him a number of feet could be heard making hard work of getting up the rampart wall. They were not the confident boots of soldiers or men of action. Unable to desist from analysis, even to the end, Adam postulated the climbing efforts of scholars and the unfit middle-aged. The nearest pikemen, only a few yards away, seemed to find the area behind Adam fascinating. Then someone put their arm close around his neck and tried to pull him back. He could just glimpse a sleeve of clerical black under his chin. It was half strangling him, but at least he was going in the right direction.

To either side he felt the movement of air and Bancroft's two magicians landed on the rampart. They ignored him and dealt death to the pikemen below. A half dozen fell horribly dead or maimed and the rest drew back. Several of the Leveller wizards rushed up, outraged at the interference.

Another rush of air, and Hillaire inelegantly joined them, sliding down the inner wall on his behind. Slumped against the rampart's support, and badly out of breath, he met the fresh challenge with a conjuration.

One opposing thaumaturge clapped hands to chest, eyes widening, and stopped in his tracks. Hillaire extended his skinny arm and slowly closed his hand. The Leveller dug at his ribcage as though hopeful of removing some terrible pressure. Death came soon after.

The other magician, a hot-eyed young girl in bonnet and black crinoline, looked at her fallen companion and then pointed at the group on the rampart. Adam heard Hillaire groan. Bancroft's two wizards, the Turk and the giant, took up the struggle. The former spat a form of words and swept up his arms. The woman was forced to do likewise, her hands pinned against some invisible barrier. Meanwhile, the giant muttered something and punched forward. The Leveller's head snapped back, her cry cut short as her kindly brain limited pain and stunned her. The Turk reached out with cupped hands towards the exposed white throat and, at a distance of a score of yards, throttled her. Only then was she allowed to fall.

By now Hillaire had recovered from his thaumaturgic blow and directed a crackling bolt of blueish light towards the remaining enemy magicians. It was deflected with ease but they seemed reluctant to come closer. They had the advantage of numbers, true, but Leveller intelligence had doubtless informed them who Hillaire was. Even the most arrogant privately tutored protégé of the Levellers had the measure of what a Church-trained Assistant Grandmaster could do. They might, at long last, overwhelm him but the game would prove . . . expensive.

Grimmond observed the feeble stalemate and ordered more prosaic missiles be discharged. The arrival of cross-bow bolts and the whistled calling cards of musketry urged Father Bancroft on to more frenzied efforts to haul the frozen Adam back over the rampart. Hillaire cast a shimmering yellow screen which seemed to shield them against the worst of the barrage. The Leveller wizards tried their best to disrupt it and caused hand-sized gaps and tears to appear. Meanwhile the Turk and the giant added their efforts to their master's and the Sicarii was bodily thrown over the wall. He fell, winded but thankful, on to one of the plank palisades traversing the ditch. A few feet to either side and he would have had a softer landing on dead Tigers. The magical paralysis fled away.

Hillaire joined Adam under his own steam – literally, propelled over the rampart by some magical manipulation of air pressure. In helping the old man, gasping and retching, to his feet, the Sicarii felt the residual effect press on his face and stream back his hair. The two wizards next appeared on top of the rampart, silhouetted against the 'sky' and tugging Bancroft between them. Their master had got himself in a tangle whilst ascending, but the two's brute force soon freed him. It proved to be a waste of effort. A crossbow bolt took him in the lower back, hammering him forward and out of his servants' grasp. They took one look and recognized a hopeless task. Bancroft was left, draped over the wall, perhaps even impaled on it, and the wizards leapt out of harm's way. By chance, the priest's grey head hung down near Adam. He raised his dying gaze to the Sicarii and forced a smile on to blood-lined lips.

'For you – of all people!' he said.

'"Greater love hath no man,"' replied Adam, quoting scripture. Bancroft frowned through his pain, unappeased.

Some magic then hit him and he left the world behind. When the blue flame had ceased to crackle, Adam closed Bancroft's eyes and made the cross on his brow.

There was – just about – time for such luxuries before the Levellers regained the rampart and could shower missiles on those below. Adam and company took advantage of the opportunity to live and left in haste. Up to now, the remainder of the Tigers had at least stood their ground but, seeing their leaders emerge, diminished and at speed, they saw no reason not to likewise head in an ignoble direction. The Sicarii, Hillaire and the two wizards soon caught up and joined in the headlong retreat. From behind came the sounds of jeers and laughter.

Right, said Adam to himself, if that's the way she wants it . . .

~

The cannons spoke in unison and raised another section of rampart into the air. Adam presumed that some defenders went with it, but the gunpowder fog made that hard to judge. The barrage had gone on all 'morning' and by now the castle loomed out of a confusion of smoke and flames and screams. The keep alone remained untouched and inviolate – the Sicarii had issued strict instructions in this respect: only the outer areas could be swept with death. This artillery storm was very much an option of despair, for one unlucky shot was all it needed. Should His Majesty – or even worse, Jonah – make acquaintance with a cannonball, then everything would come to ruin.

The first job had been to dispose of the remaining Leveller gun. That was soon done and then the recital came from one side only. Afterwards, there was no obstacle to the systematic dismantling of the little haven of safety, the gate, the ramparts, the courtyard cabins, that the Levellers had constructed in this strange world.

The Tigers were ordered to stand-to all the while, for fear of a sally from the castle or a visitation from the bugs. They were in a sullen and fractious mood, conscious of their state of disgrace. Before the defences vanished into the gunpowder haze, the Levellers taunted them, waving their lost banner and dishonouring it with spit and worse. Failure and frustration led to insubordination and the officers found it advisable to hang one offender to educate the others. His body adorned the regimental gallows, swaying slightly as the cannons blasted nearby; an incongruous tree-like form in the infinite plain.

There had been no opportunity to bury the dead; they were still in the castle ditch or on the ramparts. The Levellers had made fresh cover out of the latter, piling them high, and Adam's sharp eyes had spotted the black of Bancroft's clerical gown amidst the barricade of bodies. Now, whatever transpired, the victors would be spared the task of interment duties. Between the attentions of scavenging bugs, who'd feasted noisily all 'night', and the current barrage there'd be little left to merit the trouble.

Earlier on, the Levellers had appealed to Adam's nonexistent better nature. There had been ominous signs of concerted movement on the ramparts and, in gaps in the smoke, they'd observed trussed-up captives, women and children amongst them, suspended in cages over the sides. The Sicarii had studied them with a perspective glass to check that the King of England was not of their number. He doubted the enemy were yet that desperate, but in dealing with unreasonable people it was as well to make sure. Presumably, these wretches were the remnant of the abducted castle servants and Royal entourage.

The Sicarii could offer them pity but not mercy. A swift examination of conscience confirmed to him that any sin would rest on another's shoulders. The Tiger's fierce Fenland chaplains risked coming close to shout absolution to the captives and then firing recommenced. By way of penance Adam made himself stay and see the consequences.

After a few such clamorous hours the gun crews began to tire and the rate of fire to slow. Adam judged the time right for the real purpose of the whole exercise.

He was standing a little way back from the army, not far from the lines of tents and the horse corral. Both were, of necessity, well guarded but it was as quiet a spot as he was likely to find.

'Well,' he said, addressing the empty air, 'this isn't *drama*, is it? This is just attrition!'

Suddenly the air wasn't quite so empty as before. Adam continued his prayer.

'Whilst they have those magicians, we can't get in. Whilst we have these cannons they can't get out. I don't want to bore you . . .'

She was beside him – and very close. The air dispelled by her arrival washed over him and bathed his face with peppery heat.

'You aren't,' she said in his ear. 'Not yet. I experience time passing differently from you.'

Despite her words, Adam detected a hint of sadness – or perhaps disappointment – in her voice. He seized upon it.

'Even so, mistress, it's not the *best* we can do.' He was careful to keep 'eyes front'. There was a long silence; her searing breath grew more rapid.

'You are very eager to please,' she whispered at last. 'What do you suggest?'

'The cannons for the wizards,' he answered. 'A fair exchange to break the stalemate. *Then* we might more properly entertain you.'

She pondered.

'Sicarii!' The call came from the area of the tents. 'I've detected some—'

It was the Turkish wizard, somehow alerted by his 'Talent' to the demon's presence. Seeing her he stopped in his tracks.

She looked at the newcomer. 'Him as well?'

285

Adam stifled a protest. 'If you must.'

She continued to stare at the magician, but a mischievous smile now occupied her fair face. The wizard sensed that his fate was in the balance.

'What are you . . .?' he shouted, outraged. 'No!'

'It was what you agreed,' she purred to Adam. 'You can't go back on it.'

'Very well.'

'I'll spare the Hillaire human. He's carrying something I made – but no more magic from him.'

'Fair enough.'

The Turk was whisked away, mid-protest, into nothing. At the same time the cannons began to glow, and then to melt. There were some powder explosions. Most of the crews made it away in time; others got caught in the molten flow and thrashed about briefly therein. For a moment the pool of metal was still – until the demon restocked it. All the Leveller wizards appeared there, shocked and screaming, and likewise Bancroft's two magicians, the Turk, brought back specially for the show, and the giant. They had just enough time to realize their predicament before merciful release arrived to end their dance.

The metal began to cool and solidify, freezing the twisted figures within into a grotesque tableau. Though he would rather not be, Adam was reminded of the sculptor Rodin's 'Burghers of Calais'.

'So then,' said the demon, materializing in the midst of the metal-shod dead, 'entertain me . . .'

~

'You cannot expect,' said Hillaire, 'that I should welcome the sacrifice of so many wizards. There is a kindred feeling among our type.'

'Just so,' replied Adam. 'Accordingly the Church keeps your "type" under her thumb. Otherwise, sooner or later, you'd have delusions of superiority to us mere mortals.'

'Yes . . . a collective of better-than-men: nature's aristocracy. A baseless fear, but most persistent. That's why we were burnt at first.'

'A waste. Mother Church brought people to their senses in that respect. But you can see why it might be believed – especially if magicians make comments like yours.'

Hillaire nodded dispassionate agreement. 'My words were unfortunate. Please understand that no cause transcends my proper loyalties.'

'It is understood. If it weren't so, you'd not be here alive and well.'

The Assistant Grandmaster of Magic courteously took that as a bald statement of fact rather than a threat.

'I'm hardly well, Sicarii . . .'

Adam shrugged. 'Don't knock it, wizard. Your cancer is why she spared you.'

Hillaire mused and then concurred. 'On balance I have no complaint,' he said. 'There are some research projects I would like to complete, and my successor must be found. The Grandmaster must have an able assistant.'

'There you are, then. I made the right decision.'

Hillaire was saved from framing a safe reply by the arrival of another body part from the castle. The two men fastidiously averted their eyes, waiting for someone to collect it.

The Levellers had been raining down bits of people on the army all 'morning'. With true artisan-class ingenuity, they'd constructed a great catapult, a *trebuchet* to give it its ancient name, out of spars and rope. Whilst not the most accurate of weapons, it reached the required distance. Being charitable, Adam presumed their aim was to lure

287

the bugs in to dine. If instead they hoped to revolt and frighten their enemy, they would be disappointed. The Tigers had stronger stomachs than that.

Deprived of their artillery, the besieging army could not reply. The only response was to have horsemen grab each newly arrived gift and rush it far away. It was unpleasant and dangerous work. A few did not return, victims, as intended, of bugs attracted by the scent of blood. The rest became aware that some of the butchered pieces were distressingly fresh.

Meanwhile the gallant surviving sappers were burrowing their way towards the semi-repaired Leveller defences. Adam was gearing the army up for a second massed assault and was conscious there'd be no opportunity for a third. Before then, his soldiers' morale would crack, or perhaps the demon would tire of him and do something horribly random. He needed therefore to make the best of their every advantage in the short time left to them and ease the passage in. Some barrels of gunpowder had survived the molten cannons incident and it seemed a shame to waste them.

A trench had been dug, with quite marvellous speed, straight towards the ramparts. Adam saw that there was a knack even to something as simple as spadework, and that God bestowed talent on even the lowest of his creatures. The Sicarii, though supremely fit, could not have made half that distance in the same time and would have bloody hands and an aching back besides. The sapper at the trench's head rolled forward a great gabion, a wicker basket packed hard with earth that absorbed the missiles sent to halt his progress. He, as 'sap-roller', had the honour of wearing the 'death's head burgonet', a skull-like, bullet-proof helmet of twenty pounds or more – it being occasionally necessary for him to peer round his protection to correct their path. He would have a headache for wearing it but, with luck, nothing worse.

Beside him the ground nigh-on melted away before the easy-looking stabs of two burly spademen. Behind them the trench was widened and deepened, and then protected with gabions filled with the spoil. From time to time a lucky shot got one of their number but the onward progress never ceased.

Adam didn't bother with a speech. Both the Tigers' and the calvary's standards were in enemy hands and wiping enemy backsides, and that should be sufficient incentive. The whole army assembled, just out of musket shot, in 'order of columns' and waited for the order to go. Marksmen ventured closer and practised their trade. There'd surely not, thought Adam, when his conversation with Hillaire was done, been a battle like this for more than half a millennium. Artillery and magic had been essential ingredients in the art of war ever since their discovery. It was ... odd to slug it out with only brawn and small arms. A certain elegance – and economy – was missing.

The Levellers must have heard him thinking. When the sappers had reached the half-filled ditch and were making it passable with bound bundles of grass, an element of novelty was introduced. Adam could only hope that the demon would be thereby amused, for he wasn't.

How on earth they had managed to capture and secure a live bug was beyond the Sicarii. Likewise the means of getting it into the *trebuchet*. With luck the liberated beast might have managed to slash a few captors before it was flung forth. It was certainly in a fighting mood when it landed.

A short drop into the trench was within the limited capabilities of the catapult. The creature landed on its back in the midst of the sappers and rocked furiously back and forth trying to right itself. All the time the scythe blade flickered out, detaching limbs and dividing men in half. The sap-roller was gripped in the bug's upside-down jaw and the stag-beetle-like projections chomped merrily upon him. The burgonet-laden head lolled forward.

Adam had recourse to his perspective glass – and then held his breath. In falling the sapper's captain had brought his protected head into the creature's reach. It tried to chew on the new mouthful – and didn't like it, leaving deep marks on the thick metal. The dying sapper was granted brief respite. His noble last thought was to flick the lucifer gripped in his hand and light the short fuse to the barrels he had planted.

The Sicarii saw the brawny arm lift, falter, and then painfully press on. A light sparked in his hand and travelled down a line into the ditch. The arm fell like lead, never voluntarily to rise again, and the bug found new purchase to resume its meal. Adam didn't care to watch the dead man's twitching false life under the bug's manipulation.

The delay went on so long that Adam bitterly concluded it had all been in vain. He had even turned his head to order the charge when the sapper's heroism was crowned with success. The Sicarii gladly commended the simple soul to his Maker's loving care.

The containers of plain powder had been converted to 'Beelzebubs' by the addition of nails, jagged metal and chain. The army were (just) beyond their warm embrace but they felt the passionate breath of delivery. A large slice of the defences learned to fly and the courtyard behind was plentifully hosed down with death. Of the bug (or the sappers) nothing remained to be seen.

'We go.'

The order was relayed left and right and they began, slowly at first, then gathering speed to a jog, the all-or-nothing attack. Adam's mind was now at ease; he had made his confession an hour before to one of the chaplains. The day before him was henceforth his own to enjoy. If perchance they prevailed, then there'd be time to think of kings and demons.

In the event, he was not allowed his day. 'Day' suddenly became 'night'.

'No matter,' he roared. 'Move on.'

To their eternal credit, the army merely faltered. The guillotine fall of darkness only bothered them at first. Most, after all, were Fenlanders, used to deeds done after sundown. Rear files ran back to the tents for rush torches and the emergency giant lucifers. Similar lights began to flare in the castle.

There was no saying why she'd done this. Her ways and whims were quite inexplicable. Adam surmised that it might amuse the demon to see them blunder blindly against each other and kill and die amidst confusion. However, it might equally be some other reason – or none. Light or the lack of it presumably meant little to her view of events.

Much the same could be said of the black stream of bugs that came out of nowhere to join the fray. Fighting both sides with similar relish, her playthings were there to add to the jollity of it all.

Adam's column headed in along the sapper's trench and for a while he was glad of the dark: the things he trod upon were shrouded in merciful obscurity. If there had been defenders waiting to meet them they'd been already swept away by the wave of bugs. The Sicarii and the leading porcupine of Tiger pikemen entered Guildford Castle without opposition.

For a second, light was restored so they could clearly see what they were getting into. Then, before their eyes could adjust, the inky darkness returned. The courtyard was briefly revealed as a swarming chaotic mêlée, in which to recognize a definite enemy was the greatest good fortune. Above them, growing louder and louder, came the sound of girlish giggles.

Even before they surmounted what was left of the rampart after the 'Beelzebubs', a particularly huge bug hurled itself on them. The Tigers were swift enough to lift their pikes and impale the beast, but killing it proved more difficult. Whilst they were thus distracted, a file of Leveller musketeers rushed up and took the opportunity to pour fire into the ranks. Pikeless and fancy free, Adam had no real contribution to make to this tussle and quietly slipped away. There was an opening to one side and he took it.

He was not left alone for long. A single figure bumped into him and he stunned it with his open hand. Two others, more aware and malign than the first, obliged him to use his pepper-box. It was only afterwards that he saw they were Tigers.

The waste – of friends as well as bullets – compelled him to slow down and order his thoughts. It was clear that other columns had penetrated into the courtyard. Wild, half-lit, half-glimpsed combat swirled round him. Soon numbers and quality would tell and the first stage of the battle would go to them. The bugs might kill an equal number on both sides: the demon would see to that, but she would not let them win. All that remained was to seize the castle keep.

'That's quite right,' said a soft, feminine voice in his ear. 'Round one will go to you – but I want to see you play first.'

Adam sighed, but didn't dare to argue. The goddess of this world – and possibly his own – required her pound of flesh. And what she wanted she must have.

The Sicarii looked for the centre of events. A nearby pool of light seemed promising and he entered into it. He was confronted by a double file of Levellers armed with pike and sword and they shouted a joyous greeting. Adam about turned and ran. They followed close behind – which was exactly what he wanted. Ten paces back was a farm cart which had survived the blasts and barrages more or less intact. Adam gracefully vaulted into it and waited for company. His pursuers came on the barrier unexpectedly and had to back off to heft their pikes. The sixteen-foot shafts weren't readily shifted to meet an enemy's sudden change in height and the dark doubly made a meal of it. The Sicarii had all the time he required to empty the pepper-box and at point-blank range felled four of them. A back flip then took him out of the cart and away from imminent impalement. Some of the angrier souls tried to follow him round, but they were hampered by their fallen friends and unwieldy weapons. Adam met their charge at the edge of the cart and stuck two with his short sword. The rest backed off to think things over.

Elsewhere he found a Leveller officer of sufficiently gentle birth to permit a display of sword skills. The man was good but nothing special, and Adam had to work to make it a show. Another, more bestial, 'protestant' with a halberd, the Sicarii took pleasure in disposing of with his bare hands.

'Enough, surely?' he asked.

'Hmm,' answered the purr at his ear, or perhaps inside his head. 'Nearly . . .'

Out of the noisy darkness came a bug. It reared up on

two back legs, towering above Adam and clacking its jaws.

'Oh, come on!' protested the Sicarii. 'Maybe if my gun were loaded . . .'

'It is,' came the whisper – and that was the only concession made.

He trod back a large pace and the whistling scythe blade only sliced a button off his tunic. Flopping to the ground allowed him to retain his head upon the blade's return swipe. Adam rolled on his back, recovered his gun and, more by luck than judgement, shot in one of the creature's multi-faceted eyes. It chittered horribly and then overcame its pain to bring down the scythe in a huge over-'arm' blow. Adam made sure he wasn't there to meet it and, as the thing tried to wrestle the buried blade out of the ground, he fired twice more. One bullet went he knew not where, the other shattered the bug's mouth. There was now the comfort that, come what may, at least it couldn't eat him.

The rolling, ducking and diving fight had taken them back to the farm wagon. Adam mounted it again and briefly wondered how the dead Tiger had got there. After that there was little chance for thought as a storm of angry scythe blows rained down on the blameless conveyance. The target was himself but there was room and cover enough for him to abstain from accepting delivery. Half blinded and maddened by pain, the bug's aim was wild. With oddly balletic steps, the Sicarii nimbly sidestepped the scythe and made each remaining shot count. He knocked out the other eye and put two big holes in the thing's thorax, but nothing seemed enough to kill it off. The flailing swipes continued and sooner or later one would connect.

'Good enough, I suppose,' came her voice, silky smooth and alluring. 'Let's move on.'

The bug erupted in golden light and exploded from within, a terrible last screech attending its betrayal. Adam was left gasping for breath, high up on the cart. At the same moment, 'day' returned.

He retained the strength to look around and saw that they had indeed prevailed. The dismounted cavalry and dragoons held the ramparts. Down below exulting Tigers were finishing off the wounded and dealing with stubborn elements too occupied to follow events. The remaining bugs were leaving at their mistress's behest. Then Adam raised his eyes to the castle keep and saw that a green flag still flew from its top. Its door was barred against them.

The demon, not yet sated, required a grand finale.

There was a nasty little struggle to get in and up. The Levellers were few in numbers but produced steady fire as the Tigers rallied and then surged on up the mound. Close to there was the chance to reply, to hurl grenadoes through the lower windows and use push-of-pike to keep snipers harmlessly inside. They gave pretty much as good as they got. Then the third or fourth man to try actually made it to the gate and affixed a saucer-shaped petard. There was a lull in proceedings as everyone took shelter and listened to its unhurried hissing.

Once the door was blown asunder they could make closer acquaintance. The Tigers were still keen to wash away their shame in blood. Likewise their opponents thought they were earning passage to a better place. These were the fanatical residue of the Leveller force: its 'pastors' and Gideons and the final tussle for the stairway and upper levels was very bitter.

Quite apart from the mounting casualties and the danger of inflicting harm on the King or Jonah, Adam was concerned. He played a prominent part in the pistol and short sword close-quarter work inside, but blessed, he suspected, by the demon's favour, came to no harm. Even so, his disquiet mounted. Eventually, once the outcome was put beyond doubt, he felt the need to draw aside and think.

The Sicarii had seen other last stands: a *Gibborim* tunnel complex in Palestine, a Gnostic 'forest university' in Latvia, but this was different. The belief that one could march straight to Paradise was not uncommon. Most fanatics could convince themselves of it. Worryingly, though, there was something else here; some firm substance to their air of triumph and careless self-destruction. Adam was disconcerted.

Then the vanguard of Tigers discovered their captured banner, and the joy they felt swept them up and over the remaining defences. Bodies with slit throats began to rain down the stairwell and from the upper windows.

Part abstracted by new doubts, the Sicarii ordered that one prisoner be left alive.

~

They saved him a 'pastor', a runtish specimen with hate-filled eyes and a club foot. Adam half paralysed the man with a sharp blow to the jaw hinge. Then, taking a secure grip on his clerical collar, he thrust him with all his strength against the closed door on the topmost level. It swung open and Adam swung away.

The pastor took what looked like two full blasts in the chest and, still unable to speak, died silently. Adam and his friends entered in.

His Majesty King Charles IV was gagged and bound to

a chair. Jonah stood, uninvolved, beside him. Ernest Grimmond was contemplating the smoking shotgun wired to the door handle.

'It was worth a go,' 'smiled' the Leveller General.

'A bit obvious, though,' said Adam, not unkindly.

A high-pitched humming sound came to his attention. He looked about and saw the demon was here, mere inches high, her usual face atop an insect body borne aloft on shiny dragonfly wings. She buzzed the Sicarii's head and then went to settle on the windowsill, an excited spectator.

'I shall attend on you shortly, Majesty,' Adam told the King. 'There may be something to settle first.'

'Don't expect too much,' said Grimmond. 'I'm no master swordsman; as an assassin you need nerve but no great skill.'

'Actually,' replied Adam, 'I had hopes of taking you alive, regardless of all that's gone between us. The contents of your head would be of interest.'

That same huge, bearded head nodded. 'I suspected as much, so forget it. I'm a dead man. I fear your racks and hot irons, and I've put myself beyond them.'

Adam's eyes strayed to the flask and bottle on the desk. A tiny phial, half full of some clear liquid, lay alongside. The Leveller confirmed his suspicions.

'That's right – and *swift* poison, too. You've barely time to gloat.'

Adam grimaced. 'A minor victory only,' he said. 'Your other hopes are blasted.'

Grimmond seemed happy to agree. 'Let God decide on that,' he said. 'I go from you to Him.'

Adam felt he deserved a treat after all he had been through. Drawing his sword he advanced on the Leveller.

Grimmond was strong, but lacked finesse. Adam let

him attack and effortlessly parried the blows. Were it not for the fact that time was short, the Sicarii could have spun it out all day. Lately, however, he'd also become a merciful man and mindful of the need for charity to even the most degraded. There was no difficulty about stepping inside the clumsy guard and burying his blade in the Leveller's chest. He was close enough to see the light fade from his eyes.

'So ends the tale,' Adam muttered, 'of Ernest Grimmond, Beast of Reading.'

The demon shrieked with laughter. 'I am amused!' she said, human tones distorted by an insectoid throat. Jonah groaned in misery. Then suddenly both were gone.

Adam signalled to the waiting Tigers to unbind the King. When it was done he crossed over to him and fell on one knee, brushing the regal hand with his lips. The Fenlanders likewise paid homage.

'Faithful servants,' said a rich, assured voice, 'I and the Lord thank you.'

Adam looked up – and wondered at the King's confident gaze.

'. . . so that, by now, I believe your realm should lie at peace.'

The King was once again toying with his cup of wine but not, Adam noticed, drinking from it. He seemed to detect some absorbing message in its depths.

From their high vantage point in the keep, they could see the Tigers swarming round the outer defences, effecting repairs. Others drilled around their recovered standard or finished off the burial duties. They were being kept too busy to be homesick.

A mass grave containing two hundred bodies enriched

the soil of the demon's world – and that was just the forces of Light. They had been interred with some reverence, buried deep and honoured with a single cross. The enemy dead were an easier proposition, flung into the ditch to await the bugs' attentions.

'I am glad,' Charles said at last. 'My heart was pained when I thought of my people.'

'But were you otherwise treated well?' enquired Hillaire, leaning forward over the dinner table. 'Were you accorded respect?'

King Charles again considered his response with great care.

'I was more than well treated,' he answered, measuring his words. 'I was granted all the respect that I deserved.'

Adam and Hillaire glanced at each other. This was not the Charles IV they knew by repute and had been briefed upon. They couldn't imagine this solemn man cutting a frantic swathe through ladies in waiting and actresses, or carousing all night. Nor did he seem to be enjoying his wine, though the Charles of England of normal times was said to be addicted to the stuff. Only the sardonic smile was present and correct as expected – but neither rescuer could pinpoint the precise cause of amusement.

'Are you well, Your Majesty?' persisted Hillaire. 'You seem quiet . . .'

The King raised his twinkling brown eyes to the magician. 'Never better, Master Wizard. I confess, though, that my adventure has . . . unsettled me.'

'Then if there is anything we can do to—'

Charles silenced him with a languid – yet imperious – wave of his slim hand.

'Thank you, no. Any rectification of my disquiet awaits me at home. I take it that messengers have been dispatched?'

'Yes,' Adam lied. 'Three riders. One at least should win through.'

In fact the trio of dragoons awaited the Sicarii's word in the courtyard. He wasn't yet minded to give it.

'That is good, for I am anxious to be gone from here. There is much for me to do – and undo. When do we move out?'

'Tomorrow, Majesty,' said Adam. 'If the demon permits.'

A shadow crossed the King's dark features. 'Yes ... there remains that particular problem. We must consult God's will upon our return.'

Hillaire slumped back in his chair and sighed. 'The Lord seems silent of late, Your Majesty. Both the Church's prayers and magic have proved equally ineffective.'

Charles frowned. He plainly disapproved of the magician's tone.

'Then we must find new helpmates – and pray more sincerely,' he said in an animated voice.

Adam poured himself another cup of claret. 'Laudable sentiments, Majesty, but I don't see how—'

'From what you tell me, Sicarii,' the King interrupted, 'to date you have leaned unto your own understanding, and it's been found wanting.'

'I cannot deny ...' said Adam, unusually bumbling and hesitant.

'You *cannot* deny that Godly men – whatever else we may call them – treated with the demon and bent her to their will.'

'The Leveller heretics?' gasped Hillaire, mock-incredulous.

Charles shrugged. 'How else do you explain my presence here – or the great reverses we have suffered at their hands? Their righteous converse reached her ear when

300

our priests and bishops could not. Is there not a lesson in that for you?'

There was – but not the one King Charles meant. Their prearranged double act had drawn him out.

'I see your meaning,' said Hillaire slowly, as though gingerly treading the required road to Damascus. 'Perhaps if we humbly stand before the throne of the Living God . . .'

'Without intermediaries,' prompted Charles. 'Without a clutter of saints and angels.'

'. . . we could be as successful as the heretics.'

Hillaire waved his hand to indicate the room, the castle, the world. The King did not spot the irony.

The room had once been the castle chapel but the Leveller command had made it their own. The murals and wall paintings had been whitewashed out, replaced with intimidating texts in black.

'THOU SHALT NOT MAKE UNTO THEE
ANY GRAVEN IMAGE: EXODUS 20'

occupied the wall where the altar once stood. That had been found in the courtyard, daubed with obscenities and used as a footrest. The water stoups had likewise been torn away, leaving ugly raw scars. All the pious donations of past generations had been swept away to make a new start.

Adam was happy to have aborted that beginning and turned their 'conventicle' into a Royal dining room. He'd also reintroduced an effigy of the Blessed Virgin, borrowed from a Tiger chaplain, in order to part redeem the place before proper reconsecration. Thinking on it, he recalled that Charles had not paid the figure any attention or honour.

'You seem disenchanted, sire,' he said, wresting his glance from the Mother of God. 'Is the repast at fault?'

301

Charles looked at the remnants of the hard-tack and salt pork that was all the Levellers' larder boasted. But for their annual 'communion-in-remembrance-only' ceremony, the meal would also have been devoid of wine.

'You have done your best,' the King said warmly. 'I know my captors were men of simple tastes. Truth to tell, I have come to share their appreciation of plain fare – in this and many respects.'

He once again lapsed into a reverie, idly spinning his eating clasp knife on the table top.

Adam caught Hillaire's eye. The magician sadly shook his head. The outcome they had most feared, but still prepared for, had come to pass.

The Sicarii topped up King Charles' cup with wine – and the balance of Grimmond's poison.

The Leveller creed was fervidly nationalistic. Adam's toast took account of that.

'To England!' he said. 'We've won! A toast for England's health!'

The King 'awoke' at these words and smiled.

'For England,' he echoed, and drank deep.

# From: THE JOURNAL OF A TWICE-ANOINTED SOUL

*... how ran we from pillar to post, from stock to stone, from idol to idol, from pilgrimage to shrine. How gilded we images, painted their tabernacles and set up candles before them. What confidence we had to be delivered out of the Pope's 'purgatory' – that same which we nowhere in* scripture *find – after our departure hence. Yes, though I lived never so ungodly a life, through the popish prattling of monstrous monks and the mumbling masses of those lazy chantry soul-carriers, I thought to be justified. What affiance did we put in auricular confession and in the whispering absolution of papist priests. How believed we to please God highly if at Rome's commandment certain days we abstained from a piece of gross smoky bacon or salt-withered beef and pampered our bellies with all kinds of dainty fish and other delicate fare ...*

Extract from the 1995 diary of Charles IV, King of England, Wales and Cornwall; Protector of Mannin and the Isles; Patron of the Jerusalem and Jaffa Citadels; Defender of the Faith.

Adam put the Royal diary down.

'They can't have believed their luck,' he said resignedly, leaning his arms on the parapet of the keep. 'Never mind holding on to him. He was ripe for them to slot back into place.'

'It is a phenomenon often remarked upon,' commented Hillaire, 'that a captive comes to love his captors. In converting to their cause he then finds reason to forgive their actions and excuse his capture.'

'One hoped that a King might prove a little more ... robust,' replied the Sicarii, staring from the flat roof into the starless 'sky'. 'It says little for his grounding in orthodoxy.'

'To start with he believed in nothing,' observed the magician. 'In crisis, a man who believes in nothing will believe in anything. There are no implications for our faith in his story.'

'You think not? The matter ends with him?'

'Wizards understand the human mind since they delve therein so often. He was a man who had neglected the spiritual aspects of his being. Once that dam was breached he was washed away – and into ruin. His life is over: we mourn and then move on.'

In their minds' eye they both considered the chapel, where under honoured guard his late lamented Majesty awaited shipment to final rest in Canterbury. The army had been properly informed of the Levellers' dastardly slow poison which had deprived them of their King.

'There's the matter of a regency to arrange,' Adam reminded Hillaire. It was the Sicarii's business to report and recommend, but he welcomed suggestions.

'Neither Archbishop,' the dying man replied. 'London's in disgrace. Canterbury's tainted by his long silence. I think it's got to be a Papal Legate: any race or nation – except perhaps a Scot.'

Adam nodded his agreement. 'I've also need to compile a list of our requirements; how many farmers and wives, the ratio of priests and monks and nuns; the appropriate library of texts; whether we need bring iron ore and timber. It requires careful thought.'

'And so do I,' said the demon.

Adam slowly turned. He'd hoped his deliberate neglect would bring her running.

'I did not hear *my* name in your little list.' Her voice was whiney-threatening. 'That's not very nice.'

Hillaire, unable to help himself, shrank away from her. The lesson she'd taught him in his Guildford hotel room was not easily forgotten. Then Jonah also appeared out of thin air and blocked his escape. The clothier seemed possessed with hatred and fear. His eyes rested solely on Adam.

'You were always on my mind,' said the Sicarii, quite truthfully.

She appraised him coolly from head to foot. 'And I have been thinking of you,' she said, her tone suddenly becoming sultry and provocative.

Jonah bared his teeth and charged. Adam had spared a fraction of his vigilance for the clothier and so wasn't taken by surprise. However, his fighting stance proved unnecessary; Jonah never met the intended crippling blow. The demon froze him in mid-leap. He was aware but quite unable to move. Tears coursed down his wrinkled face.

The Sicarii was disappointed. He would not have dared kill him, but to inflict real harm might have been useful. If it *did* come to a time of choice between the two of them, she'd be less likely to select a damaged pet.

'Impetuous creatures,' she lisped. 'I shall enjoy ruling your kind.'

'No,' said Hillaire in a voice of horror. She looked at him and he sank to the ground. The torches round the roof of the keep flared into golden starbursts.

'Why not?' she asked. 'Is what you possess so much better? You'll have a more ... responsive God. I feel fully awake now. I can be my proper self in your world as well as this. You'll come to like it.'

'No,' said the prone magician, his faith supplying courage.

'You will,' she said firmly, and then ignored him. 'See?' she told Adam. 'I can be merciful. I shall be worshipped. The demon paused. She'd undergone one of her dramatic mood swings. 'So, what can *you* give me?' She frowned at Adam.

He went down on one knee and gazed doe-like up at her. 'Everything,' he answered.

'And what about *you*?'

Jonah's face was freed to reply. 'Love,' he said, amidst his tears.

She wrinkled her brow, exaggeratedly serious, like a little girl choosing between two toys.

'I think,' she said hesitantly, 'I prefer "everything". Do you mind?'

Jonah was given no chance to say. She pointed an elegant forefinger in his direction. He stared, uncomprehending, at the black-painted fingernail – and then burst into flames. For a while the human torch ran madly around the top of the keep screaming like a banshee. Mercifully the parapet eventually tripped him and he went over the side. A ragged cheer came up from the soldiery below. They might not know who it was but they approved of the spectacle.

It was very instructive. The way she prolonged Jonah's agony suggested what life would be like under her rule.

The Tigers' cheer foreshadowed man's likely acceptance of it.

Adam, as always, kept his feelings to himself. 'Madam ...' he said, in unctuous homage.

'Hello!' she replied, bright and fresh as though they'd never met. 'What shall we do now?'

'Whatsoever you wish,' he said. 'That is the sweet prerogative of a god.'

'It is, isn't it?' She smiled, staring at him. 'Though I *still* detect your old creed in you. Why cling to it? What *can* you be hoping for? Let's convince you otherwise. Wait here while I go to your world and ... wipe out a race. That should start us off on the right footing.'

Adam desperately wondered if he could – or should – dissuade her. He had risked all to gain this position of influence, however slight. It was very early to try and exercise it. His moderating suggestions had to be used sparingly, but an entire race ...

'Why shouldn't I?'

The Sicarii first thought she was speaking to him, but then saw that was not so. The demon was in conversation with some unseen third party. She seemed agitated.

'Oh, don't be like—' Her voice trembled. Something was interrupting and overruling her. 'Please?' She shook her head in fury and drummed her fists against empty air – or an invisible chest. 'I've only just arrived,' she pleaded. 'I'm only playing. They don't mind – do you?'

She looked desperately at Adam, tears of frustration welling in her eyes, causing the black tints around them to run.

The Sicarii didn't answer. For the first time since his blighted childhood Adam was at a total loss. Up to now he'd been a stranger to fully answered pleas and ... joy.

The demon staggered back and sobbed. It seemed the visitor was gone.

'I'm stuck here,' she howled. 'I *can't* be a god! I can't even harm you.' An admission was unwillingly wrung from her. 'You and your prayers! He won't *let* me!'

~

'It's not too late to join us,' said Adam. 'I'm in charge here; I can okay it.'

Fred Pelling studied the vast stream of wagons coming unopposed through the portal into the Demon's realm. The settlers looked cheerful enough and there was, he admitted, some appeal in starting a complete new life.

'I don't think so,' Fred said with a smile. 'Surviving this long in your company is achievement enough. Best not to push my luck.'

Adam smiled in return. 'You're missing an opportunity. I have high ambitions for this place. We might actually dispense with original sin. It could be Utopia at last. Man's not had such a fresh start since Noah.'

'Amidst the bugs?' asked Pelling. 'Don't be surprised, I heard about them.'

Adam expressed unconcern. 'They'll keep us lean and fit – and thankful for our blessings. Humans need an enemy in order to shine.'

'And what about *her*? That's another "blessing" you neglected to mention.'

'She's tamed.' The Sicarii sounded completely assured. 'She can watch us but not intervene. I quite enjoy her visits now.'

Again it was brought home to Pelling that he and Adam were made of different stuff. Though earth-side magicians said her influence was now removed, the demon

308

still stalked Fred's dreams, in them, at least, quite undiminished in her power.

Those passing, however, the picked recruits of the Sacred College of Propaganda and the Congregation for Evangelization of the Nations, saw less difference between the two men. Their association had caused them to converge. Fred was slimmer now, more martial, more tempered by experience. His eye patch lent him a sinister edge. Outwardly Adam remained the same, but within new thoughts were entertained – and even made welcome.

Conversation lapsed as they watched an array of holy banners and a huge figure of Mary enter from the Guildford side, borne aloft on a palanquin. A little way off mass was being concelebrated by the mission's priests on a mobile altar and incense was issuing from the altar boys' censers to sweeten and bless the new world. The larger wagons rumbling by contained the sections of prefabricated buildings, amongst them this land's first church. Within a week services would be held in Guildford Castle amidst the settlement of 'New Guildford'. Within a year new villages were planned, spreading out in a neverending network all over 'New England'.

'So what did happen to the King?'

Adam tried to look suitably grave. 'He was poisoned.'

'Leveller scum!' spat Pelling. 'They deserved what they got: here and in England.'

'I'm told the hangings are still going on.'

'Not for much longer,' said Fred. 'English blood runs high, but we'll be at peace soon: proper peace. England'll be a better place.'

Adam was surprised at Pelling's new sternness. It seemed the genuine item.

'Fairer, certainly,' he half agreed. 'Was it very bad in Guildford? I can't go and look for myself.'

'No, you're stuck here, aren't you?' grinned Fred. 'It was bad enough. You were right: we held the walls for about five minutes. They were all over us. The pre-humans were hungry and went straight for the townsfolk to feast.'

'Is that when you—?' Adam tapped his own left eye.

'That's right. Last I saw of it was on the end of a *disva*'s claw.'

'Still, you survived.'

Pelling nodded. 'And did some good work, too. Once we abandoned the defences our fighters were free to escort people away. We saved most. Then we could sneak back at night and snipe at 'em. That's the way it was till the army arrived.'

'The Levellers camped round the portal, I suppose.'

'But she wouldn't let 'em in. Those that tried it were spat out in flames. You should thank her for that. Otherwise you'd have been fighting on two fronts.'

'I may mention it next time I wake up in bed with her.'

Pelling raised his remaining eyebrow. 'Like that, is it?'

'Sometimes.'

'Rather you than me. When does the portal close?'

'We'll be warned. Very soon, though.'

'Never to open again?'

'So she says. She's very insistent about that and allowed to have her way apparently. It doesn't matter: we've got a bishop – the apostolic succession won't be broken. It's her world, I suppose, and we're just guests. Fortunately we're *honoured* guests. Madam got to meet our patron. She can observe us and do us favours – but no more than that. She told me.'

310

Pelling considered the infinite green plain. 'You could have ended worse,' he said.

Adam looked in the same direction. 'I *expected* to end worse,' he replied.

There was a noise like the greatest gong ever filling the sky. It sounded again and again, angry and impatient.

'That's it, I think,' said Adam cheerily.

Pelling stared at him. 'I'd like to say—'

The Sicarii shook his head. 'Don't. No sentiment, please. Just say good luck.'

'I thought you made your own.'

'I do, but I'd still like your blessing.'

'Good luck, then – and God go with you.'

Adam smiled. 'Don't worry, Fred. He will.'

They shook hands as the last few carts and settlers hurried through. Then Adam mounted his horse and rode off to the front of the column without a rearward glance.

Fred Pelling's last sight of him, as he backed through the portal, was of a tiny figure at the head of a tide of humanity. Adam, who no longer had any other name, was signalling his people forward to build Jerusalem.

# The BSFA takes you beyond your imagination

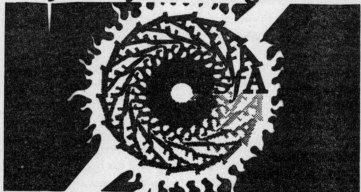

# CRITICAL WAVE

## THE EUROPEAN SCIENCE FICTION & FANTASY REVIEW

"CRITICAL WAVE is the most consistently interesting and intelligent review on the sf scene."
- Michael Moorcock.

"One of the best of the business journals...
I never miss a copy..." - Bruce Sterling.

"Intelligent and informative, one of my key sources of news, reviews and comments." - Stephen Baxter.

"I don't feel informed until I've read it."
- Ramsey Campbell.

"Don't waver - get WAVE!" - Brian W Aldiss.

CRITICAL WAVE is published six times per year and has established a reputation for hard-hitting news coverage, perceptive essays on the state of the genre and incisive reviews of the latest books, comics and movies. Regular features include publishing news, portfolios by Europe's leading sf and fantasy artists, extensive club, comic mart and convention listings, interviews with prominent authors and editors, fiction market reports, fanzine and magazine reviews and convention reports.

Previous contributors have included: MICHAEL MOORCOCK, IAIN BANKS, CLIVE BARKER, LISA TUTTLE, BOB SHAW, COLIN GREENLAND, DAVID LANGFORD, ROBERT HOLDSTOCK, GARRY KILWORTH, SHAUN HUTSON, DAVID WINGROVE, TERRY PRATCHETT, RAMSEY CAMPBELL, LARRY NIVEN, BRIAN W ALDISS, ANNE GAY, STEPHEN BAXTER, RAYMOND FEIST, CHRIS CLAREMONT and STORM CONSTANTINE.

A six issue subscription costs only eight pounds and fifty pence or a sample copy one pound and ninety-five pence; these rates only apply to the UK, overseas readers should contact the address below for further details. Cheques or postal orders should be made payable to "Critical Wave Publications" and sent to: M Tudor, 845 Alum Rock Road, Birmingham, B8 2AG. Please allow 30 days for delivery.

*Recent titles available in VGSF*

Prices correct at time of going to press (March 1995)

# A Dangerous Energy

## JOHN WHITBOURN

London, 1967. In an England where the Protestant Reformation failed, and in which magic is an integral part of the mighty Catholic Church's armoury, there are plenty of opportunities for a talented young necromancer like Tobias Oakley. From his early initiation into the dark arts by an elvish witch, he progresses steadily into a career as a Church magician.

In such an exalted position, Tobias finds not only the power he craves, but also the time to indulge in other, secret, and more satisfying, pursuits – such as drug-running, debauchery, demonology – and murder.

*A Dangerous Energy* was chosen as the winner of the BBC Bookshelf/Victor Gollancz First Fantasy Novel Competition by a panel which included Terry Pratchett, Mary Gentle and Nigel Forde.

'He doesn't soften the edges. A well-textured alternate history' – Mary Gentle

£4.99   0 575 05576 6

# Popes and Phantoms

## JOHN WHITBOURN

From his villa in Capri, Admiral Slovo looks back on a past full of dark magic, corruption, and random violence: as a brigand on the high seas, or as emissary to the Borgias, or even Mr Fix-it to the Pope, Slovo has lived life to the hilt – but now it is time to pay . . .

'A masterly sense of fantastic landscape and baroque plotting, with the added bonus of a rounded cast of exotic characters' – *The Dark Side*

'Wreaks stylish havoc on Renaissance Italy' – *Time Out*

'Everything you never knew about history but were afraid might be true. Machiavelli, the Borgias, Martin Luther – what is *really* down there in the crypt of St Peter's – at last, secrets buried for centuries brought to light! Don't wait for the Illuminati cover-up, buy it now!' – Colin Greenland, author of *Take Back Plenty*

£5.99   0 575 05763 7

# Aztec Century

## CHRISTOPHER EVANS

In her dreams, Princess Catherine could still see
London burning, and the luminous golden war-
ships of her enemies, the Aztecs, as they added yet
another conquest to their mighty Empire . . .

Sweeping from occupied Britain to the horrors
of the Russian front and the savage splendour of
Mexico, *Aztec Century* is a magnificent novel of
war, politics, intrigue and romance, set in a world
that is both familiar – and terrifyingly alien.

'A sacrificial *feast* of a story – highly original sf
from the first page onwards, an intriguing and
compelling thriller to the end' – Robert Holdstock

'Christopher Evans is particularly brilliant at mix-
ing a cocktail of the everyday and the wonderful
to make a magical alternative history' – Garry
Kilworth

'Intelligent, finely written, and towards the end,
absolutely nail-biting' – Iain M. Banks

£4.99   0 575 05712 2

# The Gates of Noon

## MICHAEL SCOTT ROHAN

*'East of the sun and west of the moon . . .'*

. . . you may find a freighter carrying ivory to Hy Brasil, mammoth tusks to Tartessos and Ashkelon, spices from Cathay to Lyonesse. Another world, of infinite strangeness and high adventure, yet never far from our own; round a corner, through a door into a harbourside inn and you may find yourself there.

Steve Fisher had been there once, had sailed the cloud archipelagos on a desperate quest to Hispaniola. Or had he? The memories have faded . . . was it only a dream? Then, in Bangkok, as he struggles to arrange a shipment of vital supplies to the endangered paradise of Bali, Steve finds himself catapulted back into that world, through the eerie gates of the Spiral – and into terrible dangers. For out there is *something* that wants him stopped, at any cost.

£4.99   0 575 05531 6

# Cloud Castles

## MICHAEL SCOTT ROHAN

The Spiral: where past and present meet, where myth and legend infiltrate the mundane world, where Hy Brasil and Babylon are a short voyage away from Liverpool or Hamburg – via the cloud archipelagos.

You can't always find it – but it can always find you. And when it once again calls lonely business-man Steve Fisher he discovers that in the heart of hi-tech Europe a denizen from the dawn of time is reaching out to ensnare one of humanity's most sacred emblems. If it succeeds an apocalyptic struggle that has raged for millennia will be resolved – and a new, eternal dark age will begin.

*Cloud Castles* is fantasy on the grand scale, sweeping across Europe's past and present in a dramatic, panoramic story – a magnificent novel from the bestselling author of the *Winter of the World* trilogy.

£4.99    0 575 05778 5

# A Land Fit For Heroes
## Vol I: Escape to the Wild Wood

## PHILLIP MANN

*Britannia 1993.* In a world where the Roman Legionaries never left Britain a man can walk from the walls of York – or Eburacum – to the southern seas without leaving the shade of the greenwood, inhabited by wildcats, wolves and bears, as well as by the descendants of the folk who built Stonehenge. Solar-powered air cars journey along straight roads that connect the Roman settlements – and link them to the cities of a global empire.

Eburacum is dominated by the Battle Dome, a vast hemisphere enclosing the artificial landscapes where the Games – as brutal, deadly and colourful as ever – are held. And it is here that the destinies of three young people, two British, one Roman, are entwined when a jealous feud forces them to take refuge in the forest – and discover that here, the assumptions of rational city dwellers no longer apply . . .

'Quite beautiful . . . Mann has given this book a mythic quality that augurs well for the rest of the series' – *New Statesman*

£4.99   0 575 05716 5

# A Land Fit For Heroes
## Vol II: Stand Alone Stan

## PHILLIP MANN

In this world Rome never fell to the Barbarians, the legions never left Britain and now, in the late twentieth century, Rome is the capital of a vast global civilization. Three young people, drawn together by a malign fate, were forced to flee Eburacum when a jealous feud led to murder. They took refuge in a village deep in the forest where they began to learn the ways of an older Britain. But Rome's arm is long and even there they are not safe.

The young Roman, Viti, and the two young Britons, Angus and Miranda, are soon on the run again after the Romans attack their village. This time, their destination is Stand Alone Stan, a community built on the Yorkshire Moors. And it is here that their paths, at last, diverge, and begin to hint at the very different destinies that await them.

*Stand Alone Stan* is the second volume in a hauntingly beautiful and compelling trilogy by one of our finest writers.

£5.99   0 575 05932 X